MURDER
at
ELM HOUSE

BOOKS BY HELENA DIXON

6

HELENA DIXON
MURDER
at
ELM HOUSE

bookouture

Published by Bookouture in 2021

An imprint of Storyfire Ltd.
Carmelite House
50 Victoria Embankment
London EC4Y 0DZ

www.bookouture.com

ISBN: 978-1-80019-541-7
eBook ISBN: 978-1-80019-540-0

This book is a work of fiction. Names, characters, businesses,
organizations, places and events other than those clearly in the
public domain, are either the product of the author's imagination
or are used fictitiously. Any resemblance to actual persons, living or
dead, events or locales is entirely coincidental.

Murder at Elm House is dedicated with much love to all my caring, nursing and medical colleagues who have pestered me for years to write a book that featured a hospital or nursing home. I'm not sure that this is quite what they had in mind.

The public are reminded not to approach Ezekiel Hammett who is wanted on suspicion of the murder of Denzil Hammett in Exeter before Christmas. An attempt to capture the wanted man narrowly failed during a recent police raid on an address in Brixham. A chase took place during which shots were fired by the fugitive, which narrowly missed the pursuing police officers. Any person with any knowledge of Hammett's current whereabouts is urgently requested to contact Inspector Greville at Torquay Police Station or Inspector Pinch at Exeter Police Station.

A substantial reward has been offered by Miss Kitty Underhay of the Dolphin Hotel, Dartmouth, for information which may lead to the arrest and conviction of any person suspected of the murder of Mrs Elowed Underhay in June 1916. It is believed that Hammett may be implicated in this crime. The late Mrs Underhay's remains were discovered in November after a box was passed to her daughter containing vital documents providing clues to the hiding place of her body.

CHAPTER ONE

Spring, Dartmouth 1934

Kitty's grandmother looked up from her perusal of the local newspaper with a grave expression. 'I really don't like this at all, Kitty. To shoot at the police. It's extremely fortunate that no one was hurt, or worse, killed.'

Kitty was seated at the table in the large leaded bay window of her grandmother's salon in the Dolphin Hotel. The promise of warmer days that had briefly appeared at the end of February had vanished leaving behind a grey and chilly afternoon.

She had to agree. The report in the newspaper had left her feeling very uncomfortable. Brixham was a little too close to Dartmouth for comfort. It was a good job that her grandmother was unaware of the threatening note signed EH that Kitty had received during the Christmas period whilst staying at Enderley Hall, her aunt and uncle's home near Exeter. Although with the intervening weeks of silence with Hammett still at large she had begun to lose hope of an arrest.

She had been grateful that her friend, Captain Matthew Bryant, had been with her when she opened it. His past experiences working for various government departments and now as a private investigator helped her to rationalise her thoughts and calm her nerves.

'It does sound as if the net is closing in on Hammett though, Grams.' Kitty replaced the cap on her fountain pen. She had almost completed all the letters that she wished to send.

'I hope so. It makes me very uneasy, very uneasy indeed. What are your plans, my dear, for the rest of the day?' her grandmother asked as Kitty gathered up the small pile of envelopes ready for posting.

'I've caught up on the hotel accounts and the ordering so I thought I would meet Robert Potter for my first proper motoring lesson.' A frisson of excitement danced through her veins at the thought. Matt had gifted her a car as her Christmas present. A small red Morris Tourer, exactly the one she had been admiring for weeks in various advertisements.

Since her return from Enderley she had been too busy with her work at the hotel to do more than visit it and sit briefly in the driving seat. A few weeks of bad weather had also delayed matters for longer than she would have liked. Robert Potter, the son of her regular taxi driver and owner of the Daisybelle touring coach, had agreed to teach her to drive. Today was to be her first lesson.

Kitty's grandmother's brow creased in a faint frown. 'I'm still not sure about this motoring business. I really cannot see what is wrong with Mr Potter's taxi. You will take care, my dear, won't you?'

She smiled as her grandmother rose from her seat and began to gather her things together. 'Of course, Grams. Robert is a very careful person. He's already insisting that I read the instruction booklet and is being really quite old womanish about tyres and oil.'

Mrs Treadwell secured her hat with a pin and adjusted the fur collar of her coat. 'Well, speaking of Mr Potter's taxi, I'm off to Torquay to visit Millicent. I shall return in time for dinner. And at least Robert Potter has some care about these matters, Kitty. You know my views on this insistence of yours about learning to drive.'

Kitty was quite familiar with her grandmother's opinions on her car and ignored the latter part of her statement. 'How is Mrs Craven?' Her bête noire, the formidable Millicent Craven, her grandmother's dearest friend, was convalescing at Elm House, a nursing home in Torquay, following a minor operation.

'I spoke with the nursing sister briefly this morning and she said she was much improved but seemed in low spirits, so I have a selection of treats to cheer her up.' Mrs Treadwell picked up a small wicker basket that appeared fully laden with flowers, chocolates and fruit. She peeped out of the window. 'I see the car is here. I shall see you later, Kitty dear, and do please, please be careful.'

As soon as her grandmother had departed Kitty tidied away her things and put on her own coat and hat, before collecting the smart scarlet kid leather driving gloves and silver key ring with her initial and car key that had been part of her gift from Matt.

Such a generous present had been quite unexpected as it had been her intention to purchase a car herself. Indeed, she had requested that Robert Potter look out for a suitable vehicle for her. She had only been officially walking out with Matt for a few weeks when he had gifted her the motor car and while she loved the sentiment, it had left her with a slight sense of obligation. Robert was in the foyer talking to Mary, the receptionist, when Kitty arrived downstairs.

'Are you ready for your lesson then, Miss Kitty?' he asked.

Robert was a pleasant, round-faced man of about twenty-four, a similar age to herself.

'All set.' She couldn't help noticing that he seemed rather nervous. 'I've read the car manual from cover to cover in readiness for our lesson.' Not that she had understood much of it, but she was sure that wouldn't matter once she began motoring. Hopefully her confident tone would reassure him that she was taking the matter seriously.

'Very good, miss.' They made their way out of the hotel to walk the short distance together to the large wooden shed that Kitty had rented from one of the boat owners. The air blowing from the river was cool and the pavements and road were still damp from the small downpour of rain from earlier in the day.

Kitty unlocked the padlock that secured the bolt on the front of the shed and Robert rolled the heavy wooden door back. Her heart gave a leap of pleasure when she saw the gleaming scarlet snub nose of her car.

'Now you've taken care of all the paperwork, Miss Kitty, tax and insurance?' Robert stood at the entrance to the shed twiddling his brown cloth cap anxiously in his hands.

'Yes, I've done everything just as you said. I have my license and I've read all the papers you gave me.' Kitty unlatched the car door and slid into the driver's seat impatient to get going. She was itching to start the engine and set off.

Robert climbed in and took his place in the passenger seat. 'Right then, Miss Kitty, I reckons as the first thing you should learn is what these here dials is for and what pedals is what.'

Kitty sighed, it appeared that learning to drive would be a little less exciting than she had imagined.

*

Captain Matthew Bryant took a seat opposite Inspector Greville. The policeman's compact office was, as usual, piled high with Manila folders and sheafs of papers awaiting the inspector's attention. The air was tinged slightly blue with cigarette smoke and a faint air of damp permeated the space.

'I saw from the newspaper that Hammett escaped your officers in Brixham. I presume you are confident that it was Hammett?' Matt asked.

Inspector Greville extinguished his cigarette in the small over-flowing tin ashtray on his desk. 'Yes, we'd had a tip off. Anonymous, of course, but seemingly reliable. The local constable checked it out and confirmed that the address was known to have links with Hammett's sister, Esther.'

'It was fortunate that the shots missed the constables pursuing him.' Matt frowned.

Greville nodded. 'It wasn't known that Hammett was armed. He got out of an upstairs window and fled across the roof of a nearby outhouse before dropping into one of the alleyways. It was a close-run thing. For a man known to have an impediment with his foot he moves like a cat.'

Matt could see the inspector was irked by his failure to capture the wanted man. 'Do you have any idea where he may have gone next, sir?'

The inspector leaned forward in his seat. 'It's unlikely he is still in Brixham, and all of Exeter is on the alert. Inspector Pinch is still of the opinion that he may head to Plymouth and try for a ship.'

'Do you share his opinion, sir?' Matt asked. He wasn't certain if the two inspectors were on the same page when it came to predicting Hammett's next move.

'I must admit that I wish I shared his confidence. Truthfully, Hammett is a slippery customer, and his sister is no better. She is denying all knowledge of her brother's whereabouts despite the house in Brixham being in her name.' The frown on the inspector's brow deepened. 'She told Pinch she rented it out in good faith through her lettings agent. Says she had no idea it was being used as a house of ill repute. Pah!'

Matt knew from information he and Kitty had received whilst at Enderley that Esther Hammett was thought to have a chain of such houses. 'Then you think her brother may be at another of her properties?'

Inspector Greville glanced at him. 'It seems likely, but she has an extensive portfolio, some in her own name and some under various company names.'

'Where does Esther herself reside?' Matt was curious to discover how close to Kitty Esther might be. The threatening note Kitty had received at Enderley could have come from a source dangerously close to Dartmouth.

'She gave Inspector Pinch an Exeter address not far from the waterfront. All butter wouldn't melt in her mouth apparently. Not that Pinch was buying it, mind you,' Greville replied. 'Where is Miss Underhay today, by the way? I half-expected her to be accompanying you. I spoke to her briefly on the telephone after the incident but had little news to give her at that point.'

'Kitty is taking a motoring lesson. She has acquired a car.' He didn't tell the inspector that he had bought her the Morris, or that Kitty was unaware of his visit to the police station.

The inspector's brows rose, and his moustache twitched at the news that Kitty was about to become a lady motorist. 'Will you be retaining your motorcycle, Captain Bryant?'

'Absolutely,' Matt responded.

'A description of Hammett has been widely circulated, as you know, and the public warned not to approach him if he is sighted. A discreet watch has been set on the sister's address in Exeter.'

'Thank you, sir. I shall pass this on to Kitty. She is quite concerned, the note she received at Christmas, which we believe was from Hammett threatening her, has I fear been playing on her mind.' The main reason Matt had decided to call on the inspector was to try to gain more information in order to ease Kitty's concerns. The note signed EH had warned Kitty to back off after she had advertised a generous reward hoping to uncover more of the circumstances which had led to her mother's death and interment in the cellar wall of the Glass Bottle public house some seventeen years earlier.

'Inspector Pinch is actively following up all the information he has received up to now. Should you or Miss Underhay discover anything new at all, then please pass it along as soon as possible.' The inspector sighed and straightened the fountain pen on his desk to line up with his partially completed report. 'Pinch is in overall charge of the case. However, if Hammett is discovered to still be in the bay then it will fall to me, and I think time is of the essence if we are to be successful in his apprehension.'

'Of course, sir.' Matt stood and offered his hand to the inspector. 'Kitty and I very much appreciate the assistance you have given us. Hammett is a dangerous man and, by all accounts, his sister may be more so.'

Inspector Greville nodded, his expression grave. 'I fear you may be right. Please advise Miss Underhay to take care.' His gaze locked with Matt's for a moment.

'I will, sir, I believe she is very aware of the need for caution.' Matt bade the inspector farewell and made his way along the whitewashed corridor and out of the police station. The business with Hammett made him very uncomfortable and he could only hope the man would be captured soon.

The shadowy figure of Esther Hammett was another cause for concern. When he and Kitty had met with a woman who had offered some information in Exeter shortly after Christmas, she had seemed more frightened of Esther than of Ezekiel.

Matt donned his cap and straightened his thick, woollen muffler around his neck before mounting his Sunbeam motorcycle. The weather had begun to close in, and the afternoon light was already fading. Kitty would be at the Dolphin by now and he wanted to discover if her driving lesson had been all that she had hoped it would be.

CHAPTER TWO

Her grandmother hadn't yet returned from visiting Mrs Craven when Kitty arrived back from her driving lesson. She requested tea to be sent to her grandmother's salon and made her way up the grand oak staircase to the first floor. Her head ached from all of the instructions Robert had given her. It seemed that learning to drive was to be more difficult than she had envisioned.

Kitty barely had time to remove her smart navy hat and warm coat when a knock sounded at the door. She quickly checked that her blonde curls were tidy in the mirror and opened the door to find Matt smiling at her.

Her spirits lifted. 'Come in, I wasn't sure when you would get here. I thought you were the maid with the tea.'

His lips were cold on her cheek as he greeted her with a swift kiss.

'I wanted to see how the driving instruction had gone and I've been to see our friend Inspector Greville.' Matt unbuttoned his leather greatcoat.

Kitty waited impatiently until he hung his coat on the small, bent wood stand and removed his scarf and cap. She was too eager to hear what he had discovered to be cross that he hadn't thought to ask her to accompany him. 'What did the inspector have to say? Do they think they know where Hammett might be? Are they any closer to capturing him?'

Matt dropped down on the chenille-covered sofa beside her, grinning at her eager questioning. 'Inspector Pinch feels that

Hammett may have fled the immediate area. Esther apparently has an Exeter address near the waterfront, and they are observing her and her house there.'

Kitty breathed a sigh of relief that Esther Hammett was some miles away. She had secretly been dreading that the woman might be more local. The discovery that Hammett had been only a few miles away at Brixham had been most unnerving. 'That makes me feel a little easier. Although I suppose Ezekiel could be at another of his sister's properties.'

'Inspector Pinch is following up all the information he has received. Hopefully, they will catch Hammett soon. I feel that to shoot at the police was a grave mistake on his part. They will be very eager to ensure he is caught now.' Matt gave her hand a reassuring pat just as the sound of cups jingling in the corridor announced the imminent arrival of the tea trolley.

Matt opened the door for the smartly uniformed maid to wheel in the trolley. Once the girl had been dismissed Kitty busied herself setting out the cups.

'So, tell me all, the motoring instruction, how was it? Am I to see you haring through Churston soon?' Matt asked, his eyes twinkling as she passed him his tea.

'Robert Potter is an old maid,' she declared as she helped herself to a piece of shortbread to accompany her drink.

Matt laughed. 'Why? What happened?'

'We did not even leave the shed! He had me practising something called double declutching and using the trafficators until my eyes were crossed.' She huffed as she took her place back beside Matt.

'I take it that becoming a lady motorist is a little more difficult than you had thought?' Matt tried and failed to hide his grin behind his teacup.

Kitty glared at him. 'I'm sure I shall master it.'

The door to the salon opened and Kitty's grandmother entered. 'Good afternoon, Matthew. I thought I spied the Sunbeam parked outside.'

Kitty prepared a cup for her grandmother while the older woman removed her outdoor clothing.

'Thank you, Kitty dear.' She accepted her tea and sank down on the armchair beside the fire with a tired sigh.

'How was Mrs Craven?' Kitty asked, concerned at the weariness on her grandmother's face.

Mrs Treadwell took a restorative sip from her cup. 'Truthfully, Kitty, I'm really not sure. I'm glad you're here, Matthew, as Millicent wishes to see you as soon as possible. She feels that there is something not quite right at the nursing home. And she suggested that it would be better if Kitty were to accompany you as she doesn't want anyone to believe it is a professional consultation.'

Kitty refrained from rolling her eyes at this. 'I see. Did she say what she thought might be wrong? I thought Elm House had a reputation as one of the best convalescent homes in the bay.'

'It does, my dear. Doctor Marsh, who took it over during the summer, has spent a great deal of money ensuring that there is the very best of everything. Apparently he was in Harley Street before and is highly regarded, I believe. Millicent was behaving very oddly. I was tempted to enquire with the nursing sister if it might be a side effect from her medication, but Millicent was so jumpy I thought better of it.' Mrs Treadwell took another sip from her cup.

'How very peculiar.' Kitty helped herself to another piece of shortbread.

'Mrs Craven isn't usually given to fanciful imaginings,' Matt agreed. 'Perhaps we should visit tomorrow afternoon?'

Kitty looked at her grandmother. 'I can arrange my duties here if you can spare me for a couple of hours?'

Her grandmother nodded. 'Of course, my dear. I would feel much easier if you would both visit Elm House and judge the situation for yourselves and decide if there is any substance in Millicent's concerns.'

After finishing their tea Kitty accompanied Matt downstairs to the lobby. 'I wonder what's going on with Mrs Craven?'

'It sounds rather peculiar. I didn't like to ask in front of your grandmother in case it might be a delicate matter, but what is Mrs C recuperating from?' Matt asked as they paused at the foot of the staircase.

Kitty laughed. 'She had a bunion correction. It has been rather painful, I believe, and it would have been difficult going up and down the stairs at her home, so she decided it would be better to stay at Elm House for a few weeks to convalesce until she is more mobile.'

Matt grinned. 'Poor Mrs C. I'm glad it wasn't for anything too serious though. I'll see you tomorrow then, Kitty.'

She glanced towards the reception desk where Mary was pretending not to watch them. 'I'll call for you on my way. Hopefully I shall be driving myself soon, if Robert Potter ever permits me to leave the shed.'

The dimple flashed in Matt's cheek as he placed a swift farewell kiss on her cheek. 'Until tomorrow.'

Kitty blushed as he strode away calling a cheery farewell to Mary as he left the hotel.

Mr Potter senior called for her promptly the following afternoon. He tugged his cap politely as he assisted her into the back of his cab, before resuming his place in the driver's seat.

'I reckon as you'll be taking yourself places soon then, Miss Underhay. Robert says as your little car is proper smart.'

Kitty adjusted the warm blue tartan travel rug over her knees. 'I hope so, Mr Potter. It's not that I don't love using your taxi, but it would be nice to be independent. Robert is being very patient with me. I must admit that I hadn't realised driving was quite so tricky.'

Mr Potter steered his motor through Dartmouth's narrow streets towards the ferry ready to cross the river. ''Tis only practise, miss.'

Kitty hoped he was right. She had been feeling a little deflated following her first lesson. They were soon across the Dart and speeding up the hill towards Matt's house near the golf club at Churston. It was a grey, cold day and the wintery sun rarely managed to show its face through the clouds.

Matt had clearly been looking out for her to arrive as he came out of his house as soon as the car pulled up. Since he was not riding his Sunbeam, he was attired in an olive-green Harris Tweed overcoat and a matching trilby hat. Kitty thought he looked most distinguished.

'Good afternoon, Mr Potter,' he greeted the driver as he joined her on the back seat.

'Well, let us go and see what is ruffling Mrs Craven's feathers.' Matt smiled at Kitty.

'Hmm, it's very strange for Mrs Craven to be so perturbed. I do rather fear though that she has acquired a taste for detection after the incidents at the Pavilion Theatre and the Imperial Hotel last year,' Kitty remarked as they drove along the seafront heading for Mead Lane and Elm House Nursing Home.

The convalescent home was a large building in the Victorian gothic style with a small, high rounded turret at one end of the red brick building. It had a prominent position overlooking the bay with tiered gardens leading down toward the seafront. Kitty imagined that in better weather it must look rather splendid.

Mr Potter pulled to a stop on the gravel forecourt outside the imposing mock medieval metal-studded oak front doors.

'If you could return for us in an hour and a half, Mr Potter,' Matt instructed as they clambered out of the taxi.

Kitty screwed up her nose. Personally, she would have said an hour of Mrs Craven's company would probably have been sufficient.

They obeyed the notice at the entrance to push open the door and found themselves inside a small but smart square reception area with a fine oak parquet floor. An intricately carved arts and crafts staircase led to the upper floors, and a brisk looking middle-aged woman in a dark green dress stood behind the oak reception desk.

They approached the receptionist. 'We're here to visit Mrs Millicent Craven.' Kitty smiled at the woman as she spoke.

She received a tight smile back from the receptionist in response. 'Very good. Your names, please?' The woman produced a burgundy leather-bound book from beneath the desk.

Kitty gave their names and the woman directed them to one of the two corridors leading off from the lobby. 'Mrs Craven is usually to be found in the public rooms at this time of day. I shall arrange refreshments for you.'

Kitty exchanged a glance with Matt, and they made their way along the cream painted corridor adorned with rather gloomy paintings to a large room with splendid views of the sea. The other walls were lined with bookcases and the ceiling was panelled in carved ornate oak squares. A roaring fire blazed in the huge imposing fireplace. Comfortable burgundy leather upholstered chairs were placed in small convivial groups around the room. Everything spoke of comfortable opulence.

Mrs Craven was seated with a view of the sea. Her affected leg was raised on a low stool covered with a tartan patterned woollen rug, while a newspaper lay open on her lap. They had scarcely had chance to step into the room when her clarion tones reached them.

'Matthew, Kitty, over here.'

An elderly gentleman with a military moustache who had been dozing peacefully in a chair beside the fire opened an eye to glare at them as they walked past him.

Mrs Craven set her newspaper aside and straightened up in her seat as Kitty and Matt each took a chair, one on either side of her. She leaned towards Matt. 'Matthew, I'm so glad you're here. I have something I need to discuss urgently with you.' She glanced around furtively after she had spoken, but there was no one else besides the man they had already seen present in the room.

'Grams said you were worried about something?' Kitty adopted the same low tone that Mrs Craven had used.

A very young maid in a dark green uniform with white apron and cap approached carefully steering a laden tea trolley. Something about the girl's features and curly auburn hair beneath the cap seemed oddly familiar.

'Dolly, Dolly Miller?' Kitty asked as the girl stationed the trolley beside them. 'Alice's sister?'

The girl flushed to the roots of her hair. 'Yes, miss.' She poured the tea carefully from a silver-coloured teapot and passed out the floral-patterned china cups.

'I hadn't realised that you were employed here. How lovely.' Kitty smiled at the girl.

'I just started here a few days ago. Will there be anything else, miss, sir?' Dolly asked, clearly very self-conscious in her new employment.

'No, thank you, this all looks splendid. I shall tell Alice that I've seen you,' Kitty reassured her.

Dolly smiled nervously and hurried away.

'Alice said that Dolly had left school and was taking a live-in position. I hadn't realised it was here,' Kitty remarked to her companions.

'Hmm, well if I were her, I would look for another position elsewhere,' Mrs Craven remarked. She took a sip of tea and pulled a face. 'Ugh, I shall be glad when this wretched foot is healed, and I can return home. That is if I make it out of here in one piece.'

'Whatever do you mean?' Kitty asked. She could see why her grandmother had been concerned.

'There is something wrong here. Very wrong.' Mrs Craven glanced around her once again to ensure they were not overheard. 'There have been strange noises in the night, people appearing and disappearing, and then there are the deaths.' She nodded her head for emphasis.

Kitty looked helplessly at Matt.

'What do you mean by deaths? I suppose in this kind of establishment that there must inevitably be some deaths,' Matt said.

Mrs Craven fixed him with a steely gaze. 'I am well aware of that. No, I'm talking about murder. These deaths were not expected, and I am not the only person here who has noticed.'

'You feel there are suspicious circumstances around some of these deaths?' Matt asked. 'Do you have details?'

'Lady Wellings, she passed away the day before yesterday. The woman was perfectly well though. One of those ladies that enjoys bad health, complains of nerves and neurosis, liked plenty of fuss, and of course she could afford it. Her late husband, Lord Wellings, was the Wellings, you know, of Wellings water biscuits. Well, she had been in here playing cards with myself, General Ackland and Mrs Fisher and was perfectly well, as fit as a flea. She'd had an argument the day before with that useless nephew of hers, Roderick Harmer. He'd been begging for money yet again. Then pouf, the next day she was dead.' Mrs Craven settled back in her seat. 'So, what do you think of that?'

Kitty exchanged another glance with Matt.

'I understand your concern, Mrs Craven, but Lady Wellings could easily have had a serious underlying health issue that you may not have been aware of. I take it that she was not a young lady?' Matt said.

'Poppycock! The woman told me herself that physically she was perfectly fit. She was here for a nervous ailment. That nephew of hers wanted to get his hands on her money and she refused him. She told us so herself. Gaming debts; she was considering changing her will.' Mrs Craven nodded sagely. 'Then the next thing you know, well.'

'You suspect her nephew of harming her?' Kitty asked.

Mrs Craven glared at her. 'Not him personally. He arranged for her death.'

'What do you mean?' Matt beat Kitty to the question.

'Roderick Harmer paid to have his aunt killed before she could disinherit him,' Mrs Craven said.

Kitty frowned. 'If you know this then surely the police—'

'I have no proof. That's where you come in,' Mrs Craven cut Kitty's sentence off.

'What makes you think this is the case then? You must have a reason for your suspicions?' Matt asked.

'Roderick Harmer spent quite some time with Sister Carmichael and with that dreadful, sneaky little orderly, Dodds, before his aunt passed away. I only overheard bits and pieces of the conversations, but it was enough to worry me when I thought about it after Lady Wellings died.'

Kitty's expression must have betrayed her thought that this whole affair was probably the result of Mrs Craven's imagination.

The elderly woman glowered at her and continued. 'And why did Doctor Marsh give up his Harley Street practice, hmm? Something fishy there too. Not to mention these so-called patients that arrive late in the evening with no luggage and then are gone again before dawn without so much as a by your leave.' She folded her arms and looked at Matt with a steely glint in her eyes.

'Have you spoken to Doctor Marsh or the sister in charge about Lady Wellings's death?' Kitty asked.

'That Sister Carmichael is involved in this scheme up to her scrawny neck. I wouldn't be at all surprised if she and Doctor Marsh were more than just professionally involved from what I have observed. And he is a married man too, not that his wife is exactly a lady from what little I've seen of her, for all her airs and graces.' Mrs Craven pursed her lips in disapproval.

'Gracious.' Kitty was at a loss.

'Good afternoon, Mrs Craven, I see you have visitors.'

Kitty, startled at the unexpected male voice, spilt a little of her untouched tea into the saucer. She twisted in her seat to see a tall, bearded man in his late forties, wearing an immaculately tailored grey suit emerge from the shadows to greet them.

'Forgive me, dear lady, I fear I surprised you.' He inclined his head towards Kitty.

'Doctor Marsh, may I present my friend's granddaughter, Miss Underhay, and her friend, Captain Bryant.' Mrs Craven performed the introductions in a stiff tone.

'I'm delighted to meet you both. Mrs Craven here is recovering splendidly but I fear her spirits have been a little low these last few days?' He made a show of checking Mrs Craven's pulse, holding her wrist between his thumb and forefingers and timing her heart rate against his awfully expensive-looking gold wristwatch. A thick gold ring was on his wedding finger.

'Yes, I'm afraid she has been rather low of late. I fear that her friend, Lady Wellings's, unexpected demise has greatly upset her.' Kitty seized the opportunity.

Doctor Marsh released Mrs Craven's wrist. 'Ah yes, dear Lady Wellings, a sad loss to us all. A sudden loss, but alas not unexpected. The poor lady had an underlying heart condition.'

'Oh dear, I expect her nephew will be terribly distressed. He visited her quite often, I believe.' Kitty gambled on Mrs Craven's information about the nephew being correct and she was keen to see Doctor Marsh's reaction.

Doctor Marsh's ready smile vanished for a second. 'I believe he is. Mr Harmer was quite devoted to his aunt.'

Mrs Craven made a noise that sounded rather like a snort, which turned into a cough.

'Sister Carmichael will attend to your dressings on your foot again later, Mrs Craven. Now you must all please excuse me while I speak to Mr Spears.' Doctor Marsh glided silently away in the direction of the elderly man beside the fireplace.

CHAPTER THREE

'That man is far too pleased with himself,' Mrs Craven muttered once Doctor Marsh was out of earshot. 'Creeping around the place, snooping, eavesdropping.'

'He sounded quite satisfied with the cause of Lady Wellings's death,' Matt remarked. He too had taken a dislike to the man, but he couldn't quite say why.

'Well, he would be, wouldn't he? After that no-good nephew, Harmer, argued with Lady Wellings about her will, I saw him having a very cosy tête-à-tête with Doctor Marsh tucked around the corner of the building. I suppose they thought themselves unobserved, but I was taking a handkerchief from my drawer and peeped out of my window and saw them.'

Matt could see that Mrs Craven was not to be deflected.

'What would you like us to do?' he asked.

'Investigate, of course. Find out about Doctor Marsh and look at the deaths. Lady Wellings, Mrs Palesbury and Miss Wordsley. They have all passed away in the last two months. Miss Wordsley was only a young girl, not quite twenty-one. Then there are the mysterious visitors.' Mrs Craven glanced around her. 'As soon as I can walk with a cane I shall be out of here. At least no one has a financial motive to benefit from my death. My only sister, Regina, is in Argentina and is a wealthy woman in her own right.'

'Are you sure you don't wish to speak to the police?' Kitty asked.

Mrs Craven snorted. 'As if Inspector Greville would take any notice. Besides, Doctor Marsh would convince him that I was deranged and ready for the funny farm. No, proof, that's what is required before the police are involved.'

Matt bowed to the inevitable. 'Very well, if it will put your mind at ease, I shall make a few discreet enquiries.'

'But please do be careful, Mrs Craven. Doctor Marsh and Sister Carmichael may be very unhappy if they feel you are making… um, well, still as yet unfounded allegations about them,' Kitty warned.

Mrs Craven scoffed at her. 'I assure you I shall take every precaution. Now, if I uncover anything further, I shall pass the information on to your grandmother, Kitty, when she visits or if I can get to a telephone, I may call you.'

Dolly reappeared beside them. 'Begging your pardon but there is a taxi waiting for you outside, sir, miss.'

'Thank you, Dolly dear.' Kitty smiled at the girl and they took their leave of Mrs Craven.

Kitty was silent until they were safely ensconced on the rear seat of Mr Potter's motor car and heading back towards Galmpton.

'Well, what did you make of all that?' Matt asked. He was keen to know Kitty's thoughts. She had, after all, known Mrs Craven for far longer than he had. 'Do we think a murder has been committed?'

'She is clearly concerned about arrangements within the home. It does seem somewhat far-fetched though to think Lady Wellings may have been murdered.' Kitty frowned. 'Although, I must admit I didn't take to Doctor Marsh at all. I wonder what Sister Carmichael is like?'

'I think I'll ask Doctor Carter if he knows anything about Doctor Marsh. After all they are in the same profession so he may well have some connections,' Matt said. He wasn't really sure if any enquiries would come to much or if it was all a bit of a mare's nest inspired by Mrs Craven's overactive imagination. Doctor Carter often assisted the police and they had come to know him well during the other cases they had been involved with.

It could all just be down to Doctor Marsh's unfortunate manner. The man had been perfectly polite and there was nothing to suggest anything was amiss. The talk about Lady Wellings's intentions of disinheriting her nephew may simply have been a coincidence. He decided to ask Doctor Carter about the other deaths at the home that Mrs Craven had mentioned too. He might as well be thorough about the matter since he knew Mrs Craven would be unlikely to let the matter rest without a great deal of convincing.

'I shall speak to Alice though. If there is something wrong at the home, I wouldn't wish young Dolly to be caught up in it all. She's only just turned fourteen.' Kitty frowned. 'I know Mrs Craven can get odd ideas in her head from time to time but I have never known her to be like this and she did seem to be genuinely frightened.'

Matt nodded. He too thought he had detected fear behind Mrs Craven's bravado, especially when Doctor Marsh had suddenly appeared beside them in the lounge. 'I agree. Does your grandmother intend to visit Elm House again tomorrow?'

'I think so. I'll warn her to be on her guard and tell her a little of what Mrs Craven has said. Then if she learns anything new, she can pass it on to us.' Kitty shivered as she looked out of the car window at the fading light across the bay. Her face pale under the brim of her navy hat.

'I'll call on you tomorrow evening, we can compare notes. And perhaps a night out might be in order? I'm sure Alice will be able to recommend a film at one of the picture houses,' Matt suggested.

Kitty's elfin features immediately brightened. 'That sounds lovely. Perhaps a fish supper too?'

He laughed and they parted at his home. He stood at the door and waved as Mr Potter turned his motor car to take Kitty back to Dartmouth.

He shivered as he stepped over the threshold into his hall. The evening was rapidly turning damp and a mist was already starting to form over the common. His housekeeper had left a cottage pie in the oven for his supper and had banked the fire so that the house was warm.

Later that evening Matt took his supper on a tray while listening to the radio. Although his house was warm and snug, he couldn't help feeling lonely with Kitty back at the Dolphin. In the years after the war, he had welcomed time spent alone. The death of his wife and child had been grievous and when not working he had done his best to shut himself away from society, burying himself in his work.

Now, since he had met Kitty, things had changed, and he found himself increasingly missing her company when they were apart. The conversation with Mrs Craven continued to play on his mind. He decided to telephone Doctor Carter in the morning to try and find some background information on Doctor Marsh and Elm House. After washing his plate in the kitchen, he checked the doors and windows were secure and headed upstairs for an early night.

Matt woke suddenly, unsure of what had disturbed him. The room was still in darkness and he lay still for a moment allowing his sight to adjust while he listened. Outside the window a tawny owl called for its mate and the wind gusted around the chimney pots.

The luminous hands on the dial of his bedside clock gave off a faint glow and he squinted to read the time. Two thirty a.m. Matt was about to close his eyes and settle back under the comforting warmth of his eiderdown when he heard it again. A faint sound from the downstairs of his house.

Every sense was now on the alert as the loose floorboard near the bureau in the sitting room where he kept his papers emitted a familiar creak. Matt sat up and carefully slid open his bedside drawer. The cold metal of his service revolver was soon within his grasp. He silently extracted the gun and closed the drawer.

He continued to listen. Someone was downstairs and he guessed from the sounds, they were conducting some sort of search. He recognised the scrape of his bureau drawer opening and the squeak of the hinge on the cabinet door.

Matt reached for his dressing gown and tugged it on before sliding his feet into his slippers. The revolver firmly in his grasp he picked his way carefully across the bedroom floor avoiding the loose boards that might alert the intruder.

He made his way silently down the stairs in the dark. Ahead of him, visible in the hall, he saw the faint flickering of a light through the open door of his sitting room. He moved down another step and a board gave a betraying creak under his weight. Matt grimaced and held his breath as the light in the sitting room was immediately extinguished.

He tightened his grip on the handle of the revolver.

'Who's there!' he called out, wishing, not for the first time, that he had a dog in the house.

A male figure, clad from head to toe in black, darted from the sitting room into the hall and on into the dining room with Matt in pursuit.

'Stop or I'll shoot!' Too late, the intruder ran out through the open French door and over the hedge into the blackness of the common beyond.

Broken glass crunched under Matt's feet as he stood, frustrated at the open door, the cold night air swirling about him while he caught his breath. He picked his way carefully to the light switch to turn on the light and see the damage.

The burglar had smashed one of the small panes in the French door and forced the latch in order to gain access. Shards of broken glass were strewn over the parquet tiles and embedded in the Turkish carpet. Matt walked through to his sitting room and turned on the light in there. He had expected to discover missing items. He had a small collection of silver trinkets and some nice objet d'art but they were all still in place in the cabinet.

The roll-top of the bureau was open, however, and it was evident his papers had been moved. Matt reached for his cigarette case and lit up. Had he disturbed the intruder before he could steal anything? Or was this a very different kind of break-in, and if so, for what purpose?

He poured himself a small tot of whisky and picked up the telephone to alert the police.

CHAPTER FOUR

Kitty arrived at Matt's home shortly before ten, at the same time as his housekeeper. He had telephoned telling her of the break-in at breakfast time, knowing that she was an early riser. The police had already attended, and Matt had contacted a glazier and a locksmith to repair and secure the door.

'Goodness me, Captain Bryant, whatever is the world coming too?' His housekeeper, a comfortable, elderly lady tutted and shook her head when she saw the damage.

'It's awful. It must have been horribly unnerving hearing someone in the house.' Kitty surveyed the broken pane with a critical eye. She was concerned for Matt. The lack of sleep had left him with dark shadows beneath his eyes and he looked dreadful.

She accompanied him into the lounge while the housekeeper went to make coffee and deal with the tradesmen.

'Did you get a look at the intruder at all?' Kitty asked as she perched on the edge of the sofa and drew off her gloves.

Matt shook his head. 'Not much, he sprinted out of here quite quickly when he heard me on the stairs. Male, medium height, dressed in dark clothing.' He paused and shrugged. 'It's very strange.'

'And nothing at all was taken?' Kitty asked. Matt had a few nice small pieces of silver and a couple of ornaments that surely would have been stolen if money were the motive behind the robbery.

Matt shook his head once more. 'Even the small amount I keep in the bureau drawer to pay the window cleaner and the gardener was left untouched. Yet I think he would have had time to put things in a bag or his pockets before he was disturbed. The only things that appeared to be of interest were my papers. He seemed to be searching for something specific, but I have no idea what it could be.'

Matt's housekeeper carried in a tray of coffee and placed it on the low polished table in front of them. 'The locksmith is here now, sir, and the glazier has finished the repair. I've asked him to send the bill.'

Matt thanked her and the woman returned to her duties. Kitty poured them both a cup of coffee from the tall, slim silver pot.

'Do you think this intrusion may be to do with a case you're working on, or have worked on recently?' she asked as she handed him a cup.

'Perhaps, but I don't keep any business things here. They are in the filing cabinet at my office.' Matt ladled sugar into his cup and gave his drink a brisk stir. 'The last cases I worked on were for some of the hotels in Torquay who were having problems with petty thefts. The cases have been to court and dealt with already.'

Kitty frowned as she added a generous serving of cream to her coffee. 'It seems that someone believes you have something that they want. What about your office? Do you think they may try there?'

Matt's office was above a gentleman's tailoring establishment in Torquay town centre. It shared a landing with a company that manufactured dentures. She knew he was at his office most weekdays for at least part of the day to see clients, make and receive calls and to attend to clerical tasks.

Matt sipped his drink as he considered her question. 'I don't know. I can't think for the life of me what they may have been after.'

'You don't suppose it could be connected with our visit to Mrs Craven, do you?' Kitty asked. It would be odd, but if someone had thought their visit was initiated by a tip-off, or that Matt had uncovered some evidence of wrongdoing, then they may have believed he would have documents in his house.

'It's possible I suppose.' Matt set his cup down and sighed. 'I'll telephone Doctor Carter as I had intended after lunch and I'll see what he knows about Doctor Marsh.'

Kitty returned her own cup to the tray. 'I had better return to the Dolphin. Try and get some rest, and I shall see you later?'

'Of course, I'm looking forward to our evening. Thank you for coming.' He gave her a weary smile as she stood and tugged on her gloves.

'The bus is due in a few minutes. I shall be so pleased when I can drive myself,' she declared as he walked her to the front door.

Matt dropped a kiss on her lips. 'Take care, and I'll see you tonight.'

The stop for the bus was a short walk from Matt's house, and it arrived promptly. Kitty was soon on her way back to Kingswear to take the passenger ferry back across the river, her head stuffed full of romantic daydreams. The bus was quite full, and she found herself wedged against the window by a large middle-aged lady with a wicker shopping basket perched upon her knees.

'Weather is brighter today,' the woman observed.

'Yes, much better,' Kitty responded politely as the basket slipped and jabbed her leg when the bus rode over a pothole.

'I don't usually take this bus, but I've been run off my feet the last few days what with my mistress being took bad,' the woman confided. 'Now she's gone to that posh new nursing home in Torquay and her son has given me a massive list of things he wants fetched for her. As if I haven't got enough to do already, what with sorting out the house and her clothes and things.'

Kitty's ears pricked up. 'Which home has she gone to?'

'Elm House, up top of Mead Lane. I have to get all these things and then go back before lunchtime as the missus's son can take them to her. I was going to go to Paignton but one of the things on the list I can only get in Dartmouth.' The woman adjusted her basket again.

'A friend of my grandmother's is at Elm House now,' Kitty said. It struck her as quite a coincidence.

'Him as runs it is from London, so missus's son said. Not as I trusts Mr Leonard's word much. Between you, me and the gatepost he's a bit of a one. I was surprised as he encouraged his mother to go there, knowing how pricey it is. Fond of the money is Mr Leonard, especially spending other people's money, but the missus has been proper low. Pneumonia. Her got caught in that cold spell over Christmas and never picked up. Then Mr Leonard's friend recommended this 'ere home.' The woman's round, pleasant face creased with concern.

'Oh dear, I do hope she recovers her health soon. What is your mistress's name? My grandmother's friend may know her,' Kitty asked.

'Mrs Pearson, of Bourne House,' the woman replied promptly. 'A nice lady she is but her husband, he were no good, God rest his soul, and Master Leonard takes after his father. Given her years of worry he has with his wild ways. Ah well, best hope as this here Doctor Marsh is worth his coppers and my poor mistress comes home soon.'

The bus jolted to a halt beside the stop and the passengers began to disembark ready to board the ferry. Kitty's loquacious companion was claimed by an acquaintance and she went off talking happily with her friend.

Kitty followed at the back of the queue pondering on the coincidences of hearing about Elm House again so randomly.

When she arrived back at the Dolphin Kitty paused to ask Mary to send Alice to come and see her, before entering her small office at the rear of the reception desk. The conversation with the woman on the bus had been oddly unsettling. It had also reminded her that young Dolly was at Elm House. Combined with the attempted burglary at Matt's home she felt curiously ill at ease.

She settled herself at her desk and opened her accounts, ready to start reconciling the invoices. Kitty had scarcely drawn the cap from her fountain pen when there was a tap at the door and Alice's beaming face appeared.

'Mary said as you wanted me, Miss Kitty?'

'Yes, come in, Alice, and close the door.' She smiled as she spoke so her friend would realise that she was not in any kind of trouble.

Alice took a seat on the chair opposite her, straightening the strap on her white apron as she did so.

'I bumped into your sister, Dolly, yesterday at Elm House when I was visiting Mrs Craven,' Kitty said.

Alice's expression changed to one of mild anxiety. 'Is she all right? How did she look? Fourteen is full young to take a live-in post even if it is only across the bay. Mother would have preferred her to stay at home really.'

Kitty rushed to reassure her. 'She seemed very well and looked very nice in her uniform. I hadn't realised where the post was when you said she had found employment.'

Alice relaxed. 'It were all a bit sudden really. She had registered with the servants' employment agency in Paignton. Mother went with her and they said as they had a request for a maid-come-kitchen help. Mother was a bit concerned at her leaving home as I said but, well, space is tight, and the pay were all right including board and lodgings. She gets a half day off every Tuesday and every other Sunday as she can come home. Mother said as the head housekeeper who did the interview seemed nice and the room was good so she give Dolly her permission.'

'The home does seem to be very luxurious. Do you know if your mother met Doctor Marsh, the owner at all?' Kitty asked. Mrs Craven's concerns had made her curious about the owner of Elm House.

Alice shook her head, loosening one of the copper curls from under her cap. 'No, miss. She did see a Sister Carmichael though. She's over the nursing staff so Dolly said. Is Mrs Craven doing all right, miss? Getting better?'

'I believe so. She did say though that she had noticed a lot of visitors to the home, coming and going at odd times of the night. It was bothering her that it seemed peculiar.' Kitty had given some thought about what to say to Alice. She didn't wish to worry her friend unduly or to place little Dolly or her position in any kind of jeopardy.

'Hmm, that sounds a bit strange, miss. You would have thought as visitors would come during the day or early evening. Shall I ask our Dolly to keep her eyes and ears open?' Alice asked.

'If you would. I'm sure it's nothing but I wouldn't wish your sister to run into any problems if it does turn out that something is amiss. There have been a few deaths there lately too, which may be normal for that kind of establishment, but, well, Matt's house was broken into last night too. It may not be connected but we can't be certain,' Kitty said.

'Oh dear, miss. Is Captain Bryant all right?' Alice's eyes widened in shock at news of the burglary.

'Yes, nothing was taken, but it's worried us both just in case there is a connection with Elm House,' Kitty said.

'Dolly'll be home Sunday, miss, for her dinner and to see us all. I'll have a word with her then and see what she says. I know what you mean, miss. Our Dolly is a bright girl, she'll keep a watch out. I'm glad as nothing was taken from Captain Bryant. Whatever is the world coming too?' She could see her friend turning things over in her mind. 'I'll not mention anything to Mother or Father. You know what Mother can be like.'

Kitty smiled. Mrs Miller had already visited Kitty a few months earlier to express her concerns that Alice had become entangled in various murders alongside Kitty. It had taken all of her powers of persuasion to get Mrs Miller to agree that Alice could continue accompanying her as her maid as occasions demanded.

'It's probably nothing. The burglary may well simply be an ill-timed coincidence. And you know what Mrs Craven can be like. No doubt with time on her hands and her foot being so painful she may simply have fallen prey to all kinds of irrational imaginings.'

Alice returned her smile. 'Most likely, miss.' She stood ready to take her leave.

'Oh, there is one more thing. Captain Bryant and I intend to visit a picture house this evening. We thought it might take our minds off everything. Is there a film that you think we would enjoy?' Kitty knew Alice loved attending the various picture houses. She read all the magazines and could give chapter and verse on the love lives of various film stars.

'*No Funny Business* is showing again with Laurence Olivier and Gertrude Lawrence. That was a good one, a comedy. You might like that. That's on in Dartmouth, save you going across the river to Paignton,' Alice said.

'That sounds perfect. Thank you.' Kitty felt a little light relief might be welcome after Matt's stressful night and the strange visit to Elm House.

'I hope as you'll both enjoy it, miss.'

Alice disappeared back to her chores and Kitty forced herself to focus on her own work, only breaking off for a cheese sandwich at her desk for lunch. It had grown quite dark and she was finishing the last of her notes by the light of her desk lamp when her grandmother returned from her visit to Elm House.

'Kitty darling, are you still working? Do stop now, dear, you'll strain your eyes. Mary is sending up a tea trolley, come and take a break.'

'I'm just finishing, Grams.' Kitty recognised she had been summoned and wondered if her grandmother had further information from Mrs Craven.

She checked the column of figures she had been working on and closed the accounts register before switching off her desk lamp and leaving her office, locking the door behind her.

By the time she entered her grandmother's salon the trolley had arrived, and her grandmother was seated beside the fire.

'It is turning very cold out there. A breeze is blowing in from the estuary,' Mrs Treadwell complained as Kitty took the vacant armchair opposite her.

'Matt and I are planning an evening at the picture house tonight. Alice has recommended a film and Matt has promised me a fish supper.' Kitty smiled at her grandmother. 'At least I hope he feels up to it after the disturbance at his house last night.'

Her grandmother had been present when she had taken Matt's telephone call at breakfast.

Mrs Treadwell took a sip of her tea. 'I take it you've heard nothing more? Matthew was lucky that nothing was stolen and that he wasn't attacked. Some of these fellows can be desperate if one is to believe all one reads in the newspapers. Robberies, motoring accidents and petty thefts.' She tutted over her teacup.

'How was Mrs Craven today?' Kitty changed the subject before her grandmother could switch from the dangers of housebreakers to the perils of motoring.

Her grandmother's brow creased in a frown. 'Truthfully, Kitty dear, I'm really not sure. She tells me that her foot is healing although it is still quite painful. She has managed to take a few steps using a cane for support. She remains very troubled by Lady Wellings's death too.'

'Matt is making some discreet enquiries so perhaps he may be able to reassure her on that point soon. Coincidentally I met a woman on the bus to Kingswear today who said her mistress had just been admitted to Elm House to recover from a pneumonia. A Mrs Pearson of Bourne House near Paignton.' Kitty helped herself to a finger of fruitcake from the trolley.

'Pearson, Pearson, oh where do I know that name from? I'm certain Millicent will know,' her grandmother mused.

'She has a son called Leonard.' Kitty hastily plucked a stray currant from her skirt before her grandmother could reprimand her for making crumbs.

Mrs Treadwell's expression cleared. 'Yes, I know her, she attends the lady's guild. A very quiet, respectable person, widowed. The son, I believe, is rather wild and keeps unsuitable company. She may provide a friendly face for Millicent. Perhaps she may even help to distract her.'

Matt called for Kitty that evening as arranged and they set off from the Dolphin together to walk the short distance to the picture house. Her grandmother had been right when she had warned of the cold wind sweeping up the river from the sea. Kitty was more than glad of the fur collar on her best black coat and her warm fur-lined gloves.

'I had thought you might wish to cancel our outing after last night,' Kitty said as they rounded a street corner in order to cross the road.

'I do feel a little tired, but I think an evening out would do us both good.' Matt smiled at her as they joined the small queue at the ticket office.

'Did you make any progress with Mrs Craven's concerns today?' Kitty asked as Matt handed over the money for their tickets.

'A little. Nothing of much interest. I'll tell you after the film. Let's just enjoy ourselves for a while.' He grinned at her as they made their way further inside the building to take their seats in the auditorium.

Kitty settled back in her seat next to Matt to enjoy the film. As Alice had promised it was a light comedy. Matt however soon had his eyes closed and much to Kitty's amusement he slept throughout the programme. He roused only at the end when the lights in the auditorium came on and everyone began to move.

'I'm so sorry, Kitty.' He looked sheepishly at her. 'I must have been more tired than I thought.'

'It's quite all right. You had so little sleep last night I'm not surprised you nodded off.' Kitty laughed as she stood ready to make her way back along the row and out of the cinema.

Matt straightened his hat and tucked her hand into the crook of his arm. 'Let's go and get our fish supper. I promise I'll make it up to you.'

The pavements were busy outside the picture house and it seemed many others were also headed for the fish and chip bar.

'Now then, tell me what you learned from Doctor Carter?' Kitty asked once they were in the small queue for the counter.

Matt checked that no one appeared to be paying them any attention. 'Doctor Marsh did indeed have a small practice in Harley Street but apparently has had some health issues himself. Congenital heart problems, Doctor Carter thought from what he remembered hearing at the time. He used to know him quite well. They trained at the same hospital in London, but Marsh was junior I believe to Doctor Carter. Anyway, apparently Doctor Marsh was married in the summer shortly before he decided to purchase Elm House and move to Torquay for his health. He was very involved with the medical students at the hospital in London and seems to have been well thought of.'

'Oh.' Kitty was oddly disappointed. 'It seems we have maligned the man then and Mrs Craven may be confused.'

Matt grinned. 'It would seem so.'

'Well, I blame it upon my acquaintance with you. I never used to view people with such a jaundiced eye, suspecting them all of wrongdoing and criminal intent.' Kitty's smile widened as she spoke. She did feel a trifle ashamed that she had allowed an irrational dislike for Doctor Marsh to have coloured her view of him.

'I don't suppose he said anything about the, um, patients who have passed away?' Kitty murmured as they took a few steps closer to the server. Her stomach rumbled as the delicious aroma of hot chips filled the steamy air.

'He said he would look into that.'

Matt broke off the conversation to give their order to the man serving behind the counter. A few moments later they stepped back out into the chilly night air clutching their hot parcels of fish and chips wrapped in newspaper.

'Let's go back to the Dolphin. We can eat these in the dining room,' Kitty suggested.

They hurried back to the hotel and slipped along the corridor to the kitchen to collect cutlery and plates before finally taking a seat in a tucked away corner of the hotel dining room. A wall lamp illuminated their table with a soft pinkish light while the rest of the room remained in shadowy darkness.

'At least we can put Mrs Craven's mind at ease about Doctor Marsh,' Kitty said as she cut into the crisp batter encasing her fish. She savoured the scent of the vinegar on her chips as she ate.

'Perhaps this lady you were telling me about, the one the woman on the bus is employed by, she may provide Mrs C with some companionship. It might help to distract her from her suspicions of wrongdoings by the staff at the home,' Matt suggested.

'Alice is asking Dolly to keep her eyes and ears open for anything unusual. I don't think we can do much more.' Kitty speared a fat, fluffy chip with her fork.

'No, I agree. We'll see if anything comes to light in the next couple of days and then report back to Mrs C,' Matt said. 'I was thinking too about Hammett.'

Kitty paused, her fork halfway to her mouth. 'Oh?'

'I know that you want more information about what happened to your mother and the news of the reward has been widely circulated.' Matt looked at her, concern in his dark blue eyes. 'Perhaps it might be as well to let things lie for a short time. Just until he is captured and behind bars. You can ask him all the questions you wish then, if he will answer them. I'm concerned about this shooting at the police when he made his escape from Brixham.'

Kitty placed her fork down on the edge of her plate and eyed Matt curiously. 'What has brought this on?'

Matt sighed. 'I called in at my office this afternoon. I decided to check that all was secure in the light of the break-in at my house.'

Fear settled like a stone in the pit of her stomach putting her off the rest of her supper. 'Was everything all right?'

'Not quite. The business that shares my landing said they were approached by a man claiming to be from the electricity company saying that he required access to my office. They said they didn't have a key and suggested he telephone me, and I would arrange for him to enter.' Matt's eyebrow raised as he spoke.

'I take it you have not received such a call?' Kitty said. 'You think this person was a fake?'

'I checked with the company and they have no workmen scheduled to visit,' Matt said.

'And you believe this may be connected with Hammett somehow?' A cold trickle of apprehension ran along her spine.

Matt ran his fingers through his hair. 'I don't know for certain. I've checked all my case files for anyone who might be interested in any of the ones I've been involved with since starting the business. No one stood out at all. The majority of those convicted are still in prison. Now whoever broke into the house focused their attention on the bureau where my personal documents are kept. Then there was this attempt to gain access to my office. It occurred to me that Hammett or his sister might want to know what information we had on him so far, or indeed on her.'

Kitty shifted uncomfortably on her seat. 'But beyond that note I received at Enderley I've had no further threat from him.'

'The continued offer of the reward has focused the attention of the public firmly back upon him once more. He may have been hoping that the longer he stayed free the better his chances of evading capture. His sister is bound to recognise that she and her address at Exeter are being watched and we know the woman we met who gave us information was more scared of Esther than of Ezekiel.' Matt scowled at his dinner plate. 'I just don't think we can rule out that all these things may be connected.'

Kitty removed her linen napkin from her lap and began to gather up their plates. 'So, what do you suggest? I cannot undo the offer of the reward, and nor do I wish to. I want this man caught and I want to find out what he knows of my mother's death.'

'Perhaps speak to Mickey, your maintenance and security man. Have all the staff alerted in case they attempt to contact you here or try to obtain access in some way,' Matt suggested.

She knew his suggestion made sense, but it did not sit well with her. 'Do you think this person may try to gain entry to the Dolphin?'

'We would be foolish not to consider the possibility,' Matt said.

Kitty sighed. 'There is of course another possibility.'

'Oh?' Now it was Matt's turn to appear surprised.

'Your former employment and the incidents at Enderley Hall with my uncle's work for the ministry.' Her tone was a little sharp. She was still somewhat disgruntled that Matt had been involved in a secret mission at her uncle's home at Enderley last Christmas and had not shared it with her. Then there had been the other similar incident at the Hall in the summer.

'It is not impossible I admit, but I feel it is very unlikely. I have not been active for Whitehall, apart from that small affair at Enderley, for quite some time. And, believe me, that was not of my own choosing.' The corner of his mouth quirked upwards and she knew her annoyance amused him.

'Then we shall simply have to wait and see if anything else occurs.' She rose and picked up the plates ready to carry them into the kitchen.

Matt leaned back in his chair. 'Just please be careful, Kitty. Stay alert, if these incidents are somehow connected to Hammett then I think he may well try again.'

'I shall, I assure you. Besides which, I am far too busy for Ezekiel Hammett and his sister with their nonsense at the moment. I have another motoring lesson with Robert tomorrow.' She headed toward the staff door leading to the kitchen. 'Who knows, he may even permit me to drive my car out of the shed this time.'

Matt's laughter rang out as the baize door closed behind her. She didn't want him to see how much his words had worried her. She still had bad dreams about Hammett where she woke in a cold sweat, the smell of the charred timbers and stale ale still in her nostrils from where they had explored the cellars of the Glass Bottle after the fire.

CHAPTER FIVE

Robert Potter drove Kitty's car out of the shed the following day and up the hill out of Dartmouth past the Naval College to a flatish straight stretch of road well outside of the town.

''Tis better you get the feel of your motor here, Miss Kitty. Them roads in town is too steep for your first attempt at driving her. We don't want you stalling and rolling back into the milk cart.' Robert chuckled at his joke.

Kitty didn't feel quite so amused at his attempt at humour. She gritted her teeth and exchanged seats with Robert while she tried to remember all the things he had shown her. An hour later as she steered her car cautiously back into Dartmouth, she felt a small twinge of triumph.

'Well done, Miss Kitty. Another couple of sessions and I reckon as you can go it alone.' Robert smiled at her as she slid the shed door shut and secured the padlock.

'Thank you, Robert. You've been very patient with me.' She was very grateful. Before long she would be able to travel where she liked, whenever she liked, as a modern independent woman. Right now though she felt completely exhausted from concentrating so hard, and in need of some lunch.

She agreed a time for her next lesson and parted from Robert ready to walk the short distance back to the Dolphin. The weather had turned milder and Kitty was in something of a reverie as she strolled along past the ferry stop.

The pavements became more crowded as she drew closer to the shops. The change in the weather had tempted more people abroad into the town to take the air beside the river. She had stepped to one side to allow a woman pushing a perambulator to pass by when there was a sharp tug on her shoulder.

'Hey!' Kitty whirled around in time to see a male figure darting away along the busy street carrying her handbag. 'Stop, thief!'

She started to pursue the robber, but the crowds buffeted and bumped her hindering her progress and she soon lost sight of the man. Frustrated, she immediately patted her coat pockets, thankful that she had slipped the keyring holding her car key and the key to the shed inside her pocket.

Annoyed, she hurried back on shaking legs to the Dolphin so she could telephone the police. There was only a small amount of money in her purse and a few personal items in her handbag. The most vexing things were the loss of one of the few precious pictures of her mother and the bag of sweets she had bought the day before.

When she entered the hotel lobby, she realised that she had in fact been carrying one set of keys in her bag. The set for her office and to her bedroom.

'Mary, do you have the master key to let me into my office? I've just had my handbag stolen in town.'

The receptionist gasped in horrified surprise. 'Of course, Miss Kitty, are you all right, miss?' The girl selected the key from the bunch she wore on her waist and opened the door to the small room at the rear of the reception desk.

'I'm a little shaken but I'm quite unharmed,' Kitty assured her.

Once inside her office Kitty wasted no time in telephoning the police station. Assured that a constable had been dispatched and was on his way, she asked Mary to send Mickey to see her.

Mickey's crinkled face was concerned when Kitty explained what had happened. 'I can get you some new keys cut, miss, no trouble but do you want to change the locks? It might be safer. I can't believe as someone would be so bold as to rob you in broad daylight with all them folk around you.'

'It happened awfully quickly. He was away before anyone really saw what was happening. I tried to chase him but lost him in the crush and I think he disappeared into one of the alleyways. Perhaps new keys for now and then ask the locksmith to call as soon as he's free? With the burglary at Captain Bryant's house and now this, I feel rather uncomfortable.' Kitty shivered. The reality of what had just happened had begun to set in.

Mary tapped on the office door bearing a tray of tea with a plate of biscuits. 'Here, Miss Kitty, have yourself a cup of tea with plenty of sugar in it. You look proper pale. 'Tis an awful thing to have happened. Mrs Treadwell will be right concerned when she comes back from Torquay.'

'Thank you, Mary.' Kitty obediently took a sip of the very sweet tea and shuddered at the taste of the hot, sweet liquid.

'I'll get on to see about the locks.' Mickey hurried off on his errand while Mary returned somewhat reluctantly to her post at the reception desk.

The constable arrived as Kitty was finishing her tea.

'And you didn't get a good look at his face, miss?' he asked as he wrote in his notebook.

'No, I'm afraid not, it all happened so quickly. A man in a dark jacket, a dark grey flat cap pulled low over his face, slim build, that was all I saw. I lost him in the crowds heading towards the Butterwalk,' Kitty said.

'And what was in the handbag?' the constable asked.

'My keys to this office and my room. A photograph of my mother, my purse which had a couple of pounds and some shillings, a comb, a bag of sweets.' She had already described her bag.

'Very good, miss. We have a few folks as I know as might be up for something such as this. I'll go aknocking on some doors and see what I can find.' The policeman returned his notebook to his breast pocket and stood ready to take his leave. 'I'll let you know straight away if I finds anything out, miss. 'Tis a shame as you didn't get a look at his face.'

'Thank you, Constable.' Kitty saw him to the office door just as Matt hurried into the lobby.

'Kitty, are you all right?' Matt asked.

'I'm quite all right now I think. How did you hear what had happened?' She glanced at Mary who promptly blushed bright pink. 'Never mind, I think I can guess. I was just about to telephone you.'

Matt followed her inside her room. 'You weren't hurt?'

Kitty waved him to a seat. 'No, I was just shocked.' She explained what had happened and Mickey's suggestion to change the locks.

'I don't like this at all, Kitty. It could simply be that you were unlucky, but coming so soon after the other things I think Mickey is right to suggest changing the locks.' He stroked his chin as he thought. 'The constable didn't say if there had been any other reports of similar robberies?'

Kitty shook her head. 'No. There have been a few incidents recently in the market when purses were lifted from shopping baskets but not like this. He said he would try some people who had records for similar offences and would let me know if he made any progress.'

'I take it Mickey is going to step up security here?' Matt asked.

'Yes, you know he is very good. My poor grandmother is going to be so upset when she returns from Elm House. She is visiting Mrs Craven again and knows nothing of this.' Kitty rubbed the tops of her arms trying to dispel the horrid feeling of gooseflesh.

Matt stood and wrapped his arms around her, enveloping her in a hug. 'We'll get to the bottom of this, Kitty.'

She sniffed. 'I'm quite cross about my handbag. It was rather a nice one and I expect it's probably floating in the river by now.'

She felt the rumble of laughter in his chest. 'Good to know that you have your priorities right.'

There was a tap on the office door and Matt released her as Mickey popped his head in. 'I've spare keys here for you, Miss Kitty, and the locksmith sent word he will be over tomorrow afternoon to change the locks.' He nodded at Matt and placed the new keys on the corner of Kitty's desk.

'Thank you, Mickey.' Kitty knew she would feel more secure when the locks had been changed.

''Tis my pleasure, miss. Mrs Treadwell has just come in and gone up to her suite, miss. Thought as you would want to go and see her.' He ducked out of the doorway.

'We'd better go up and tell her what's happened. She may have more news from Elm House too.' Kitty collected the spare keys and she and Matt headed up the staircase to her grandmother's suite.

Mrs Treadwell was tidying her hair in front of the mirror when Kitty knocked on the door and entered.

'Darling, I was about to ask Mary to send you up. Matthew, how very fortuitous, I've just come from Torquay.' Her grandmother moved to take her place in the armchair beside the fire.

Kitty and Matt took their seats on the sofa as Kitty explained what had happened to her in the town.

Her grandmother pressed her fingertips to her lips in shock. 'Oh, my dear, how perfectly awful. Whatever is Dartmouth coming too? I hope the constable is going to act? You are not hurt though?'

She reassured her grandmother. 'I'm sure they will do their best to catch whoever it was. Mickey has arranged for the locks to be changed and for extra security in the hotel.'

Her grandmother appeared slightly mollified by this. 'A burglary at your home, Matthew, and now this. These are not connected, I hope?'

Kitty exchanged a glance with Matt. 'We can't think why they should be, but it does seem like a very odd coincidence.'

Her grandmother pursed her lips. 'I can't say that I'm not concerned. Ever since your poor mother was finally laid to rest, I've been worried that man, Hammett, would come after you.'

Kitty swallowed. 'I know, Grams, but we have no proof that any of this could be connected with him or his sister.'

'That's true, Mrs Treadwell. Precautions have been taken and he surely cannot elude capture by the police for much longer,' Matt hastened to add his reassurance to Kitty's. 'Please do not allow it to prey on your mind.'

Her grandmother sighed. 'Very well, I hope you are right. I've just been to see Millicent again. She is still firmly convinced that something is amiss at Elm House. She and General Ackland, another patient there, have had their heads together over it.'

'I can find nothing untoward with Doctor Marsh's background,' Matt said.

'Well, Millicent is convinced the man is a blackguard. He has always appeared perfectly pleasant to me when I have been visiting. Most solicitous, in fact.' Mrs Treadwell shook her head. 'But she will not have it.'

'Oh dear, and has she seen Mrs Pearson? The lady I told you about?' Kitty asked.

'Yes, she is recovering from a pneumonia and is rather run-down. Millicent is of the opinion that a break from living with her son is probably all she requires to set her right. This son of hers is a friend of Lady Wellings's nephew. He recommended the home apparently.' Mrs Treadwell tutted. 'It says it all if they run in the same circles.' Her tone was disparaging.

'Is Mrs Craven's foot continuing to improve?' Kitty asked.

'I believe so, my dear. Nurse Hibbert, a very nice young woman, assured me that Millicent was doing well. She certainly appears to be in less pain. I do think the sooner she recovers enough to return home the better it will be.'

'We shall visit her again tomorrow and hopefully persuade her that all is well,' Matt said and earned a grateful smile from Kitty.

'I do hope so. I know Millicent can get very fixed ideas.'

Kitty raised her eyebrows at this. Mrs Craven had always seemed to have fixed ideas about both Kitty and Kitty's parents.

Matt took his leave a while later, declining Mrs Treadwell's invitation to stay for dinner. 'I have a few things to attend to. I'll call for you tomorrow afternoon, Kitty.'

'Hopefully by next week I shall be able to drive us. Robert says I've made good progress today.' She stepped outside the door of her grandmother's suite to say farewell.

'Now there's a thought.' Matt gave a smile before his expression sobered. 'Stay alert, old girl. I don't like this incident today.'

'No, it's all very worrying,' she agreed.

He placed a tender kiss on her lips. 'Until tomorrow.'

Kitty finally retired to her bed somewhat later than she had intended. A combination of soothing her grandmother's concerns and having to deal with an unwell guest had taken rather a long time.

She made herself a mug of milky cocoa and took it up to her room, hoping the drink would help her to relax. The air in her room had grown chilly and she shivered as she undressed for bed. The small cuckoo clock on her wall sounded a reassuring double melodic cuckoo to sound the hour.

The burglary at Matt's and the loss of her handbag was still playing on her mind as she turned the duplicate key in the lock of her bedroom door. She would be happier once the locksmith had been and the replacement made.

For her own peace of mind, she dragged one of the armchairs from her small seating area and wedged it under the door handle before draining her cocoa and turning out the light. Despite her precautions and the milky drink, she lay awake for some time in the darkness, unable to settle.

She had just started to drift off when she heard a sound in the corridor outside her room. Kitty lay rigid under the eiderdown, ears pricked listening for any other noises. No one else was on her floor as her room was at the top of the hotel. Most of the doors were to store cupboards, with a couple of rooms used to house staff or friends occasionally if the hotel was full. No one else had any reason to be on her floor.

Just as she had convinced herself that she had imagined the sound she heard it again. A soft footfall in the corridor. Her staff would have no cause to be on her floor at that time of night and it was unlikely to be a guest.

Kitty carefully eased herself silently up on her pillows. Her eyes had just adjusted to the dim light in her room when she saw the polished brass handle on her door twisting slowly. She had left the new key in the lock after securing the door. The movement stopped and she listened as whoever was on the other side of her door attempted to insert what she assumed was the key stolen along with her handbag.

Kitty's heart thumped against the wall of her chest as she heard the scraping sounds of an attempt to dislodge the key on her side of the door. She looked around her for a suitable weapon, mentally cursing at the lack of heavy objects close to hand.

There was a small metallic ping as the intruder managed to dislodge her key causing it to drop to the floor behind the chair that she had wedged under the door handle. Kitty slid out of bed and stepped quietly to the side of her dressing table to retrieve a long pearl-headed steel hatpin from the china tray.

She knew that when the intruder opened the door, they would have to put their hand through to try and move the chair. The boldness of it alarmed her. She crept to the side of the door, flattened herself against the floral wallpaper and waited. The intruder's key scraped in the lock and she held her breath as the door handle turned once more. As soon as the door began to open it encountered the back of the armchair.

Kitty held her breath, the pearl end of the hatpin firmly in her grasp. Sure enough a hand snaked through the narrow gap and around the door to feel for the obstruction. As soon as Kitty saw the hand appear, she stabbed down with the pin as hard as she possibly could.

There was a howl of pain and the hand retreated swiftly, followed by the sound of running feet along the corridor heading towards the back stairs normally used by the staff. Kitty pushed the chair aside and set off in pursuit.

She lost him on the first floor and instead turned and hurried along the corridor and down the main staircase to alert the night porter.

Bill, the night porter, was at his post behind the reception desk peacefully completing his crossword when Kitty ran breathlessly into the lobby.

'Quickly, Bill, there's an intruder in the hotel. He tried to get into my room. I think he's headed into the kitchens.' She slipped behind the desk and picked up the telephone receiver to call the police as Bill sprinted down the hall towards the kitchens at the very far end of the ground floor.

Kitty had just finished speaking to the desk sergeant when Bill returned puffing and panting to the desk. 'I'm sorry, he got away from me, miss. He'd broken a pane of glass to get in through the kitchen door and it looks like he'd used some bolt cutter on the padlock to the yard gate out back.' The older man wiped his hand across his brow to clear the sweat. He was clearly disappointed at his failure to capture the intruder.

'Perhaps it's as well, Bill, he could have been dangerous if you had managed to corner him.' Kitty's hand trembled as she replaced the receiver on its cradle. Bill wasn't in the first flush of youth.

'I can't understand it. I never heard a thing, miss.' Bill frowned. 'He must have gone straight up the back stairs. The kitchen door was wide open and there's broken glass all over the floor.'

Kitty shivered, suddenly aware that she had bare feet and no dressing gown over her pyjamas. 'The police will be here in just a moment. I'll just run up and get my gown.'

Bill nodded and Kitty hurried away back to her room. With her feet ensconced in her slippers and her warm flannel dressing gown securely fastened she hurried back down to the reception desk.

The constable had arrived already and was talking to Bill. Both men looked up as she re-entered the lobby. Kitty explained what had happened as the man made notes in his pocketbook. A smile tugged at the corners of Bill's mouth when she recounted stabbing the intruder's hand with the hatpin. She was glad that the kerfuffle hadn't disturbed her grandmother.

'And you didn't get a look at his face, miss?' the constable asked.

Kitty shook her head. 'No, I'm afraid not, it was dark on the landing and he was someway ahead of me. Did you see him, Bill?' she asked.

'No, miss, just the back of him running as fast as he could out the yard and off along the embankment,' Bill said. 'I did think though as he had a bit of a limp as he was moving. A gammy leg like.'

The cocoa Kitty had drunk an hour or so earlier swirled in her stomach threatening to make a reappearance. 'Are you sure, Bill?'

The older man scratched his head. 'Yes, Miss Kitty, he had a sort of a hop and drag as he moved. Not that it slowed him down at all, mind you.'

The constable eyed her curiously. 'Are you all right, miss? You've gone quite pale. Do you think you might know this person?' He and her night porter assisted her to a nearby chair.

'It may be nothing, Constable, but the wanted man, Ezekiel Hammett, has just such a disability and he has some reason to try to intimidate me as I have offered a substantial reward for his capture.' Her mouth dried at the thought that the intruder could have been Hammett and she licked her lips in an attempt to moisten them.

'Hmm.' The constable made a note in his pocketbook. 'Thank you, miss. P'raps as you could show me where this man gained access.'

'Certainly, Constable. If you'd like to come with me.' Bill started to lead the way.

Kitty immediately got to her feet and followed after them, earning her a concerned look from the police officer.

Bill had left the light switched on in the kitchen revealing the smashed pane of glass in the small window beside the back door. Shards of glass crunched under the constable's boots as he examined the door and the window.

'It looks as if he smashed the pane to get to the catch, then realised there was a bolt as well.' He drew closer to the heavy brass bolt that the kitchen staff used to doubly secure the door when they closed the kitchen for the day.

'Now then, what's this?' He carefully extracted something from the edge of the bolt.

'Have you found something, Constable?' Kitty came forward, eager to see what the man had discovered.

'Mind where you'm stepping, miss, in your house shoes, with this here glass,' the constable advised. 'A bit of thread. Looks as if our man got his coat cuff snagged on that bit of metal when he reached through the hole to slide the bolt back.'

Kitty peered at the few dark threads. They looked as if they had come from a coarse cloth such as might be used for a man's overcoat. The policeman stowed them carefully in a small brown paper envelope that he produced from the back of his pocketbook.

'Now then, where is this yard gate?' The constable directed his question to Bill. 'Best as you keep inside, miss. 'Tis cold out there.'

Kitty could already feel the icy draught coming from the open door, so she remained in the kitchen as the others went to look at the small gate leading to the service yard. The men were back within a few minutes.

'The padlock has been cut through,' the constable confirmed. He placed his notebook back inside his breast pocket. 'I'd best go back to the station and make my report.'

'Can you ensure that it is passed to Inspector Greville at Torquay and Inspector Pinch at Exeter, please. If it should turn out to be Hammett who is behind this then they need to be made aware,' Kitty said.

'Very well, miss,' the constable agreed.

Kitty accompanied Bill and the constable back to the lobby and saw the policeman leave.

'I dunno what your grandmother will think of all these goings on, Miss Kitty.' Bill scratched his chin, a worried frown on his forehead.

'No, neither do I,' Kitty replied ruefully. 'I'd better go back to bed. Can you secure the kitchen door for now, please, Bill? I'll ask Mickey to get the repairs sorted when he comes in. It will be another job for the locksmith.' She stifled a yawn with the back of her hand.

'You get off upstairs, Miss Kitty. Don't you be worrying about anything, I'll sort things out down here,' Bill assured her.

Kitty made her way wearily back up the stairs to her room and wondered what her grandmother and Matt would have to say about this latest incident.

CHAPTER SIX

The black Bakelite telephone in Matt's sitting room rang out early as he was about to set off for his office in Torquay.

'Hello.' He listened intently as Kitty recounted the events of the night.

'Are you all right? You weren't hurt?' His heart clenched at her description of the incident. Although the tale of the hatpin drew a rueful smile to his lips. As she told him more about the man with the altered gait his feelings quickly returned to concern for Kitty's safety.

Despite her assurances that she was quite all right he felt bad that he was unable to put off the meetings he had arranged for the morning in order to go straight to the Dolphin.

The news of an attempted forced entry into Kitty's room concerned him deeply. It certainly seemed that the break-in at his house, the theft of Kitty's bag, and the raid at the hotel were all connected. And behind it all hovered the shadowy figures of Ezekiel Hammett and his sister.

The meeting at his office was to discuss a potential new case involving a number of businesses in Torquay that had been targeted by a fraudster. He was relieved to discover his office was as he had left it. With the trouble at the Dolphin and a failed attempt by someone to gain access to his office, he hadn't known what to expect when he'd unlocked the door.

He lit the fire to take the chill from the room and awaited his clients. Fortunately, they arrived promptly, and the meeting was soon concluded with Matt agreeing to take on the case. After his new clients had gone and he had stowed his notes away in the small wooden filing cabinet beside his desk, he began to extinguish the fire ready to lock and head out for Dartmouth.

There was a tap at his door as he was preparing to leave. With the events of the last couple of days at the forefront of his mind he was somewhat cautious when opening the door.

'Bryant, old chap. Makes a change for us to meet somewhere without a corpse in between us.' Doctor Carter looking every bit like a cheerful, chubby middle-aged cherub in a tweed suit was on the other side of the door. 'Bit of luck catching you in. I thought I'd chance it as I was on my way past your door.'

Matt ushered the doctor into his office, curious as to what could have brought him there.

'Please come in and have a seat. I take it you have some new information about Doctor Marsh or the deaths at Elm House?' Matt resumed his own seat behind his desk.

Doctor Carter's habitual smile diminished for a moment. 'Yes, as a matter of fact I did some more probing. If you remember you asked me about the nature of the recent deaths over there?'

Matt nodded. 'Yes, Mrs Craven furnished a few names Lady Wellings, Mrs Palesbury and a Miss Wordsley. I believe they were the most recent ones.' He wondered what the doctor had discovered.

The doctor templed his hands together and surveyed Matt with a level gaze. 'Hmm, well, I must admit when you first asked me about Doctor Marsh and Elm House I was surprised. He took the place over about eight months ago, as I'm sure you know, and has spent a fair bit of money on it. It has always seemed quite popular, especially as a place for those suffering with nervous ailments or recuperating from minor surgery.'

'That was what Mrs Craven told us.'

'I looked back at the deaths since Doctor Marsh took ownership and number-wise they seem to be what one would expect.' The doctor paused.

'I sense a but?' Matt suggested.

Carter sighed. 'Indeed. It was the people that you named and the causes of death that might be considered, well, worrying. Miss Wordsley was a young woman, almost twenty-one, and from London. She had one relative, her guardian. I believe he inherited her estate when she died.'

'Twenty-one is very young.' Matt frowned.

'Miss Wordsley unfortunately had a drug habit, cocaine. She was at Elm House to be weaned away from the habit. It was thought that this was successful, and she was making good progress. Then, somehow, she managed to obtain a supply and sadly took too much. There was an inquest. The coroner asked questions about where the drug could have come from but there seemed to be no definitive answer. The orderly from Elm House, a Mr Cyril Dodds, gave evidence about an unknown visitor approaching Miss Wordsley in the gardens when she was taking the air. He assumed it was a romantic liaison, so he didn't question it at the time. The conclusion was drawn that this visitor must have been the source, but he was never identified.' Doctor Carter blinked. All of this was in the records from the inquest.

'I take it Miss Wordsley's estate was worth a considerable amount?' Matt asked.

The doctor smiled. 'Several hundred thousand pounds. The girl would have come into the lot in a few months' time. The guardian was rumoured to have some financial problems, so the inheritance was a bit of a windfall for him. I checked on your behalf with the coroner for any extra details and he remembered the case well.'

'Hmm, I see. And the others?' Matt asked.

'I have the telephone number for Mrs Palesbury's physician.' Doctor Carter passed over a slip of paper containing the number.

Matt gave a rueful smile. 'You have certainly been busy.'

Doctor Carter smiled back at him. 'My curiosity was roused. Now, Lady Wellings, Mrs Craven's other name. As you know her nephew, Roderick Harmer, has quite a reputation locally as a gambler and a lady's man. He had been "borrowing" money from his aunt for years. I know them well socially. This was the death that puzzled me as you told me that Doctor Marsh had said the lady had an underlying heart condition.'

Matt shifted forward a little in his seat. 'Yes, that is what he said when Kitty broached the subject.'

'And indeed, that is what was on the death certificate. However, about twelve months ago I attended Lady Wellings myself when she was unwell at a dinner party I was attending. She was not taking any medication for her heart at that point and I did not hear any issue when I examined her.' Doctor Carter looked troubled. 'I understand that notorious nephew of hers is set to inherit?'

'Yes, so Mrs Craven said. His aunt had been talking of disinheriting him just before she died. What are you saying about her death? Is Mrs Craven right and there is something suspicious about it?' All of Matt's detective instincts had been aroused. Perhaps Mrs Craven was right after all.

The doctor sighed. 'I am unhappy about it, and now you've told me about Roderick Harmer inheriting then it leaves a sour taste in one's mouth. I intend to speak to Inspector Greville to gain his opinion about all this. We could be adding two and two together and coming up with five of course. So may I ask that you please keep it to yourself for now, but should you or Miss Underhay learn anything further then I would be interested to know.'

'Of course, and thank you for calling in,' Matt said. He glanced at the telephone number the doctor had given him. Once he had found out more about Mrs Palesbury's death then he too would be contacting the inspector.

The doctor glanced at his wristwatch. 'I must be off; I want to catch Greville before he goes for lunch.' He stood and shook hands with Matt and left.

Matt remained in his seat for a moment thinking about what the doctor had said. He and Kitty would have to decide how much of this they could share with Mrs Craven. He had no wish to place the elderly woman in danger whilst she was still resident at Elm House. If indeed something was afoot there.

He picked up the telephone and dialled. A few minutes later, after a little persuasion, Mrs Palesbury's doctor's receptionist informed him that the lady had some kind of nervous complaint that affected her stomach and had been at Elm House for some three or four weeks before she collapsed and died. The cause of death had been documented as a ruptured gallbladder.

With encouragement Matt discovered from the now quite gossipy receptionist that Mrs Palesbury had been a wealthy woman in her own right having inherited a large sum of money from her mother. His informant's opinion was that Mrs Palesbury had controlled the purse strings in her marriage. Mr Palesbury had always appeared a most solicitous husband and the couple had no children having met later in life.

Matt asked if the receptionist knew anything about an inquest but was told the cause of death had not been considered suspicious.

'And the husband?' Matt was curious to hear if the receptionist knew what had become of him.

'Engaged to a young lady who was his secretary, I believe.'

*

Kitty discovered when she went to take breakfast with her that her grandmother had already heard about the intruder.

'Mickey came to see me, first thing this morning. Obviously, Bill had told him all about it,' her grandmother said as Kitty took her place at the breakfast table. 'I find the whole thing horribly distressing, Kitty. Just think of the hotel's reputation for one thing and then you could have been killed, pursuing the man like that.'

Kitty helped herself to toast and marmalade. 'He was well ahead of me, Grams, and I did give him quite a stab in his hand with my hatpin though.'

'And what if he had succeeded in his attempt to gain entry to your room? He had obviously snooped about to discover where your room was located within the hotel. We must assume he was intent on discovering your whereabouts. No other rooms were disturbed so far as we can tell.' Her grandmother fixed her with a steely glare.

Heat crept into Kitty's cheeks. She didn't wish to worry her grandmother, but it was hardly her fault that this man had decided to try and gain access to her room. 'I'm sorry, Grams.' She hoped her grandmother hadn't connected the break-in with Ezekiel Hammett.

'I must admit I wish Millicent had not involved you and Matthew in this absurd investigation of Elm House. Obviously, it is Matthew's employment, but I do feel, Kitty, that perhaps you should stop your involvement in any further investigations. You were in great danger several times last year.' Her grandmother stopped speaking and appeared to be attempting to compose herself.

'Oh, Grams.' Kitty got up from her seat to hug her grandmother. 'I promise I shall be more careful, but I have no idea why my bag was taken or why someone would have attempted to rob Matt's home or the Dolphin.'

Her grandmother patted her hand and shooed her back to her seat. 'I fear this is all connected with your mother's death. I have lost Elowed, I have no wish to lose you. Perhaps you should focus more on the affairs of the hotel for now and leave the detective work to Matthew.' Her grandmother then swiftly changed the subject back to the everyday business of running the hotel.

After breakfast Kitty went to her office to start her day's work. Despite trying her best to focus on organising the staff rotas her thoughts kept wandering and she found it hard to concentrate. After making yet another error she threw her pencil down in disgust.

What could the intruder have hoped to find either in Matt's home or amongst her possessions? She glanced at her wristwatch and discovered it was already mid-morning. Matt would be arriving shortly, and she had accomplished virtually nothing with her day so far.

She decided to abandon her work for now and freshen herself up ready for her lunch date with Matt and their visit to Elm House. She locked the office and headed to her bedroom. Kitty took a seat on the stool in front of her dressing table and tidied her hair. The carved ivory string of rosary beads that had been gifted to her by Jack Dawkins hung from the mirror.

It had been Jack's legacy of an old wooden cigar box filled with newspaper cuttings that had enabled Kitty to finally locate her mother's remains. She frowned as she looked at the rosary. Father Lamb had said it had belonged to Jack's mother and had been hugely important to him. He had also said that Jack had been insistent that Kitty receive the cigar box and its contents when he had been dying.

Could that be what Hammett was after? The battered old box and its contents? She had been through the clippings with a fine-tooth comb and had seen nothing of any interest, apart from the ones where Jack had made a few pencilled comments in the margins.

Suppose she had missed something though? The news reports of the discovery of her mother's body had mentioned that she had followed an idea sparked from inheriting a box of papers. Perhaps that was it.

Kitty hastily applied her lipstick and a fresh dab of perfume to her wrists and jumped up from the stool. Hammett had to believe that Jack had left her a clue to something else in that box. Something he didn't want anyone to know about.

The cigar box and its contents had been placed in a small wooden chest in the tiny reading room she had created that was linked to her bedroom. She hurried through the narrow archway and knelt on the floor to lift the lid of the chest.

Jack's box was inside, along with a few things that had belonged to her mother and a pressed flower from a small bouquet that Matt had given her just after they had decided to take their friendship to a different level.

Kitty lifted out the cigar box and moved to sit on the same armchair that she had used during the night to help secure her bedroom door. She placed the box on her knees and lifted the lid. The scent of old tobacco mixed with print greeted her.

Her pulse speeded as she started to look through the cuttings once again. This time alert for anything that might have some connection with Ezekiel Hammett or his sister, Esther. There was one old cutting that she had seen before about a fine levied on the landlord of the Glass Bottle, but she didn't think that was significant.

After looking at all the cuttings she leaned back in her chair baffled. She had been so certain for a moment that the box held the key to Hammett's interest in her and Matt. The cuckoo clock in her bedroom softly sounded the hour. Startled, the now empty cigar box slid from her lap onto the floor, landing with a sharp crack where the corner struck the polished wooden floorboards.

Kitty bent to retrieve it, hoping the fall hadn't damaged it. She knew it was ridiculous to feel sentimental about an old balsa wood box that had no intrinsic value, but she couldn't help it. It was one more small thing that linked her to her mother and the past.

To her relief the box initially appeared intact. It was only as she set it back on her lap to replace the cuttings inside it that she could see that the base appeared loose. She set the box down again for a moment while she collected her paperknife from the tray on her dressing table.

Kitty took her seat and examined the box more carefully wondering how she hadn't noticed the glued in wooden base before. She ran the tip of the paperknife carefully under the wafer-thin sheet of balsa noting that it had only been secured with a small dab of glue in each corner to hold it in place.

Her heartbeat increased as she eased the wood clear of the base of the box exposing several slightly yellowed thin sheets of paper folded in two. Kitty set down the paperknife and lifted the notes from the box. Her hands trembled slightly as she opened the papers and smoothed them out so she could read the contents.

The papers appeared to have been torn from a notebook of some kind. The first sheet was divided into columns and Kitty quickly realised that some of the entries were in code. The far column however was in pounds, shillings and pence with various amounts completed.

Her curiosity piqued; she lifted the page to look at the other two pages. They all had similar entries with different dates all from the previous year. Kitty frowned. These pages were clearly important enough to have been hidden away and the ripped edges on the one side showed they had been torn from their original book. If Jack had taken them it must have been done at some risk to himself. Why else would they have been hidden?

She realised that Matt would be arriving soon, so she replaced the base of the box and the cuttings before putting it back inside the chest. She kept the notebook pages and tucked them carefully inside her purse ready to show Matt when he arrived.

He walked through the door of the hotel just as Kitty rounded the foot of the stairs to enter the lobby.

'Are you ready for lunch?' He smiled at her and her spirits lifted. She couldn't wait to see what he would make of her discovery.

'Absolutely, I'll just get my hat and coat from my office.' She collected her things and reminded the receptionist that she would be late back as they were visiting Elm House immediately after lunch.

'Very good, miss. I should have your new keys for your office when you get back. The locksmith is with Mickey now looking at the kitchen door,' Mary said.

Kitty tucked her hand in the crook of Matt's arm as they stepped outside the Dolphin into the mild March day. The sun was out, and the breeze had gone, leaving the air feeling mild and spring-like.

'Would the tea room at Bayard's Cove suit you?' Matt asked.

'That sounds very acceptable. I have so much to tell you,' Kitty replied as they strolled along.

'That sounds interesting. I've a lot to tell you too. I had a visit from Doctor Carter at my office this morning.' He peeped at her as he spoke.

'Really?' Kitty's pulse jumped and they halted temporarily at the edge of the embankment looking out across the Dart as Matt told her what the doctor had said.

'Oh dear, that does appear to place a different complexion on things, although it still could all simply be well, normal, for a place like Elm House. I suppose families do have these complex relationships,' Kitty mused as they walked on towards the tea room.

'Doctor Carter intends to discuss everything with Inspector Greville. I called myself too and left a message for him.' Matt held open the door of the tea room to allow Kitty to enter.

'I suppose he is the best person to decide if there is a case to look into,' she agreed.

A waitress wearing a black uniform with a starched white cap and apron came to greet them and sit them at a vacant table near the large stone inglenook fireplace. The tea room was fairly busy and there was a pleasant hum of chatter in the room mingling with the scent of coffee and fresh bread.

Once they were seated and their order given for crab sandwiches and a pot of tea, Kitty produced the papers from her purse and passed them across to Matt explaining what she'd found.

'How did we miss this before?' Matt frowned as he looked at the notes.

'I don't know, except the base was sealed down at each corner and we were both focused on the newspaper cuttings while we looked for clues to find my mother.' Kitty stopped talking while their waitress set a china plate of sandwiches before each of them and placed a matching teapot, milk jug and cups onto the table.

'Do you think these might be what Ezekiel was after, if it was him? It seems odd that all of this is happening after the *Herald* ran that article and mentioned the box?' Kitty placed the tea strainer over a cup and poured the tea.

'It looks as if these were torn from some kind of informal accounts ledger. It's interesting that the entries are in code. I wonder where Jack got these from?' The frown lines on Matt's brow deepened.

'Perhaps payments received from businesses?' Kitty suggested. 'Some kind of protection racket? Heavens, I sound like Alice when she's watched too many films at the cinema.'

'That suggestion may not be as far-fetched as you think. It could be, or it could be revenue from orders for smuggled goods. It could implicate a lot of people in all kinds of things if one could crack the code.' Matt helped himself to the milk jug, tipping a small amount into his tea.

'Enough to get Ezekiel concerned about any other contents in Jack's box then?' Anxiety swirled in Kitty's stomach.

Matt met her gaze, his expression sombre. 'Unfortunately, I fear you may be right.'

CHAPTER SEVEN

They took Mr Potter's taxi directly from the tea rooms to Elm House.

'I think we should be careful to ensure our conversation with Mrs Craven is not overheard,' Kitty said as they exited the taxi, having arranged for Mr Potter to return for them in an hour and a half's time.

'I agree, it would be safer to be cautious. It's a pleasant day today. Perhaps we may be able to persuade Mrs C to take the air. The grounds here are very lovely and there appears to be several sheltered spots,' Matt suggested looking at the broad gravel paths that wound between the palm trees and the formal beds.

The same stern receptionist that had greeted them on their previous visit was in position again. She produced the leather-bound visitor ledger for them to sign in. Kitty noted that Roderick Harmer's name and that of Leonard Pearson were together in the morning's entries.

A slim woman in her late thirties with chestnut hair under her white frilled cap and wearing a navy nurse's uniform approached the desk as Matt signed his name below Kitty's.

'Where might we find Mrs Craven today?' Kitty asked the receptionist.

The woman exchanged a glance with the nurse that had approached the desk. 'Sister Carmichael here will be happy to show you, I'm sure.' She closed the ledger once Matt had signed in and stowed it away under the desk.

'Of course.' Sister Carmichael gave a tight-lipped smile. 'I'm sure Mrs Craven will be glad of the company. Are you friends of hers?' she asked as she led them along a different corridor to the one they had used previously.

'My grandmother is one of Mrs Craven's oldest friends, she visits regularly, Mrs Treadwell?' Kitty said.

'Ah yes, from the Dolphin Hotel, I believe.' Sister Carmichael paused in front of a heavily carved oak door. 'Mrs Craven is in the reading room.' She gave them both another tight smile and left.

The corner of Matt's mouth quirked upwards as he looked at Kitty and she gave a slight shrug. Sister Carmichael did not appear to be very friendly.

Kitty pushed open the door to find herself in what appeared to be a library. Bookshelves lined two of the walls from floor to ceiling. A large round table was in the centre of the room covered in copies of the daily newspapers and a selection of periodicals. Wine-coloured leather winged armchairs with deep button backs were grouped around the room and a fire blazed in the carved marble fireplace.

Mrs Craven was seated beside the window, a newspaper lying open on her lap. She turned her head towards them at the sound of the door opening and beckoned them over with an imperious wave of her hand.

She folded up the newspaper as they approached and dropped it down on the small table next to her.

'Oh, I am so glad to see you. Well? What have you discovered? Come on, sit down and tell me all about it.' She looked expectantly at them.

Kitty saw Matt scan the room to see who else was there. A couple of other patients were seated not very far away and a male orderly of oriental appearance in a white jacket was ostensibly tidying some of the books back onto the shelves.

'We thought as it was such a nice mild day outside that you might care to take the air for a short while. The gardens look super with the view of the sea and it's really very sheltered,' Kitty said.

Mrs Craven gave her a shrewd look. 'Very well, excellent idea if Matthew would do the honours and push my chair?' She looked at Matt.

'Of course, I should be delighted.' Matt went to the orderly to request his assistance.

Within a few minutes Mrs Craven was bundled up in her coat with a rug across her knees and Matt steering the wooden framed rattan caned wheelchair. They had declined the orderly's assistance, something he seemed a little vexed about.

Matt pushed the chair through the reception area and out to the side of the building onto the broad terrace, before steering the chair down to the next tier away from the house.

'Thank goodness we are stopping. This ghastly thing jolts one about so. I shall be glad when I am permitted to use my cane more and can leave this chair behind,' Mrs Craven complained as they rumbled to a halt next to a small wooden bench in a sunny, sheltered spot.

Kitty refrained from commenting and took a seat on the bench. The sea sparkled in front of them in the sunshine and a couple of white sailed boats were visible on the horizon. Matt took a seat next to Kitty and gave Mrs Craven a brief outline of their discoveries to date.

Mrs Craven listened intently; her lips pursed in disapproval at what she heard. 'I knew it! I said there was something fishy about all of this.'

'We don't yet know that for certain, only that Doctor Carter has some questions and is placing the matter before Inspector Greville for his thoughts on the matter,' Matt cautioned.

Mrs Craven flapped an ivory-coloured kid gloved hand about dismissively. 'You know my opinion of the local police. There is a case to be answered here I'm certain. Poor Miss Wordsley, such a nice girl and to die just before her birthday, such a tragedy. She had such plans, you know, for when she became of age. She intended to travel to Madeira to stay with an old school friend. They wanted to open a sanctuary for donkeys.'

'Donkeys?' Kitty queried, wondering if she had heard correctly.

'Yes indeed, the poor girl was devoted to animals and after all she had gone through, you know, she wanted to live away from temptation, devoting herself to good works.' Mrs Craven shook her head sadly.

'Doctor Carter said an orderly from Elm House gave evidence at the inquest for Miss Wordsley. Was that the man we saw earlier, the one who assisted with the chair?' Matt asked.

Mrs Craven gave a small nod. 'Yes, that would be him. He is quite distinctive. Cyril Dodds. I understand his mother was English, but his father was Chinese I believe.'

'I noticed Roderick Harmer's and Leonard Pearson's names were in the register today when we signed in,' Kitty said.

'Thick as thieves those two. Birds of a feather, and all that. I saw Leonard visiting his mother. He had some papers he wanted her to sign. I didn't see his friend, however. Perhaps he was with Doctor Marsh.' Mrs Craven gave a disapproving sniff.

'I think we are being observed,' Matt murmured. 'There is someone at the window of the house watching us. Perhaps we should show interest in the view for a moment.'

Kitty obliged, shading her eyes and pointing as if to indicate interest in the sailing vessels. 'Did you see who it was?' she asked.

'Sister Carmichael, I think. The dress was dark, and I glimpsed the white of her cap.' Matt frowned and twisted slightly to risk another discreet peep back at the home.

'There were more of those shady visitors here again late last night too.' Mrs Craven also pretended to be studying the horizon.

'You said they arrive very late in the evening without luggage and then are gone in the early hours of the next day?' Matt, like Kitty, had refocused his attention on the view of the bay to allay the suspicions of any observers.

Mrs Craven wriggled herself more upright in the wheelchair, taking care to ensure her bandaged foot was on the rest. 'Yes, a black motor car drops them off at the rear of the home towards midnight. General Ackland's room is overlooking that side and he was disturbed by the arrival of the cars. He said the headlamps are switched off and they only stay long enough for these mysterious people to get out and enter the home. Then, early in the morning, only a few hours later at about one thirty they are picked up in the same manner, but this time they are carrying bags and packages. He has looked out and seen them.'

Kitty looked across at Matt. 'That certainly does sound very suspicious. Whatever could they be doing? Smuggling something, perhaps, but what? And why here at Elm House?'

'I think there is something hidden in the linen closet at the end of my landing. Since poor Miss Wordsley's death I am the only patient resident in that section. The cupboard is facing you as you come out from the elevator and turn in the direction of my room.' Mrs Craven leaned closer to Matt, a glint in her eye. 'They keep it locked and I've only ever seen Sister Carmichael and that man, Dodds, enter. I tried to see inside once when Sister Carmichael was entering it and Nurse Hibbert was pushing my chair. As soon as she realised that we were approaching Sister Carmichael closed the door though and she appeared quite flustered.'

'And did you see anything?' Kitty asked.

'No, just empty shelves and possibly some towels, but I'm certain that there is something hidden there. I hear people going past my room late at night. The same nights when these people come. There's no one else at that end of the corridor. Mine and Miss Wordsley's are the very last rooms at that end of the landing,' Mrs Craven insisted. 'I have an idea.'

She fumbled under the rug that was draped across her lap and produced a key attached to a wooden fob with a room number. 'Here, take the key to my room. You can pretend you are fetching something for me. The cupboard will be locked I'm sure, but you can snoop around. Have a look and see what you can find.' Mrs Craven pressed the key into Kitty's hand.

Kitty opened her mouth ready to protest and closed it again just as swiftly. Perhaps a bit of a nose around might provide a clue to whatever was going on at Elm House.

'Very well, but if we are being observed then, perhaps, we should move to where we are less visible and I shall try to gain entry without the receptionist spotting me,' Kitty suggested.

Matt stood and pushed Mrs Craven's chair further along the path and down another tier while Mrs Craven gave Kitty the directions to her room.

'Now, the number is on the key. I suggest you bring back a book or handkerchief or something as cover,' Mrs Craven instructed.

'Do be careful, Kitty.' Matt didn't look at all happy about Mrs Craven's idea as Kitty checked to see that their watcher had moved before hurrying back up through the gardens to the home.

A glance through the front entrance showed her the receptionist talking to someone at the front desk. Kitty hesitated for a moment then headed around the building towards the tradesmen's entrance at the rear. She was relieved to see the rooms appeared empty on that side of the building and in her black coat and hat she would be less likely to be noticed.

To her delight as she peeked in through a side window, she spotted Dolly carefully preparing some tea trays. Kitty tapped softly on the glass and waved to attract the girl's attention. Dolly immediately stopped her work, wiped her hands on her apron and scurried to open the tradesmen's door.

'Miss Kitty, what are you doing round here?' the girl asked, a bewildered look on her face.

'Is anyone in there with you?' Kitty asked in a low voice.

'No, miss. Cook has gone with one of the nurses to do something so I'm on my own.'

'Do me a favour, Dolly, please, let me in and don't say anything to anyone. I need to go upstairs to Mrs Craven's room unobserved.' Kitty hoped that Dolly would prove as quick on the uptake as her sister. 'Don't worry. If I get stopped, I shan't mention you at all,' she hurriedly reassured her. The last thing she wanted was to get the girl in trouble.

'Mrs Craven's room is upstairs, miss, on the second floor. You'd be best up the servants' stairs if you don't want no one to see you.' Dolly opened the door wider and beckoned to Kitty to follow her.

Dolly led the way through a maze of service corridors that ran through the kitchen and laundry. The air smelt of soap and stale cabbage. Kitty could hear voices in one of the rooms as they hurried quietly past. Dolly halted at the foot of a narrow flight of stairs.

'Go on up two flights, miss. That will bring you out on the right floor, then Mrs Craven's room is right at the far end.'

'Thank you, Dolly. You are a star.' Kitty beamed her thanks at the little maid making the girl flush to the roots of her hair.

Kitty hurried away up the narrow flight of stairs listening carefully as she went in case any of the other staff might be approaching from one of the floors. She paused at the top of the second flight to catch her breath, her hand on the door as she listened for any signs of life on the landing.

Once she was satisfied that it was safe, she pushed the door open and entered the corridor. The soles of her shoes sank into the plush pile of the carpet runner that extended in a delicate muted floral pattern all along the landing. The bedroom doors on either side of the corridor were numbered and she checked the key in her hand to make sure she knew where she was going.

Kitty walked briskly, keen to reach her target before any of the staff could appear and ask her what she was doing in the bedroom area of the home. She passed the elevator and the head of the main staircase that led up from the floor below. Again, she could hear the distant rumble of domestic activity and guessed the maids were cleaning.

She released a breath, trying to steady her heart rate and pressed on. The end of the corridor was rapidly approaching, and she saw that Mrs Craven had been correct. She had the last room on one side of the corridor while Miss Wordsley had occupied the room opposite. Facing her was a blank cream painted door, which had to be the one Mrs Craven was convinced held some kind of contraband.

There was still no sign of anyone else in the corridor. Kitty checked behind her in case someone had entered unnoticed. She took another breath and tried the door handle of the cupboard. Unsurprisingly it was locked. Kitty decided that she really needed to get Matt to teach her how to pick locks with the little device he carried in his pocket.

The sound of footsteps on the stairs alerted her to someone approaching from the floor below so she darted to Mrs Craven's door, unlocked it swiftly and slipped inside. She kept the door open just a crack so she could see who might be entering the corridor. Her heart pounded in her chest even though technically she considered that she had every right to be in Mrs Craven's room.

Kitty put her eye to the tiny opening between the door and the frame to peep out while she listened hard for some clue to determine which direction the owner of the footsteps may have taken. She stifled a gasp as Sister Carmichael passed the door clearly heading towards the locked cupboard.

She glanced around the large and comfortable bedroom with its plush dark pink velvet curtains and stylish décor looking for an item she could use as her excuse for being in the room. She spotted a book on the bedside table and picked it up.

When she judged that Sister Carmichael would have had time to open the cupboard, Kitty silently opened Mrs Craven's door and stepped out into the corridor. Sister Carmichael had her back to Kitty and appeared to be looking at the shelving that covered the one wall of the closet. A few towels were folded on the shelf but otherwise the cupboard appeared bare.

Satisfied that she had seen as much as she could, Kitty deliberately closed Mrs Craven's door with a sharp click. Sister Carmichael immediately closed the cupboard door and locked it with a key secured on a long chain that was fastened to her waist.

'Miss Underhay, isn't it? Can I help you? I understood you were outside with Mrs Craven.' Sister Carmichael's tone was sharp.

Kitty detected a tinge of red in the woman's cheeks and was privately amused at her discomfiture. 'Mrs Craven sent me up to her room to fetch her book.' Kitty waved the volume she had ready in her hand.

'Oh, I see. You should really have asked a member of staff to collect it for her. We try to discourage visitors from entering this floor unless visiting a patient in their room. For security purposes.'

Kitty could see that despite the polite nature of the sister's words the woman was unhappy with Kitty's presence on the landing.

'Of course, I'm terribly sorry, Sister. I really didn't want to cause the staff any trouble. I'll be sure to bear that in mind for the future.'

Sister Carmichael gave a stiff smile. 'I shall walk back downstairs with you, Miss Underhay. I expect Mrs Craven will need to return inside now. It is only March after all, and it must be turning chilly.'

Kitty was forced to fall into step beside the sister and make her way back down to the entrance hall via the main staircase.

'Have you known Doctor Marsh for some time?' Kitty attempted to make conversation in order to dispel the nurse's ill humour.

'Yes, indeed. Doctor Marsh is most well thought of. He still retains an apartment in London and goes back there to teach at the hospital.'

Sister Carmichael's face softened as she spoke and Kitty surmised there had to be some strength in the sister's attachment to her employer.

The receptionist appeared most surprised to see her accompanied by Sister Carmichael.

'Miss Bowkett, please can you send Dodds to the gardens to assist Mrs Craven back inside, and can you remind visitors that our staff will assist them should they require items from patients' rooms.' Sister Carmichael gave the receptionist a frosty glare. There was no doubt in Kitty's mind that the sister was blaming her for Kitty's presence upstairs.

*

Matt resisted the urge to check his wristwatch again. It felt as if Kitty had been gone for an eternity. He'd spent the time in her absence telling Mrs Craven of the things that had been happening back in Dartmouth and at his house.

Mrs Craven had naturally been deeply shocked and demanded to know what the police were doing about these events. He was then forced to listen to Mrs Craven's opinion of the police, 'quite useless', the chief constable, 'incompetent' and finally Inspector Greville, 'beyond the pale'.

To his relief he heard quick light footsteps on the gravel pathway and Kitty appeared. She was accompanied by Mr Dodds, the same orderly who had assisted Mrs Craven into her wheelchair.

'I'm sorry to have taken so long, Mrs Craven. I met Sister Carmichael and she feels that you should return to the home now before you become chilled. Mr Dodds here has been dispatched to assist us.' Kitty waved the book in her hand.

'Thank you, my dear, so very good of you to fetch that for me. Once we are inside then I shall show you the part I meant.' Mrs Craven smiled at Mr Dodds as the man moved to come behind her chair ready to push it back up the sloping pathway.

'Mr Potter will be here to collect us soon, I think. Next time we visit I shall hopefully be driving my own car,' Kitty said as they followed behind the wheelchair.

'Are you sure, Kitty? Is that wise? One has to be so careful with motor cars,' Mrs Craven called over her shoulder as they re-entered the house.

Matt did his best to hide his amusement as Kitty rolled her eyes behind Mrs Craven's back. Once Mrs Craven was installed back in an armchair in the lounge and Dodds had disappeared, Kitty gave a quick whispered update about her adventure.

'I knew it!' Mrs Craven smacked the arm of her chair with her hand in triumph. 'That woman is up to no good I tell you.'

'Mrs Craven, please be alert and do not put yourself in any danger. We don't know quite what is happening here at Elm House but keep your suspicions to yourself for now,' Matt urged.

'Very well. General Ackland is the only other person here who is also concerned about these matters. We shall both be discreet,' Mrs Craven reluctantly conceded.

Matt looked up to see young Dolly approaching them.

'If you please, miss, sir, your taxi has come for you.'

'Thank you, Dolly dear.' Kitty smiled at the little maid as she tripped away back to her duties. 'Such a good girl. I do hope she will be all right in all this if it does turn out to be suspect.'

'Come, we had better not keep Mr Potter waiting. We shall call again soon.' Matt made his farewell to Mrs Craven. Kitty followed suit.

He noticed the receptionist appeared to have gone from frosty to glacial as they signed out of the building.

'I don't think that we have won many friends here today,' Matt observed as he held the taxi door open for Kitty.

'No, but then I don't think I would wish to be friendly with any of them,' Kitty remarked as he climbed in after her.

He noticed her shoulders visibly relax once they were down the hill and following the coast road back towards Paignton. 'What do you think Sister Carmichael was doing in that cupboard?'

Kitty's brow creased as she considered his question. 'I couldn't see anything that looked unusual, except it seemed to me that I would have expected that cupboard to be deeper. It was large enough for a person to stand inside it but I thought it should have gone further back. When I was on my way back downstairs with Sister Carmichael it struck me that the cupboard must back onto the area of the home with the turret. I didn't see a way into the turret from the servants' stairs or the main staircase.'

'You think there may be an entrance from the cupboard to another area of the building?' Matt asked.

Kitty shrugged. 'It's possible, isn't it? It would account for people going past Mrs Craven's room. It looked as if Sister Carmichael was feeling along the shelf for something.'

'Hmm, it could be a concealed catch.' Matt could see all kinds of possibilities if Kitty were correct in her supposition. 'Well done, old thing. You did a super job.'

She returned his smile, but he could see something was troubling her. 'Grams wishes me to stop assisting you in your investigations. This business of the break-in has made her very concerned.'

'Ah, would you like me to speak to her?' he asked. He was cautious of offering to help knowing Kitty's passion for independence, but he guessed she had already tried and failed to reassure her grandmother on this particular score.

'It might help allay her worries. Although until Hammett is captured, I'm afraid she will remain anxious about my safety.'

'I'll do my best,' he assured her. He could understand Mrs Treadwell's concerns. The break-in at his own home and the attempted entrance into his office was worrying. The papers Kitty had discovered in Jack Dawkins's box crackled inside his breast pocket.

Kitty was right when she said that all of these attempts had been made after the *Herald* had mentioned the box in their news report. Whatever was behind these codes had to be important even now if Hammett were prepared to go to such lengths to retrieve them.

The man was facing the noose anyway for the murder of his half-brother and would have questions to answer about a multitude of crimes over the years, including Kitty's mother's death. With nothing to lose he had nothing to be afraid of and wouldn't have any scruples about killing again. Of that Matt was quite certain.

CHAPTER EIGHT

Matt noticed Kitty shiver as they left the taxi outside the Dolphin.

'The air is turning chilly again, let's get inside out of the cold.' He held the door open for her to enter the hotel lobby ahead of him.

'Inspector Greville, this is a surprise. What's happened? Do you have any news?' Kitty exclaimed as she spied the familiar figure of the police inspector waiting patiently in a chair in the corner of the otherwise deserted entrance hall.

Matt followed behind her as she went over to greet the policeman. Inspector Greville rose to meet her and removed his hat.

'Miss Underhay, Captain Bryant, the receptionist said you were expected back shortly so I took the liberty of waiting for you.' The inspector nodded to Matt.

'Matt, please ask Mary to bring us some tea,' Kitty asked as she took a seat beside the inspector, leaving the vacant chair on the other side of the small table free for Matt's return.

He returned from his errand to see that Kitty had unfastened her coat and drawn off her gloves and was now looking expectantly at Inspector Greville.

'I called in to say that your handbag had been recovered.' The inspector reached under the table to produce Kitty's bag. It looked a little worse for wear but appeared generally undamaged.

Kitty immediately opened it to check the contents. 'The keys are gone and my purse, along with the picture of my mother.' She looked disappointed but unsurprised.

'A passer-by found it stuffed in a hedge not far from the lower ferry station and handed it in to the local constable,' Inspector Greville said.

'And no news on who may have stolen it, sir?' Matt asked as one of the hotel maids approached and set a tray down on the table before them.

The inspector's expression was grave as Kitty poured the tea. 'Unfortunately not. The constable has followed up all the local men he considered may have been responsible and has drawn a blank.'

Kitty handed the inspector his drink. 'And what of our main suspect, Ezekiel Hammett? Is there any news yet on his whereabouts?'

The inspector's moustache drooped morosely as he accepted the cup. 'I'm afraid there is nothing definite. Inspector Pinch has a watch set on the local ports and the harbour masters have been made aware of his description.'

Matt took a sip of tea as Inspector Greville helped himself to biscuits from the plate Kitty offered him. 'Have there been no recent local sightings reported?'

The inspector crunched on a shortbread before swallowing and replying. 'There have been a multitude of reports, from all over the county. The difficulty comes in sorting the wheat from the chaff so to speak. We are still very low on manpower thanks to this flu that has been circulating ever since Christmas.' He took another bite of shortbread and chewed, spilling crumbs down his tie. 'The rest of my men are involved in a big operation with Scotland Yard.'

'Oh?' Kitty asked.

Matt bit back a smile, he could see her interest perking.

'I'm afraid I can't say anything more about that, Miss Underhay. Hush, hush, best to keep that to yourself.' The inspector tapped the side of his nose with his forefinger and looked sorrowfully at the now empty plate of biscuits.

'I take it nothing has come from Inspector Pinch's observation of Esther Hammett's property in Exeter then?' Matt asked.

Inspector Greville brushed the stray biscuit crumbs from his tie. 'Not as yet. There is no sign of Hammett approaching the house or of her meeting with him anywhere. We are still investigating her so-called business links and associates.'

'We made a discovery that we should like you to see, Inspector.' Kitty looked at Matt and he took the sheets of paper she had found in Jack Dawkins's box from his breast pocket and placed them on the table.

'They were hidden under a false bottom in the cigar box that Father Lamb gave me. They were the property of Jack Dawkins. We wondered if the recent attempts to gain entry here and at Matt's house might be somehow connected to these papers. The *Herald* mentioned the box and its contents in its most recent report,' Kitty said as the inspector studied the notes.

'Hmm, these have clearly been torn from some sort of accounts record, I should say. Payments received or made. I presume Dawkins considered them important if he hid them so well but there is nothing to connect these with Hammett unless you can crack the code and link the dates at the top of the pages with something significant.' The inspector frowned and passed them back to Kitty.

Matt could see that she was a little put out about his apparent lack of interest as she refolded the papers and stowed them away in her handbag.

'Has Doctor Carter spoken to you, sir? About Elm House and his concerns, especially focusing on the death of Lady Wellings?' Matt asked.

'Yes, I also received your message regarding Mrs Palesbury. I have called for a review and contacted the coroner about Lady Wellings. The funeral has not yet taken place so I am waiting to hear if there will be an autopsy to confirm the cause of death. Doctor Carter seemed to think that the certificate issued by Doctor Marsh may not be appropriate. It is most likely simply a difference in diagnosis. Doctor Marsh appears well regarded, even Doctor Carter agreed upon that point.' The inspector drained his teacup.

'I expect then that the coroner will make a judgement on the matter. There is however something else, sir, besides the deaths.' Matt glanced at Kitty. He was unconvinced by the inspector's ready dismissal of the issues they had raised and annoyed that his own information was being brushed aside.

'Do go on?' The inspector looked puzzled.

Matt told him of the mysterious visitors and of Mrs Craven's concerns.

The inspector gave him a sceptical glance. 'I can see why you might think there is something odd, but it could simply be visitors not wishing to disturb the residents at the home with noise and lights. If they have travelled a distance and can only stay a short time, then that would surely explain it. And, I have to say, Miss Underhay, the business with the cupboard sounds highly fanciful. Many buildings are altered over time and Elm House has not long been refurbished.'

'You are inclined to dismiss it all then, sir?' Kitty asked.

'Mrs Craven has nothing else to occupy her mind whilst she is recovering and is seeing issues everywhere,' the inspector replied soothingly.

Matt could see by the glint in Kitty's eyes that she was not convinced.

'Well, thank you for returning my handbag and for updating us on the progress on the search for Hammett.' Kitty placed her empty teacup back on the tray.

'If we have any further news, Miss Underhay, we shall of course be back in touch.' The inspector rose and gathered his hat ready to leave.

'I'll see you out, sir.' Matt accompanied the inspector to the door of the lobby. 'Before you go, Inspector, do you feel it likely that Hammett might try again if he is trying to retrieve those papers?' He glanced back towards Kitty.

Inspector Greville followed his gaze. 'I think it is unlikely, especially as the attempts so far have been unsuccessful, but I would urge you both to continue to be on your guard. The man is highly dangerous, and, it seems, increasingly reckless.'

*

Kitty narrowed her eyes as she watched Matt talking to the inspector at the main entrance. Normally she had great respect for Inspector Greville, but on the matter of Elm House and on the papers she now had tucked inside her handbag, she was convinced he was wrong.

Matt bade the inspector farewell and returned to rejoin Kitty.

'What do you think about all of that?' she asked.

'I suspect the inspector is feeling under pressure with the men from Scotland Yard and the shortage of manpower. The longer Hammett remains on the loose, then the worse it will appear for both Greville and Inspector Pinch. Elm House will be very low on his list of concerns, and hence I suspect his wish to dismiss it as a problem.' Matt smiled at her. 'Chin up, old thing, I know that wasn't what you wished to hear. I do agree with him on one point, however. We must remain vigilant.'

Kitty collected up both her handbags and her gloves. 'We best go and see Grams and tell her everything. She intends to visit Mrs Craven again tomorrow.'

Matt fell into step beside her and they walked up the stairs together.

'Whatever may or may not be happening at Elm House, I hope Alice's sister will be out of harm's way,' Kitty said.

'I'm sure she will be. If our suspicions are correct then it would seem that it is the more senior staff that are involved in some kind of skulduggery,' Matt reassured her as she tapped on her grandmother's door before entering.

Mrs Treadwell was seated at her bureau dealing with her correspondence when they entered. She replaced the lid on her fountain pen and set it down.

'How is Millicent today? I do hope you have eased her mind of those fancies of hers?' Mrs Treadwell remarked.

A guilty flush heated Kitty's cheeks as she hung her coat and hat on the coat stand. Matt gave her grandmother a succinct explanation of their discoveries playing down Kitty's adventure so as not to alarm the older woman.

When Kitty took her seat next to Matt on the sofa, she could see her grandmother was not impressed.

'I heard that Inspector Greville had stopped by the hotel too?' her grandmother asked. Kitty might have known that she would have heard about the inspector's visit. A fly could not have entered the Dolphin without her grandmother being aware of its presence.

Kitty showed her the handbag that the inspector had returned and explained what he had said.

'I see. Then they are no closer to capturing Hammett and he regards this fancy of Millicent's as being something of a mare's nest?' her grandmother remarked crisply. 'I must confess, I wish Millicent were well enough to return home. Hopefully, if she continues to improve that will be sooner rather than later. I don't like any of this, Kitty.'

Kitty swallowed. She could see that despite her grandmother's stern tone she was genuinely distressed by the information they had shared with her.

'Hammett must be captured soon. Inspector Pinch is working hard at the Exeter end of things and Hammett's description has been widely circulated. I agree that we should remain vigilant, but the inspector has said he doubts that he will risk trying again to access the hotel or my house.' Matt attempted to allay some of her grandmother's concerns.

'Well it seems to me that enough is enough, Kitty. If the inspector believes those papers of Mr Dawkins are not significant then I feel you should leave well alone. And please do not continue to encourage Millicent in her ideas. It all makes me very uneasy. It is bad enough that the man who must have had a hand in the murder of your mother is still roaming free, without you exposing yourself to more danger, Kitty. I appreciate that I cannot forbid you from continuing your involvement, but I hope you will oblige me by stepping back from all of this. And I hope you will support me in this, Matthew.' Her grandmother turned her steely gaze onto Matt.

Kitty's heart had sunk lower with each word. She could understand her grandmother's concerns. After all, Kitty herself wasn't happy that Hammett was still on the loose, but it seemed unfair that her grandmother wished her to step back from investigating the odd affairs at Elm House or from trying to solve the coded messages contained in the papers from Jack Dawkins's box.

'I'm sure Kitty will take great care not to expose herself to any unnecessary risks,' Matt said.

'I appreciate that you would do your best to protect her, Matthew, but as you know my granddaughter, like all the women in this family, can be quite wilful.' Her grandmother turned her gaze back onto Kitty.

'Grams, I assure you that I shall take every precaution.' Kitty sighed when she saw her grandmother's glare hadn't faltered. 'Very well, I shall refrain from encouraging Mrs Craven's investigations at Elm House and I shall not place another advertisement with the newspapers about the reward for Hammett's capture for the next week.'

Her grandmother appeared mollified by her promise and smiled graciously at Matt. 'I trust you will ensure that my granddaughter is not drawn back into anything further until this man is captured, Matthew?'

Kitty opened her mouth to protest but thought better of it in case her grandmother realised that she had omitted making any promise about not trying to solve the codes or about trying to discover more information about the other staff at Elm House.

'I promise that I shall do everything possible to ensure Kitty's safety,' Matt promised her grandmother.

He gave Kitty's hand a quick squeeze of reassurance and her spirits lifted slightly. After all, Matt hadn't directly said he wouldn't continue to include her in any discoveries he might make, either about Elm House or Hammett.

Matt stayed a short while longer before leaving to return to his home. Kitty walked out onto the landing with him to say goodbye.

'I'm sorry I couldn't sway your grandmother, Kitty.' He reached out to smooth a wayward curl on the side of her head.

'It's all right. I can appreciate her concerns for me. At least there are a few things that I can still do.' She smiled at him. 'I suppose I had better use my time to concentrate on my motoring skills. I have one last lesson tomorrow with Robert and then I believe I shall be fully independent.'

Matt's grin widened. 'How very exciting. We must warn your fellow motorists.'

She gave his arm a playful smack. 'How very rude. You will regret it when you require my chauffeuring assistance.'

He laughed and dropped a tender kiss on her lips before bidding her farewell and heading off down the stairs.

*

Kitty had arranged to meet with Robert Potter early the next day for her final lesson. It was still quite dark when she hurried down the main stairs to the lobby where Robert awaited her.

'Are you all set, Miss Kitty?' he asked as she tugged on her scarlet driving gloves.

'Absolutely. I can't wait to be motoring independently. You have really been the most splendid tutor.' Kitty trotted alongside him as they headed for the shed that garaged her car.

She was pleased to discover that the skills she had gained from her previous lessons were still evident as she drove her car carefully through Dartmouth and up the hill past the Naval College adhering to Robert's instructions.

An hour later and flushed with success, she reversed her car back inside the shed. The sun was out now, and a brisk, cool wind was blowing from the direction of the river.

'I reckon as you'm good to go on your own now, miss. Just remember to give her a bit more when you'm on these here hills,' Robert said as they clambered out of the car.

'I will, and thank you so much for all of your patience with me.' Kitty smiled as he followed her out of the garage and waited for her to secure the padlock.

''Tis nothing, Miss Kitty. Um, I was wondering if I might be so bold as to ask you something?' Robert's complexion, always slightly ruddy, had turned a darker shade of red and he ran a finger nervously around his collar.

'Of course, ask away.' Kitty dropped her keys into her coat pocket and wondered what Robert was about to say.

'Well, I knows how you are friends with Miss Miller.' Robert paused awkwardly.

'Alice? Yes, of course.' Kitty tried not to smile; she had a good idea what was coming. She thought she had noticed some partiality before from Robert towards her friend.

'Um, I don't suppose you might know if she had a sweetheart?' Robert asked.

Kitty took pity on the lad. 'No, I believe Miss Miller's affections are not currently engaged with anyone in particular.'

Robert appeared relieved at this reassurance. 'Thank you, Miss Kitty.'

'She is very partial to chocolates and loves attending the cinema,' Kitty added helpfully.

Robert gave a bashful smile. 'I'll bear that in mind, miss.'

They were about to part company when one of the men working on the exterior of a nearby house approached them.

'Excuse me, miss, can I ask if you have a good lock on that shed? I take it as it belongs to you?'

The man was dressed in his working gear and he had a concerned expression on his weather-beaten face.

'Yes, I do rent the shed and I keep it padlocked as I store my car inside. Is there a problem?' She had rented the shed from a local fisherman who had used it for chandlery. The interior still held the faint aroma of fish.

'Only, the reason I'm asking, miss, is there were a strange fellow knocking about the other day asking questions about that there shed. He reckoned as he were looking for a place to rent and wondered if the lady with the red car were still using it. I didn't like the look of him so gave him short shrift. I thought as he had gone but then, a bit later, I spots him a trying the door when he thought as I weren't looking. I reckoned as you should know.'

Kitty's pulse speeded. 'How odd. What was he like, this fellow?'

'Had a cap pulled down low over his brow, looked shifty. Walked a bit gimpy like.' The man considered her question. 'I told him to get out of here or I'd fetch the constable.'

Kitty hands were quite clammy inside her gloves. 'Thank you. If you should notice him again, please can you alert the constable immediately. From your description I believe he may be a person they are looking for.'

The man nodded. 'Right you are, miss.' He tugged his cap and took his leave to return to where he was working repairing a wall with another man.

'You've gone proper pale, Miss Kitty. I'll walk back with you to the hotel.' Robert offered her his arm and she accepted gratefully. The workman's warning had made her feel quite light-headed.

'Thank you, Robert.'

She released his arm when they reached the main entrance of the Dolphin.

'Are you all right now, Miss Kitty?' he asked, an anxious frown puckering his forehead.

'Yes, perfectly, thank you for walking me back. By the by, Alice usually takes her break at around eleven if you should happen to be passing around then, maybe to drop some leaflets off in the foyer.' Kitty gave him a wink and saw the tide of red surge back into his face.

'Thank you, Miss Kitty.' He gave a shy grin and walked away.

Kitty smiled to herself and went inside the hotel ready to start her day's work. Immediately after she had entered her office, she telephoned the police station at Torquay and left Inspector Greville a message about the latest possible sighting of Ezekiel Hammett.

Matt wasn't at home or at his office when she tried there so she had no choice except to delay telling him that Hammett had probably been sighted near her garage. It concerned her that he was obviously aware that she had a red car and stored it in the shed.

Shortly before eleven there was a tap on her office door and Alice entered bearing a tray with her morning coffee.

'I thought as you might be ready for these, miss.' Alice set the tray down carefully on the corner of Kitty's desk.

Kitty saw that Alice had thoughtfully included a small plate containing a couple of jam tarts. 'Oh lovely, thank you, Alice. Um, are you about to have your break now?'

'Yes, miss.' Alice smiled happily. 'I've a half day today too, I'm going to meet our Dolly in Torquay this afternoon to take her for a tea at Bobby's café.'

'That sounds lovely. She did me the most enormous favour yesterday, she's a very bright girl.' Kitty hoped that no one at Elm House had discovered how she had managed to get to Mrs Craven's room without being seen.

'She is that, miss. She wants to go to secretarial school. Always good at her letters and numbers she was, so she's saving all her wages up so as she can get a place and then she can have an office job,' Alice said.

'That's very enterprising of her.' Kitty took a bite from one of the small jam tarts and savoured the delicious tang of strawberries.

'Yes, proper clever she is. Can solve the puzzles in Father's paper faster than anyone.' Alice beamed as she sang her sister's praises. 'Why don't you come with us this afternoon, miss? If you're free. You've had some nasty things happen lately, what with your handbag being took and then the break-in here. We can go for tea all together and take in a film. It'd be nice.'

The idea of an afternoon out doing something pleasurable certainly appealed. The hotel was always quieter in March so she could be spared for a short time.

'I can drive us if you're sure that I shan't be in the way. It will give me the chance to practise my motoring skills.' Kitty beamed at her friend as another idea struck her. Perhaps Dolly might be able to help her work out the codes on Jack Dawkins's papers. 'Do you think Dolly might look at a small puzzle that I have?'

'I reckon so, she loves a challenge. That sounds proper nice, miss, for us all to have a bit of a treat. I said as I'd meet Dolly by the Pavilion at half past two.' Alice prepared to return to her duties.

'Marvellous. I'll meet you here at two and we'll fetch the car together.' Kitty could hear the faint rumble of a male voice in the lobby. It had just turned eleven and she guessed that Robert Potter was loitering in the hope of seeing her friend.

'I'll see you in a bit then, miss.' Alice left the office and Kitty crept over to her tiny porthole window that looked out onto the reception area to see Alice engaged in conversation with Robert.

She grinned to herself and returned to her work determined to gently tease her friend later about her beau.

CHAPTER NINE

Kitty found she was looking forward to her afternoon outing, even if she was a little nervous about making her first solo motoring excursion without Robert's calming presence at her side.

Alice had changed from her uniform into a smart green floral frock, teamed with her best coat and hat. Kitty fluffed her blonde hair, put on her lipstick, and stowed the papers from the box inside her coat pocket. She was wary of carrying them in her handbag just in case something else should happen.

She linked arms with Alice and the two women made their way to the shed in high spirits. The workmen were still nearby repairing the wall and waved to Kitty as she carefully drove her car out and relocked the garage.

''Tis a proper nice motor, miss. Captain Bryant done you proud with it,' Alice remarked admiringly as she hopped up on the running board and into the passenger seat.

'I am rather pleased with it. I'm looking forward to the warmer weather when I can lower the hood.' Kitty pressed the starter and turned the key, taking a calming breath before easing the car forwards ready to join the slow stream of traffic on the road leading to the ferry.

Alice appeared to sense that Kitty required all her concentration and refrained from any chatter until they were safely on board the ferry.

'I reckon as you done that smashing, miss.' Alice smiled at her as the ferry rocked and swayed on its way across the Dart to Kingswear.

'Thank you, Alice. I must confess I hadn't thought there would be quite so much to remember. Robert always makes it look so easy,' Kitty said.

A hint of a blush crept into Alice's cheeks at Kitty's mention of Robert's name. 'I suppose it's because he's been motoring for a while now, miss.'

The ferry bumped to a gentle halt and a small group of foot passengers disembarked. Kitty focused her attention once more on starting her engine ready for the stewards to wave her forwards.

Once she was safely on the road again negotiating the steep hill past Coleton Fishacre, Alice glanced across at Kitty.

'What's been going on at Elm House then, miss? You said as our Dolly had done you a favour and Mrs Craven isn't your favourite person for you to visit so often with Captain Bryant. Are you investigating something? You said as you thought something might not be quite right there?'

Kitty might have guessed that her friend would want to know what was going on so as they motored along she told her everything. All the concerns about Elm House and her fears that Hammett might be in the vicinity of the Dolphin.

'Oh, my word, miss. What a time of it. You had best be extra careful. Thank goodness Robert walked you back this morning. Don't you get going to collect your motor on your own until they catch that Hammett,' Alice warned as Kitty slowed her car to look for a suitable place to stop near the seafront.

'I do so wish they would hurry and catch him. Grams has made me promise not to continue investigating Elm House during my visits to Mrs Craven. She has also made me promise not to try and get any more things into the newspaper about Hammett. She feels it may be directing his attention towards me.' She pulled her car to a halt and turned off the engine. It really was so irritating that she was being held back from finding out more information that might answer her questions about her mother's murder all those years before.

'Well, I can understand her worrying, I suppose.' Alice gathered her handbag ready to climb out of the motor. 'You done well with your motoring, miss. You only had one car sound his horn at you and I reckon as that were his fault.'

Kitty laughed as she got out and locked the car doors. 'Thank you, Alice. Come, let's go and find Dolly.'

Dolly was outside the Pavilion, tucked in a corner out of the wind. She spotted them walking towards her and raised a gloved hand in a cheery wave. Kitty stood back a little as the sisters embraced.

'I asked Miss Kitty to come and join us for a bit of a treat. I've just had a ride in her new motor car.' Alice beamed at her sister.

'Really? Oh that is exciting.' Dolly smiled shyly at Kitty.

'I do hope you don't mind me tagging along with you this afternoon? Alice said she didn't think you would object, and I do have a small puzzle that your sister thought you might possibly be able to help me solve,' Kitty said.

'Of course not, you're very welcome, miss. Our Alice has told me all the lovely things you two have done together,' Dolly said.

Kitty presumed that Alice had given her sister the edited versions and not dwelt on the times she and Alice had managed to get in various scrapes.

They crossed the road and entered the café and Kitty realised she was actually quite hungry. She had missed her lunch, as she presumed the other girls had too. The smell of coffee and fresh bread made her stomach growl as they were seated at a corner table with a side view of the pavement outside.

'Please let me get this. I owe Dolly anyway for smuggling me past that dragon of a receptionist at Elm House and it's so kind of you both to invite me on your outing,' Kitty said as they perused the menu.

Alice immediately began to object but Kitty managed to persuade her, and they ordered pots of tea and a large stand of dainty sandwiches, cakes and savoury treats from the uniformed waitress.

Kitty sipped her tea while Alice and Dolly caught up on their family news. It was pleasant to be out and having a carefree time. She and Alice had been out before a few times, but that had been before Christmas and the visit to her aunt and uncle at Enderley Hall. So much had happened since then it was lovely just to relax and enjoy herself for once.

The waitress placed a large four-tiered china and gilt stand in front of them loaded with all kinds of delicious treats and Dolly's eyes lit up with pleasure.

'Do help yourself to whatever you want,' Kitty instructed as she took a sausage roll from the stand.

Once they had all eaten their fill, the conversation returned to the puzzles that Kitty had mentioned. After checking no one was in earshot she told the girl about the box, emphasising that she was to tell no one about the papers.

'That's all right, miss. I know when to say nothing.' Dolly nodded her head vigorously.

Kitty drew the pages from her coat pocket and placed them in front of the young girl. 'They seem to be entries in some kind of account ledger, but they have been written in code. Quite how Jack came by them, or why he felt they were important, we are not sure. I've looked and so has Matt, but I can't work it out.'

Dolly opened her handbag and produced a small pair of wire-framed spectacles that she fitted over her delicate snub nose. She took a pencil and a bit of paper before frowning over the pages.

'Hmm, let me have a few minutes to think on it, miss. I have heard of different codes that people have used before. I read a book on it a while back from the public lending library.'

Alice smiled proudly at her younger sister. She turned the conversation to the film they intended to see later at the Burlington Picture House, giving Dolly time to study the sheets before her.

Kitty was about to suggest that they needed to start walking the short distance to the cinema when Dolly gave an exclamation.

'I think I have it.'

'Really? Oh how marvellous, how does it work?' Kitty leaned forward, as did Alice, to study the papers. Dolly showed them the back of an old envelope that she had been scribbling on.

'What it seems to me, miss, is that they've reversed the words. See this word here is 2g1kc1p, now replace the vowels with numbers, A1, E2, I3, O4, U5. If you turns it round look, and puts in the vowels now, it says package.' Dolly sat back and beamed at them both before removing her glasses and returning them to her bag.

'Gosh, Dolly, that is amazing,' Kitty said admiringly. 'I would never have worked that out in a month of Sundays.' She had looked at the notes several times and tried various ideas but hadn't managed to break the code. 'You are so clever.'

Dolly's cheeks flamed crimson. 'I enjoy a good puzzle, miss.' She tucked the envelope and her pencil back inside her bag.

'We must get going if we are to see the film,' Alice said, glancing at her watch.

Kitty folded the papers back up and placed them deep inside her coat pocket. As soon as she returned to the Dolphin, she intended to work out the rest of the code to see if there was a link to Ezekiel Hammett or his sister.

They left the café and walked into the town towards the picture house. Dolly and Alice walked ahead, arm in arm while Kitty followed behind. Her mind was busy thinking over the possibilities which cracking the coded papers might uncover.

The town was busy for a cool Tuesday afternoon in March and the sun had already begun to drop lower in the sky as they approached the cinema. Kitty kept her handbag close to her side and found herself keeping space around her by avoiding the more congested parts of the pavement. The snatching of her bag a few days ago had made her more cautious and aware of who might be near to her.

It was that caution that made her notice the boy. She had spotted him before loitering around near the café. He looked about twelve, in worn clothing with a dirty face and a man's cap that was too large for his small head.

Now he was outside the cinema. She wondered if he might be begging, hoping for a few coppers from the cinema patrons. Alice got their tickets from the booth and Kitty took a last look at the boy as he stood outside the entrance. For a split second their gazes locked, and the boy immediately took a step back before melting away as if by magic into a knot of people walking by.

'Kitty, come on, we've got some sweets ready. Let's go and find our seats.' Alice nudged her, then seemed to notice her expression. 'What is it, miss? Is something wrong?'

'Nothing, it's fine, my imagination is running away with me.' She forced a smile and accompanied Alice and Dolly into the auditorium. She had no desire to worry her friend with what could simply be a strange coincidence especially as young Dolly was with them.

The boy had gone now so there was nothing she could do. Instead, she took her seat beside Alice and settled down to watch James Cagney on the silver screen. With the aid of several toffees by the time the film ended, Kitty felt much more relaxed.

The girls walked back down to the seafront together to where Kitty had left her car. She kept a sharp eye open in case she saw the boy again, but he didn't appear. She had offered to take Dolly back to Elm House in order to save her a walk up the steep hill in the cold. The lamps were now lit, and the shops in the town were mostly closed for the day.

Dolly beamed as Kitty unlocked her car doors so they could climb inside. Alice taking the front passenger seat and Dolly in the back. Kitty held her breath as she started the engine and tried to remember Robert's instructions. To her delight, the car turned over on her first attempt and she signalled with her trafficators before turning around to head for Elm House.

She decided not to pull her car into the small, gravelled forecourt directly in front of Elm House as she didn't wish to broadcast any connection with Dolly. Instead, she pulled further up the lane and stopped there to allow the girl to climb out.

'Thank you ever so much for the ride, miss, and for the lovely lunch. It's been a rare day out,' Dolly said, smiling as she closed the car door. Alice and Kitty waved farewell and waited at the kerb until the girl had walked inside the entrance to the convalescent home.

Kitty followed the road around until she reached a part she recognised, then made her way back onto the coastal road.

'I'm glad Dolly enjoyed herself. She is so clever. I would never have mastered that code on my own,' Kitty said.

Alice beamed. 'She's the cleverest out of all of us. My brother, Sam, the one between me and Dolly, he's clever as well but not as smart as Dolly. He's got an apprenticeship at the bakery. Doing well, he is. I'm helping our Dolly with her savings where I can. She doesn't really like being a maid, but she gets books from the lending library and studies what she can.' Alice unwrapped another toffee and popped it in her mouth.

'Well, I'm very grateful to her. By the way when we were at the café, you didn't by any chance notice a young lad standing outside? Aged about twelve, with a cap that looked too big for him?' Kitty asked as she concentrated on steering her motor past a horse and cart.

Alice tucked her sweet into her cheek as she replied. 'Hmm, yes, I think there was a boy. A bit scruffy looking, a street urchin.'

'That's the one. I think he followed us to the cinema.' Kitty winced as she crunched her gear change as they reached the common at Churston to start the descent along the lanes to Kingswear.

'I knew something had rattled you, miss, when I was getting the tickets. Wonder what he was up to? Do you think someone paid him to spy on you?' Alice frowned.

'No one knew we were going to be in Torquay today so unless someone saw me park the car and spotted an opportunity, then I don't know what they hoped to achieve or who would do such a thing.' Kitty slowed the car to join the small queue of traffic waiting to board the ferry.

'I see what you mean, miss. It's a bit odd though, I suppose he could just have followed us hoping to beg something or steal something. He might have thought as you had money being a lady motorist. Could be one of them pickpockets as you read about.' Alice finished her sweet as they boarded the boat.

'True.' Alice could be right, and she was simply allowing her imagination to run wild.

Once the car was once more locked safely away inside the shed and everything secured, Alice walked back with her through the darkened streets to the Dolphin. Kitty knew it was irrational but seeing the golden glow of the lights spilling through the leaded panes of the ancient building made her appreciate its safety and homeliness.

'Will you come in for coffee?' Kitty asked as Alice released her arm outside the front entrance.

'Usually I'd like nothing better, miss, but I promised Mother as I'd let down the hem of our Sarah's frock,' Alice apologised.

'Of course, I've monopolised enough of your half day. Let me telephone Mr Potter. I don't want you to walk home alone in the dark, not with all these queer things happening,' Kitty urged.

'It's quite all right, miss. I've only to walk along here just a step and my uncle will be closing up his business for the day. He'll see me home all right,' the girl reassured her. 'Besides, I reckon as you have a visitor.' She grinned as the familiar sound of Matt's Sunbeam rounded the corner.

Kitty waved farewell to her friend and waited for Matt to disembark from his motorcycle.

'Was that Alice I saw slipping away?' he asked as he approached her.

'Yes, she's gone to her uncle's workplace, then he is walking her home. We've been out to the cinema in Torquay along with young Dolly. And, you'll never guess. She's solved the code.'

Matt slipped his arm around her waist to give her a quick hug. 'Really? That is good news. Come on and you can tell me all about it.'

They entered the lobby. Matt drew off his leather gauntlets as Kitty collected the new key for her office from Mary at the reception desk.

'A lady came by this afternoon, Miss Kitty, after you had gone out. She asked for you in person,' Mary said as she passed over the key.

'Oh, did she leave a name?' Kitty often had people call in, usually wanting to discuss trading with the hotel or looking for employment.

'No, miss. I asked if you were expecting her and she said no. She left a note here for you.' Mary reached into one of the small pigeonholes that were used for letters, small items and keys to the guest rooms.

'Thank you, Mary.' Kitty took the note and opened her office, turning on the green glass shaded desk lamp before taking off her outdoor things. Matt followed suit, hanging his leather greatcoat, woollen muffler and cloth cap next to Kitty's things on the small coat stand.

Once the office door was closed behind them, Kitty took out the papers from the pocket of her coat and placed them on the desk before telling Matt everything that had happened that day.

His brows raised and he released a low whistle of surprise when she told him of the man hanging around the shed where she kept her car.

'You have informed the police, of course?' he asked.

'Yes, I telephoned them immediately. He must be hiding not far away, Matt. Someone in the town must know where he is and who is sheltering him.' She went on to confess her suspicions about the young boy in Torquay. 'What do you think, Matt? Am I making too much of all this and jumping at shadows?' she asked.

Matt's frown deepened. 'I don't know, Kitty, but I don't like it. I think the sooner we work out what those pages say and then, if they are important, give them to Inspector Greville or Inspector Pinch, the better it will be. Hammett clearly harbours a grudge against you for worsening his position. While he may have quietly escaped the law for the murder of his half-brother, the offer of the reward and the potential conviction for historic crimes, including your mother's murder, would definitely see him hang.'

Kitty stared at him. She knew he was right but hearing her own suspicions voiced aloud by Matt made them all the more real and terrifying. 'What should I do? The police have not been much help so far. He has evaded them once and fired at the officers pursuing him.' She bit down on her lower lip to stop the trembling she knew would betray her fears.

'I think you are safe enough here, within the hotel. There are people all around you and I don't think he will risk an attempt again. It will be all right, Kitty, I'm quite certain. Let's crack this puzzle and then I think we should go and see Greville again tomorrow and demand that he does more to ensure your safety.' His expression was troubled as he spoke, and Kitty could see that he was turning over the possibilities in his mind for what they might do.

'He has to be caught soon, he simply has to be. It's quite absurd that he has been able to move around so freely for so long,' Kitty said.

'I agree. Chin up, darling, I promise I won't allow anything to happen to you.' Matt leaned over the desk to place a gentle kiss on her brow. 'First thing tomorrow we shall be knocking on the inspector's office door.'

CHAPTER TEN

Kitty sent for a pot of coffee and they started to decode the inscriptions on the pages from the box. They divided the task between them and worked in silence for an hour scribbling away.

Eventually Kitty leaned back in her seat, an expression of disgust on her face. 'Whew, well, I'm not certain after all that effort that any of this is helpful. I can't see what could be on this that Hammett might want.' She placed her pencil down next to her writing pad and stretched.

Matt finished the last few translations and turned her sheets round so he could read them alongside the ones he had completed.

'I don't either, let's look at them when we put them together and see if they make more sense.' His brow creased as he studied the sheets.

Kitty rose, stretching her back and came around the desk to look over his shoulder. 'Very well, let me see.'

He pointed to the first sheet. 'This seems to be a list of addresses and I assume the figures at the end might be rents.'

Kitty leaned closer, brushing his shoulder. 'That address there, Prospect Road, isn't that where Ezekiel was staying when the police almost caught him?'

'Yes, near Cobden Steps. These could be Esther's properties. Inspector Greville said the police in Exeter were finding it difficult to establish which properties she owned as some were through some kind of holding company.' Matt could see that as well as the address, which he knew to be at Brixham, there were street names he recognised in Torquay and Exeter.

'Then Ezekiel could be sheltered at any of these places. I know some of those street names and they are not in desirable areas,' Kitty said.

'What of this page? This one seems to be notes with amounts marked next to them. Fishtown package received. Redistribution arranged. Two hundred pounds.' Matt glanced up, he could see she was concentrating hard.

'For that sum of money I can't believe it to be for something that is above board,' she said.

'Fishtown?' Matt queried.

'Another name for Brixham.' Kitty smiled at him. 'Call yourself a detective.'

He grinned back at her before returning to the notes. 'This one seems to be a list of names. People, possibly, or businesses, perhaps, with figures next to them. Some seem to have paid the owner of the notes, some appear to have received money. Then there are some crossed out with void written above them.'

He felt her shiver as if something had suddenly chilled her. 'What do you think that could be? And why does this sheet have Elm House written in the column?'

'Perhaps their business is completed, and they are no longer customers? Suppliers? There is no figure next to Elm House. Just the name. Maybe Esther thought to add it to her portfolio before Doctor Marsh acquired it? If indeed these papers belong to Hammett and Esther. Or something that was purchased during the refurbishment?' Matt suggested.

He deliberately kept his tone calm and his features composed so as not to alarm Kitty. It bothered him greatly that Elm House was listed even though the explanation he had just given Kitty could very well be the truth.

'Hmm, I suppose so. It might be helpful to discover who some of these people might be. Do you think Father Lamb may know?' Kitty asked.

The elderly priest had been the person who had given Jack's box to Kitty, saying it had been the man's dying request. As priest of the Church of the Sacred Heart in Exeter he had connections in all levels of society there.

'I think it may be worth asking him. If we go along the official route, if there is something odd, then having the police poking around may tip them off,' Matt said.

'Do you think there may be a connection between these mysterious visitors at Elm House and this document? When Jack acquired these, he only had a few days to live. The date on this one is just after you went to see him at his shop. Doctor Marsh bought Elm House I believe over the summer.' Kitty stirred the papers gently with the tip of her finger, as if by touching them they might give her the answer she sought.

'It would be an extraordinary thing but there are too many coincidences lately and we have encountered many extraordinary things together before.' Matt took hold of her hand, twisting on his seat so he could face her more fully.

She held his gaze, her blue-grey eyes clouded, and he suspected they reflected her thoughts. 'The sooner Mrs Craven can return home the happier I shall be. I keep worrying about little Dolly too.'

'Let's compile a list from this page of names and then we'll telephone Father Lamb and see if any of them are familiar to him,' Matt suggested.

'Especially those crossed out ones. They trouble me, Matt. If these papers do belong to Esther or Ezekiel, then I doubt it would be a straightforward matter to cease doing business with either of them.' Kitty picked up her pencil once more and returned to her seat.

Matt glanced at his watch. 'If we telephone now, we should catch him before he has dinner.'

'Oh dear, I hadn't realised the time. Grams will be expecting me soon. Will you join us?' she asked as she picked up the telephone receiver ready to dial.

Since he had made no special plans for his evening meal Matt was happy to agree. He had considered suggesting that he move back into the Dolphin for a while until either Hammett was captured or the danger had decreased. It wouldn't be the first time he had stayed in one of the spare rooms on Kitty's floor to ensure her safety. However he wasn't sure if Kitty would welcome the suggestion and he didn't wish to further alarm her grandmother.

He listened to Kitty's side of the conversation as she gave Father Lamb the names on the list. In response to some of his replies she frowned and scribbled notes on her writing pad.

'I see, thank you, Father. That has been enormously helpful. If you do learn anything more then please do let me know.' She finished her conversation and replaced the receiver on its cradle.

Matt's chair creaked as he leaned back and looked at Kitty. 'Well, what did Father Lamb have to say?'

Kitty squinted at her writing pad. 'He recognised a few of the names I gave him. One of them is a prominent councillor in Exeter. Another one is on the board of several companies in the city.'

'What of the names that had been voided?' Matt asked.

He saw Kitty swallow, her blonde curls bobbing with the gentle movement of her head. 'He knew of two. Tappley, he believes may be a Peter Tappley, found drowned in the river in June. Haig, he thinks may be Douglas Haig, a Scotsman who owned a wine importing business by the waterfront. He perished in July in a fire at his warehouse. No one was ever caught although the police at the time apparently suspected arson.'

Matt blew out a sigh. The more they were uncovering, the less he liked it. 'I think we may have to speak to Inspector Greville again about this after all.' He ripped their notes from the pad and gathered all the papers together. He folded them up and tucked them inside the breast pocket of his jacket.

Kitty picked up the envelope that Mary had given her at the desk. 'I'd better see what this is about before we go for dinner,' she said as she slit it open with her paperknife.

The envelope contained only one sheet of commonplace cheap lined paper. He watched Kitty's complexion pale as she read it before she passed it across to him to see.

For the attention of Miss Underhay,

It seems you and your nosey detective friend cannot take a hint. Stay out of my concerns or it will be the worse for both of you.

E H

'Something else for Inspector Greville in the morning,' Matt remarked, sliding the note back inside its envelope. 'I wonder who the woman was who delivered it?' He kept his tone casual not wishing to alarm Kitty.

Colour had returned to Kitty's cheeks. 'Mary has finished for the day now. We can ask her for a better description in the morning.' She rose and walked towards the door.

Matt clicked off her desk light. 'Let's go and see your grandmother and have dinner. I think we shall have a busy day tomorrow.'

Kitty left Matt in her grandmother's salon and hurried to her room to change from her cheerful rose printed day dress into a more suitable gown for dinner. She took a moment to tidy her hair and to add a touch more lipstick before returning downstairs to join them.

'Kitty dear, you look lovely.' Her grandmother moved to embrace her before pressing a glass of sherry into her hand. 'Now, I understand you went out with Alice and her sister today? Did you have a lovely time?'

Kitty obliged her grandmother with a description of the film and their afternoon tea in the café. She omitted any mention of the man hanging around her garage or of the young boy who may have been watching them.

'How was Mrs Craven this afternoon?' Matt asked once they were all seated at the small table situated in the bay window of the salon and Kitty had served them all with a bowl of consommé for their first course.

Mrs Treadwell patted the corner of her mouth with her white linen napkin. 'She is improving. She tells me that she can walk a few steps now with her cane without too much discomfort.'

'And how is she in herself?' Kitty asked, causing a frown to appear on her grandmother's face.

'She seems brighter, but I do wish she would desist from this nonsense about Elm House. She has that man backing her up now too, you know, that general she's become friendly with. I believe he is the one egging her on with this talk of mysterious visitors and suspicious deaths.' Her grandmother took a sip from her water glass.

Kitty exchanged a glance with Matt. 'I expect she will be able to go home in a few days.'

'I do hope so, my dear. Doctor Marsh has been called away apparently, back to London. Sister Carmichael said he still does a lot of work teaching the medical students, and of course he still sees some patients there. She did not seem very pleased, however. I expect it places a lot of work on her shoulders.' Mrs Treadwell picked up her spoon to finish her soup.

This seemed to confirm the information she had learned herself from Sister Carmichael.

'Doctor Marsh must be a very busy man,' Matt remarked mildly.

'Indeed, he is. Sister Carmichael said he was very well thought of. She has worked with him for several years,' Mrs Treadwell replied.

Kitty finished her own soup. 'Goodness, you seem to have had quite a conversation with Sister Carmichael today.' She saw Matt hiding a smile behind his napkin as she gathered up the empty bowls ready to serve their second course from the trolley.

'The woman was quite talkative for once. She came over as I was about to leave. She was asking quite a lot about you, Kitty dear. Apparently, she had read that piece in the *Herald* about that dreadful Hammett fellow and the reward.'

Kitty almost dropped the serving dish of vegetables. 'Really, well I suppose it did make the headlines when he shot at those policemen.'

Mrs Treadwell offered Matt a helping of potatoes to go with the pork cutlets on his plate. 'And, of course, she had discovered that you, Matthew, were a private detective. She was most interested in your work. I said very little of that as I did not want Millicent to make more of it.'

Kitty thought it sounded as if she and Matt were not the only people who had been doing a little investigative work. With what she and Matt had uncovered it made her quite uncomfortable that Sister Carmichael may have been asking questions of her grandmother about them.

'I think that may have been wise, Grams. It wouldn't do for Mrs Craven to upset the staff caring for her,' Kitty said, picking up the white porcelain gravy boat.

Her grandmother smiled approvingly at her. 'I'm glad we are agreed on that point, my dear.'

The rest of dinner passed peacefully with the conversation on other matters related to the hotel. Once the delicious dessert of treacle tart with clotted cream had been consumed, Kitty and Matt excused themselves with Kitty pleading the need to check on the staff in the ballroom, a local female vocalist was entertaining the guests that evening.

Matt accompanied Kitty to the ballroom and waited patiently for her to complete her tasks before collecting a couple of Bellini cocktails and taking a seat next to her at a quiet, corner table.

'Thank you,' Kitty said and took a sip from her drink while looking around the room with a critical eye to ensure everything was as it should be.

'What did you think about what Grams said at dinner?' she asked.

'I wonder what has sent Doctor Marsh back to London so swiftly? I also wonder what Sister Carmichael was hoping to discover about us?' Matt said.

'I definitely think we need to speak to Inspector Greville again tomorrow and this time I hope he'll pay more attention to our concerns,' Kitty remarked.

'I think that note may help to focus his mind, combined with the information from Father Lamb. Kitty, will you be all right here at the Dolphin with your grandmother? Would you like me to stay over for a few days, just until this blows over and Hammett is caught?' Concern showed in Matt's eyes as he took her free hand in his.

For a moment Kitty was tempted by his offer. It would be quite reassuring knowing that Matt was just a few steps away along the landing should Hammett try again. However, it would also alarm her grandmother if she thought danger was so close by, not to mention that tongues would invariably wag now she and Matt were known to be a couple.

'That's kind of you, but I don't think he will try the hotel again and, as you can see this evening, Mickey has increased our security.' She looked in the direction of the entrance where a large, burly man in evening attire was working with Mickey to welcome guests into the room.

The corners of Matt's mouth curved upwards. 'Yes, I wouldn't wish to argue with Mickey's friend.'

Kitty laughed. 'Shall I call for you in the morning? You may have your first experience of being chauffeured by me.'

Matt chinked his cocktail glass against hers. 'Around nine thirty? We can go and beard Inspector Greville in his office and see what he has to say.'

Kitty rose early the next morning and took her breakfast in her office to complete some of her work before she needed to set off to collect Matt. Mary, her day receptionist, arrived at eight and Kitty stepped out of her office to greet her as soon as she heard the girl bidding farewell to the night porter.

'Mary, the lady that left the note for me yesterday, you said she didn't leave her name, or a calling card?' Kitty asked.

'No, miss. Is there a problem, miss?' The girl appeared anxious and Kitty hurried to reassure her.

'No, it's just that I can't make out her signature on the note she left. What did she look like?' She blurred the truth a little so as not to further worry her receptionist.

'Well, she was dressed quite well, fashionable like, a nice fur collar on her coat and lots of gold rings on her hands. I noticed them as she passed the letter across. She had dark hair and an expensive hat. She wore quite a lot of rouge mind, and her shoes wasn't the best quality, so I wasn't sure if she was a real lady, if you catch my meaning, miss,' Mary said diplomatically.

'Thank you, Mary, that's really very helpful. If she comes in again can you try and get her name and let Mickey know that she's here,' Kitty said. She had alerted Mickey about the visitor the night before when she and Matt had left the ballroom. He had promised to look out for the woman as well as continuing to watch out for Hammett.

'Yes, Miss Kitty.'

Kitty was about to return to her office when the reception telephone rang out.

'The Dolphin Hotel, may I… yes, Mrs Craven, one moment, Miss Kitty is right here.' Mary covered the speaking part of the receiver with her hand. ''Tis Mrs Craven, miss, she wants to speak to you urgently. She sounds all of a do.' The girl passed the receiver across to Kitty.

'Mrs Craven? It's Kitty, is something wrong?'

Mrs Craven's voice, in a loud whisper, filled her ear. 'Kitty, thank heavens. I tried Matthew first, of course, but he doesn't appear to be answering his telephone.' There was a pause. 'You have to come here right away. Something dreadful has happened. I haven't long, I'm telephoning from the guest telephone in the reception area and that ghastly Bowkett creature listens in usually to any calls, but she's run off somewhere in all this panic.'

Kitty could hear voices in the background and what sounded like some kind of commotion growing louder as Mrs Craven spoke.

'Are you all right? Are you hurt?' she asked.

'Find Captain Bryant and hurry, Kitty.' The phone went dead, and Kitty assumed she had rung off if Miss Bowkett had returned to her post.

Kitty glanced at her watch. She would be early calling for Matt if she left now but Mrs Craven had sounded quite desperate.

'I'm going to Elm House with Captain Bryant if Grams wants me. I shall be back later this morning.' Kitty gave Mary her instructions for the morning, then collected her hat and coat before hurrying out of the hotel to the shed.

The workmen from the previous day had already arrived to complete their work on the wall and she gave them a cheery wave as she drove off. The sun was just making an appearance as she boarded the ferry and she shivered in the cool wintery air.

A few minutes later she had driven through Kingswear and along the lanes to Matt's house near the golf course at Churston. She parked outside and tooted her car horn. A moment later, he appeared on the doorstep carrying a teacup and waved to her to come in, a puzzled frown on his face.

'You're early, what's wrong?' he asked as she entered the neat square hallway.

'Mrs Craven telephoned me. She tried you first but didn't get an answer. Something is wrong at Elm House.'

Matt set down his tea. 'That must have been the call I missed while I was bathing. Is she all right?' He started to pull on his hat and coat as he spoke.

'I'm really not quite sure, there was a terrible commotion going on around her. She seemed very anxious not to be overheard telephoning,' Kitty said as they hurried back out to her car.

Matt clambered into the passenger seat and Kitty started the engine and turned her key. There was more traffic around on their way into Torquay and Kitty was forced to concentrate to avoid cyclists and slower horse-drawn traffic on the road as well as the few business vehicles.

Matt had cracked the side window open slightly and a cool breeze curled its way around the interior of the car. Ever since the war he had struggled with confined spaces. An inheritance from serving in the deep labyrinth of muddy trenches which were prone to collapse and bury both men and horses alive in the sticky, heavy clay of the battlefield.

'I do hope Mrs Craven is all right. There sounded the most dreadful racket in the background, doors banging and people shouting. She said something dreadful had happened.' Kitty turned off from the coastal road and changed gear ready for the steep climb to Elm House.

'Mrs C is quite a tough old bird. I wonder what's gone on.' Matt gave her a reassuring smile and she guessed he was trying to lighten her concerns.

Kitty steered her car through the opening in the stone walls that surrounded the convalescent home and found that some familiar vehicles were already parked outside the front entrance.

'Isn't that Doctor Carter's car? And Inspector Greville's black police car?' she asked as she pulled to a halt under one of the large elm trees that bordered the gravelled space.

'Yes, I believe you're right.' Matt was out of the car almost before Kitty had a chance to pull up the handbrake and turn off the engine.

She collected her handbag and locked the car before following him to the front door at a slightly more sedate pace.

Miss Bowkett was back in place behind the reception desk, although her demeanour was more ruffled than usual.

'I'm terribly sorry, sir, madam, but we are not permitting visitors at the moment.'

'I am not leaving until I have seen Mrs Craven and verified that she is safe and well. I see Doctor Carter and Inspector Greville are present. They will vouch for us, I'm sure,' Kitty said as she swept past the woman, following the sound of voices along the corridor to where she was sure the incident was occurring.

'Wait, stop, I must insist that you return to the reception area.' Miss Bowkett hurried after them, her heels clicking on the parquet floor.

'Miss Underhay, and Captain Bryant, I might have guessed that you would be along.' Inspector Greville appeared in front of them clad in his usual dark overcoat and trilby hat.

'I tried to tell them, sir.' Miss Bowkett glowered at Kitty.

'That's quite all right. Please return to your business.' The inspector dismissed her, and the receptionist stalked away back to the lobby.

'As a matter of interest, how did you arrive here so quickly?' the inspector asked once Miss Bowkett was at a safe distance.

'Mrs Craven telephoned us requesting us to come as quickly as possible,' Matt replied. 'What's gone on here, sir?'

The inspector led them a short way along the corridor and into a small office where he offered them both a seat. 'A resident collapsed this morning in the dining room shortly after breakfast. Not an unusual occurrence in a place like this, however, the staff returned the lady to her room where she subsequently passed away. Doctor Marsh is not present, so the nursing sister telephoned a local doctor to visit and certify the death. The doctor they contacted happened to be Doctor Carter. He was not satisfied, given his other concerns about this place, and we were called in. As soon as he declined to issue a certificate pandemonium appeared to break loose.'

'That must have been when Mrs Craven made her telephone call,' Kitty said.

There was a knock at the door and Doctor Carter's cheery cherubic face peeped around the edge of the door. 'Hello, Miss Underhay, Captain Bryant.' He inserted his plump, tweed-clad frame into the tiny room. 'Just to let you know, Inspector, I left the constable taking statements from the staff and the other patients. Sister Carmichael is most unhappy about it all. She wishes to speak to you.'

'I need to speak to her too,' the inspector said.

'Inspector Greville said you were unhappy with the alleged cause of death?' Kitty phrased her question delicately. She was not yet sure who had died.

'Yes, a lady called Pearson. I know her quite well and, frankly, although she had been ill and was run-down, there was no reason for her to turn up her toes just yet. I want to do some tests, there were signs when I examined the lady that could indicate that she was murdered,' Doctor Carter explained.

Kitty gasped when she heard the name. 'She'd recently had pneumonia, hadn't she?'

'Yes, but she simply needed a break to regain her strength and to get away from that son of hers for a while.' Doctor Carter frowned. 'I take it you know the lady, Miss Underhay?'

'Not exactly, but Mrs Craven knows her, as does my grandmother, although they are more acquaintances than friends. I believe Lady Wellings's nephew is a friend of Leonard Pearson and recommended Elm House to him,' Kitty said.

'Did he indeed?' Inspector Greville muttered as he tugged his pocketbook free from his coat to scribble a brief note inside it.

There was another tap on the door. This time more peremptory.

'I expect that will be Sister Carmichael in search of you, Greville,' Doctor Carter murmured.

'Better let her in,' the inspector said as the doctor smiled and bade them all a cheerful farewell.

Sister Carmichael crackled into the office, stopping short when she saw Kitty and Matt comfortably ensconced on the other side of the polished rosewood desk from the inspector.

'Inspector Greville, I really must protest. My patients and staff are quite upset at being interrogated by your constable about poor Mrs Pearson. I must inform you that I have telephoned Doctor Marsh in London and he is making an immediate return to Torquay.' She glared at Kitty and Matt and Kitty could tell that she was most put out that they were present for this tirade.

'I assume you have informed Doctor Marsh of Doctor Carter's concerns about Mrs Pearson's death?' the inspector asked in a mild tone.

'Of course. Like myself he was most surprised and concerned. We have no reason to suspect that Mrs Pearson's death was due to anything except natural causes. My staff are most distressed at the inference that it may be due to anything else, despite what some people set upon causing mischief may have inferred.' Sister Carmichael favoured Matt with a look that would have put Kitty's grandmother to shame.

'If Doctor Carter has concerns that a death may not be due to natural causes, then he is duty-bound to report it, and I to investigate it. I must also inform you, Sister Carmichael, that we may also be revisiting the death of Lady Wellings,' the inspector said.

The colour receded from Sister Carmichael's cheeks at this announcement, leaving behind two ugly patches of red. 'Doctor Marsh will be informed of this immediately on his return. I daresay he will have strong words to say about these matters.'

'He may say whatever he wishes, but it will not affect my investigation. Please return to your patients, Sister. I shall come and find you shortly to take your statement.' The inspector appeared unperturbed by the nurse's outburst.

'And I fail to see quite why a private detective and his lady friend are here.' Sister Carmichael turned on her heel and marched off, her carriage stiff with indignation.

'We must go and find Mrs Craven,' Kitty said, rising from her seat. 'We had intended coming to see you this morning, Inspector, as we have more information about Hammett, and it may even have links to this place.'

Inspector Greville's moustache twitched at this piece of information.

'We managed to decode those sheets of paper from Dawkins's box.' Matt stood to join Kitty.

'I see. Perhaps I can call on you later today, Miss Underhay, when I've finished gathering all the evidence from here?' the inspector asked.

'Of course,' Kitty agreed. She could see that the inspector had his hands full at Elm House. If Mrs Pearson's death was proved to be the result of foul play of some kind, then he would need to ensure he had followed every lead.

Mrs Craven was seated near the window in the lounge next to a smartly attired silver haired gentleman.

'Kitty, Matthew, about time. Wherever have you been?' Mrs Craven demanded as soon as they were within earshot.

'Our apologies, we met Doctor Carter and Inspector Greville on our way in,' Matt said, and extended his hand to the man sitting opposite Mrs Craven. 'General Ackland? Good to meet you, sir.'

The general nodded an acknowledgement as Matt and Kitty took a seat on the plush covered but rather uncomfortable upright chairs nearby. Mrs Craven performed the formal introductions.

'Did the inspector tell you what had happened? I did tell you to hurry, Kitty.' Mrs Craven lowered her voice as Cyril Dodds entered the room.

'All we know so far is that Mrs Pearson was taken ill in the dining room and died shortly after she returned to her room. Doctor Carter is not satisfied about the cause of death and has notified Inspector Greville and the coroner. The inspector has also said they are going to re-examine Lady Wellings's death.' Kitty also kept her voice low as she monitored Dodds's position in the room out of the corner of her eye.

General Ackland snorted. 'Died in her room my foot. Woman hit the ground like a sack of potatoes. She was dead when they stuffed her into a wheelchair and carted her out.' He leaned forward and tapped Kitty on her knee. 'Poison, mark my words. Seen deaths like that before you know, out in India.'

'Gracious.' Kitty looked to Matt for support.

'I expect Doctor Carter will get to the bottom of the matter. Why poison though, sir? I can see that her son may benefit from his mother's demise as we've heard he was always asking her for money, but he wasn't present at breakfast surely?' Matt asked.

It crossed Kitty's mind that perhaps Mrs Pearson's son might have paid to have his mother murdered.

The general's bushy brows knitted together like two angry silver beetles. 'The Carmichael woman and that fella Marsh are speeding things along in return for a bit of a backhander. That Pearson woman was as right as rain until she tucked into her porridge and Nurse Hibbert gave her the morning medication. It was probably in the pills. Poor Nurse Hibbert is a bag of nerves. Looked like she was about to burst into tears when the constable took her out to question her.'

The general's words confirmed her own thoughts. 'You think it was her medication that may have killed her?' Kitty asked. It could be a mistake, a medication error perhaps. The wrong dose or some confusion over the tablets.

Mrs Craven looked smug. 'I told you I saw Roderick Harmer up to no good with Doctor Marsh after Lady Wellings died and Leonard Pearson has been here every day to try and get money out of his mother.'

'I presume you will tell Inspector Greville all of this?' Kitty was aware that Dodds, under the pretext of straightening up various chairs and papers, had made his way closer to their group.

'Naturally.' Mrs Craven looked at the general who nodded solemnly in agreement.

'Mrs Craven, are you quite certain that you wish to remain here?' Matt asked.

'I shall be returning home in a couple of days. My maid is holidaying at her sister's home in Scarborough and when she returns to open my home, I should be sufficiently proficient with my cane to manage the stairs in my house.' Mrs Craven looked at Matt. 'I am quite capable of taking care of myself, Matthew.'

Kitty could see that they would be unable to dissuade her grandmother's friend from remaining. Quite what her grandmother would think of this latest event she really wasn't sure. Mrs Treadwell had been quite dismissive of Mrs Craven's theories that something was wrong at Elm House. Now it appeared that Mrs Craven had been right all along.

'Well, please do be careful, Mrs Craven. If something is amiss it would never do for you to become the next victim,' Kitty said.

General Ackland gave a snort of laughter. 'Have no fears, little lady. I shall protect your grandmother's friend to the best of my abilities.'

Kitty was amused to see Mrs Craven turn quite pink and simper at the general like a young girl.

Matt seemed to bite back a smile. 'Then I can see you are in good hands, Mrs C.'

They said their farewells and left the elderly couple to enjoy each other's company.

'I do believe Mrs Craven has a beau.' Kitty grinned at Matt as they made their way back towards the reception area.

'Brave man.' Matt smiled back at her as Miss Bowkett scowled at them both from behind the reception desk.

Doctor Carter's car had gone when they stepped outside the building, but the inspector's vehicle remained.

'This is such a beautiful spot, and the gardens with the view of the bay are so lovely. It's hard to believe that we've just spent over an hour talking of poison and murder.' Kitty shivered as she looked at the sea, blue green and sparkling before them.

Matt placed his arm around her waist. 'I expect the view is even more spectacular from the top of the turret.'

Kitty turned to look back at the building, shading her eyes with her hand. 'I believe so. It actually looks as if there is a telescope up there.'

'Perhaps Doctor Marsh is an astronomer.' Matt's tone was light, but she knew it wasn't astronomy that was likely to draw mysterious night-time visitors to Elm House.

'We should get back to Dartmouth. The inspector will no doubt be across to the Dolphin when he has completed his interviews here.' Kitty hoped little Dolly had not been involved in the mayhem when Mrs Pearson had collapsed. With any luck she should have been busy washing pots in the kitchen out of harm's way.

'It's almost lunchtime. Do you want to call somewhere for lunch on the way?' Matt asked as they crunched their way across the gravel to Kitty's distinctive little red car.

'I really should return and do some work. The hotel is starting to become busier now and Grams will tell me off for not giving more attention to my tasks,' Kitty said. 'You can share a sandwich with me, if you like?'

'That sounds lovely.' Matt waited for Kitty to unlock her car.

'Psst, excuse me.' The urgent half-whisper came from a shady spot at the corner of the home. A dark-haired young nurse of about her own age, dressed in a pale blue uniform, stood shivering near the wall as she tried to get their attention.

Kitty glanced at the home to check no one was watching them from the windows and hurried over to the girl leaving Matt to keep watch beside the car.

'Can we help you?'

The nurse had red-rimmed eyes and looked anxious. 'Mrs Craven said as you and the gentleman was detectives?'

'Well, yes.' Kitty decided it wasn't worthwhile taking time to explain that it was technically just Matt who was a private investigator. The girl had obviously stepped out from her duties and no doubt would have to get back quickly before she was missed.

'I need to talk to someone, but not the police. It's about this place.' The girl peered fearfully at the building next to her.

'You must be Nurse Hibbert?' Kitty guessed.

The girl nodded. 'Yes, Eloise Hibbert. Can you meet me in the town tomorrow afternoon? The Copper Kettle tea room at half past two? I need some advice.'

'Well, yes, of course, but can you not give me an idea of what it's about?' Kitty asked.

The girl looked at the fob watch pinned to the front of her starched apron. 'Not here, I can't talk here. They watch you.' She darted back inside before Kitty could get any more information from her.

Kitty rejoined Matt at her car and unlocked the door.

'What was that about?' Matt asked as Kitty slipped into the driver's seat and unlatched his door so he could get in.

'I don't know. She said she couldn't talk here. We're to meet her tomorrow afternoon at a tea room in town. I wonder what she wishes to tell us, perhaps she did make a mistake with the medicines.' Kitty started her car.

'Even from a distance I could see she looked scared to death.' Matt opened his window a crack. 'Perhaps Inspector Greville will have more to tell us when he calls this afternoon.'

'Hmm, I hope so. That place is really starting to make me very uneasy.' Kitty accidentally crashed her gears as she pulled out onto the coast road. 'I should be glad to never have to visit it again. I shall be much happier when Mrs Craven is back at home, and I very much wish that young Dolly didn't have to work there.'

'I wonder what Doctor Carter will find when he examines Mrs Pearson?' Matt mused.

'And what Doctor Marsh will have to say when he returns from his mysterious errand in London,' Kitty added.

CHAPTER ELEVEN

Matt took his lunch with Kitty in her office as she finished off some of her tasks for the day. By mid-afternoon with no word from Inspector Greville they went to take afternoon tea with Kitty's grandmother.

Mrs Treadwell was naturally very shocked at the news of Mrs Pearson's death. 'How very extraordinary. I really wish Millicent would either find another convalescent home or agree to stay here for a while until she is fully back on her feet. It is quite worrying if Doctor Carter is concerned that poor Mrs Pearson may not have met her end by natural means.'

'Inspector Greville said he would call here this afternoon to tell us of any progress in the case,' Kitty said. She and Matt had agreed that they wouldn't tell her grandmother about there being a possible link between Elm House and the Hammetts. She was already opposed to Kitty potentially being exposed to further danger and there seemed no point in worrying her any further on that score.

Mrs Treadwell checked the time with the clock on the mantelpiece. 'He must be busy. The inspector is fond of his stomach and it is most unlike him to dally if there is the prospect of something to eat,' she observed drily.

Before Kitty could reply the telephone rang and her grandmother crossed over to her bureau to take the call.

'Lottie, my dear, I'm sorry, do slow down.'

Kitty looked up from her contemplation of an extra scone to see that her grandmother's complexion had paled. Lottie Jenkins was one of her grandmother and Mrs Craven's close circle of gals. She wondered what the woman could be telling her grandmother to make her look so anxious.

'I see. How dreadful. Yes, quite. I know, I have tried reasoning with Millicent too, but she will not give way. Perhaps she will now change her mind.' Mrs Treadwell replaced the receiver and walked slowly back to retake her seat beside the fire.

'What is it?' Kitty asked. 'What's happened?'

'I hardly know what to say. It's really quite terrible.' Her grandmother's hands trembled as she pulled her lace-edged handkerchief from her pocket.

'Mrs Treadwell, may I get you something? Some more tea? Something has clearly shocked you.' Matt exchanged a concerned glance with Kitty.

'Inspector Greville has been called back to Elm House. Lottie was visiting Millicent this afternoon when it seems there was the most dreadful accident. Poor little Nurse Hibbert—' Her grandmother broke off and pressed her handkerchief to her lips in an effort to compose herself. 'The girl is dead. She appears to have fallen to her death from the roof of the home.'

Kitty gasped aloud. 'That's horrible. We only saw her just before we left there this morning.'

'How could she have fallen? And from the roof?' Matt placed his empty cup back on its saucer.

'Why would she have been up there?' Kitty shivered as she remembered looking back at the home only a few hours earlier. The turret rose a good few feet above what she realised now must be a flat leaded area before the steep slope of the tiled main roof of the home.

'Perhaps she took her own life?' her grandmother suggested.

'Guilt? If she were responsible for the medication error that killed Mrs Pearson?' Kitty looked at Matt.

'We are going too fast. We don't even know yet how Mrs Pearson died,' Matt said.

'Nurse Hibbert said there was something she wished to tell us. She was scared that someone was watching her. Suppose she was lured to the roof and pushed?' Kitty shivered at the thought.

'Really, Kitty.' The sharp tone of her grandmother's voice recalled her to the present. Matt gave her hand a sympathetic squeeze.

'We must tell the inspector that Nurse Hibbert intended to meet us away from Elm House. She went to some trouble to waylay us before we left. If nothing else that would indicate that she was not thinking of harming herself. Not at that point,' Matt said.

'Lottie was very distressed. Millicent refuses to listen to reason and is insisting on remaining at Elm House. She really is as stubborn as a mule.' Mrs Treadwell dabbed at the corners of her eyes.

'She will not be there much longer; she is recovering well now,' Kitty attempted to reassure her grandmother.

'Well, I have made my mind up on one point at least. Kitty, I forbid you to return to Elm House.' Mrs Treadwell gave a determined sniff and returned her handkerchief to her pocket.

'Grams!' Kitty protested.

'I am well aware that you are of age, Kitty, and as such I cannot stop you if you are fixed upon continuing, but I am asking that you oblige me in this. I don't know what is going on at that place. I had thought it was just Millicent's fancifulness but now I am not so certain. You had enough narrow escapes last year, without placing yourself in harm's way now, especially with that Hammett still on the loose. This is simply too, too much.'

Kitty could see that her grandmother was determined. 'Very well, if it will give you peace of mind I shall stay away. Matt can return to check on Mrs Craven and on young Dolly.' She stifled a sigh of frustration. She would have loved to go and jump in her little car to head back across the bay to discover what had happened to Nurse Hibbert.

*

Matt arranged to meet Kitty the following morning. They needed to speak to Inspector Greville now more than ever to share what they had uncovered. He knew that Kitty was most put out over her grandmother's edict that she was not to return to Elm House. There was nothing Kitty would have liked more than to go poking about asking questions.

If anyone other than her grandmother had made such a request of her, he was pretty certain that she would have ignored them. However, the one person Kitty always obeyed was her beloved Grams. Even if it sorely grieved her to do so.

The toot of her car horn outside his house let him know that Kitty had arrived to collect him in her car. He had privately nicknamed the car the Red Peril, something that caused him to smile to himself as he donned his overcoat and hat before stepping outside.

'Good morning, you seem very pleased with yourself today?' Kitty observed as he took his place in the passenger seat.

'Just pleased to see you. You look very pretty today.'

His words caused her to blush under the brim of what he suspected was a new pale blue hat that brought out the colour of her eyes.

'Let us hope Inspector Greville is available to see us.' Kitty pulled away and they set off for Torquay and the police station.

'It's fairly early and the inspector seems to have a habit of trying to conquer his paperwork first thing before he sets out on his investigations.' Matt looked out of the partially opened side window at the view across the bay. The sea reflected the grey of the morning sky and lack of sunshine.

'If he is not tied up with his visitors from Scotland Yard. He was very reticent about what they might be doing here in the bay.' Kitty flicked out her trafficator and took the turn into the town.

'Yes, he was, wasn't he? Hmm,' Matt agreed. He had wondered what might be happening locally. Usually, he picked up whispers from his various contacts, but there had been nothing.

Kitty spied a space at the kerb near the police station and pulled her car to a halt. She slipped her arm through Matt's and they walked up the steps of the police station together.

The desk sergeant was known to both of them, now having met him many times in the past year.

'Morning, sir, miss. Is it Inspector Greville you'll be after?' the sergeant greeted them with a smile.

'If we could please, Sergeant. It's quite important,' Kitty said.

The man lifted the telephone receiver and called through to the inspector's office. Kitty wandered off to study the posters attached to the noticeboard on the wall of the station office. The most prominent was the one appealing for the public to look out for Ezekiel Hammett with an artist's sketch of Hammett's face and a description of his physical characteristics beneath it. It also advertised the reward Kitty had offered for his apprehension.

'They'll capture him soon, old thing.' Matt placed his hand on the small of Kitty's back in a gesture of reassurance.

'I hope so. The longer he is at liberty the more I fear he will escape justice,' Kitty said.

The sergeant replaced the telephone receiver and they turned to face him.

'If you would both be so good as to take a seat. The inspector will be available shortly.'

Matt took a seat next to Kitty on the plain bent wood chairs beneath the noticeboard. They had not been waiting long before the door in the wall at the back of the desk opened and two men clad in dark overcoats and hats emerged accompanied by Inspector Greville. He guessed from their demeanour that these must be the men from Scotland Yard.

He watched as they shook hands with the inspector and departed leaving the policeman appearing even more morose than usual.

'Miss Underhay, Captain Bryant, please do come through.' The inspector led the way into the narrow, whitewashed corridor to his small office. The air inside the small room was tinged with blue smoke and an old china saucer on the desk that was now serving as an ashtray was full of cigarette butts. Piles of manilla folders teetered in untidy stacks on all the flat surfaces.

They waited while the inspector moved some of the stacks of paperwork around to allow them to sit down. Matt wondered how the inspector could ever possibly get any work done amidst such chaos.

Inspector Greville lowered himself into the ancient office chair behind his desk and surveyed them with a level gaze. 'I don't suppose I need to ask if you have heard the news about Nurse Hibbert?'

'Yes, sir, we heard yesterday afternoon. One of Kitty's grand-mother's friends was visiting Mrs Craven at Elm House when the incident occurred. She telephoned the Dolphin,' Matt said.

'I presume Nurse Hibbert's death was not an accident, sir? She would have had no call surely to be on the roof,' Kitty said.

The inspector sighed. 'Initially we considered that Nurse Hibbert may have taken her own life. As you say, Miss Underhay, she had no reason to go to the roof. Toxicology reports carried out by Doctor Carter have indicated that Mrs Pearson received a fatal dose of medication, and this was presumably administered by Nurse Hibbert in the course of her duties yesterday morning.'

'You said initially?' Matt queried. 'Does that mean that you have now discounted this theory?'

'There were certain indications at the site of Nurse Hibbert's fall that were inconsistent with the idea of suicide.' The inspector's moustache twitched.

'Nurse Hibbert spoke to me yesterday lunchtime as we were leaving the home. She approached us and asked us to meet with her today at a tea room in Torquay. She appeared scared and worried. She wouldn't say what it concerned, only that she wanted advice. I tried to draw her out on the matter, but she said she was being watched.' Kitty leaned back in her seat.

'May I ask, sir, what made you inclined to discount the idea of it being suicide?' Matt asked.

'There were marks on the lead flashing which tallied with marks on the backs of Nurse Hibbert's shoes indicating she may have been dragged across the roof, possibly whilst unconscious. Her apron was torn with a fragment of material being caught on the metal railing that surrounds the area. In order to jump, she would have had to have stepped over the guard rail. This is obviously inconsistent with the lady having jumped to her death.' Inspector Greville looked deeply unhappy.

'Has Doctor Marsh returned yet to Elm House?' Kitty asked.

Inspector Greville nodded. 'He arrived yesterday afternoon, shortly after Nurse Hibbert's body was discovered on the terrace.'

Matt saw Kitty struggle to suppress a shudder and he guessed she was probably imagining the scene.

'Who discovered the body?' she asked.

'The gardener, an elderly man, a Mr Johns, he works part-time keeping the grounds tidy. He walked up from the bottom of the garden, rounded the corner and saw her.' The inspector's moustache seemed to droop even further. 'Doctor Marsh arrived at the scene shortly afterwards.'

'Had no one noticed she was missing?' Kitty asked.

'It seems not. Sister Carmichael claims to have been busy in her office and the orderly, Mr Dodds, says he was restocking the medical supplies cupboard. Neither of them has an alibi as they were not seen by anyone else, either patients or any other staff in that time.' The inspector drew out his cigarette case and offered it first to Kitty and then to Matt. They both declined and the inspector took out one for himself before returning the silver case to his pocket.

'It's a bad business.' He lit his cigarette and Matt saw Kitty attempting to suppress a cough.

'Why would anyone wish to harm Nurse Hibbert? What did she wish to talk to us about, I wonder?' Kitty mused. 'We also have other information on the other matter that may be useful, Inspector.'

'We managed to decode the sheets we showed you the other day. The ones from Jack Dawkins's box. There is a reference there to Elm House.' Matt passed across copies of the translated coded papers. He also gave the inspector the information on the names that they had gleaned from Father Lamb.

The inspector studied the papers. 'May I keep these?'

'Certainly. Does any of it mean anything to you, sir?' Matt asked.

'I'm not certain, I, ah…' He gave Kitty and Matt a quick glance. 'I'm not at liberty to say at present.'

Matt noticed Kitty's neatly arched eyebrows rise slightly at this statement. He couldn't help but wonder if this was somehow connected with the gentlemen from Scotland Yard who had just left.

'Was Nurse Hibbert local, Inspector?' Kitty asked.

'Yes, her family are from Brixham. Nurse Hibbert lived-in at the home but saw her family regularly.' Inspector Greville gave Kitty a keen look.

'I wonder if I might call on them, to express my condolences. I feel awful about her death, thinking I may be one of the last people she spoke to. They may also have an idea of anything that might have been troubling her.' Kitty turned her wide blue-grey eyes on the inspector.

Matt suspected that Inspector Greville was not taken in by Kitty's innocent expression. Nonetheless he pulled a sheet of paper from one of the tottering stacks on his desk and scribbled an address for her.

'Anything you may learn, Miss Underhay, I expect you to tell me.'

'Naturally, Inspector.' Kitty looked injured that he might believe she would do anything other than present any evidence she might uncover to the police. 'I don't suppose you have any further news regarding Ezekiel Hammett?' she asked.

Inspector Greville's brow creased showing his frustration. 'I'm afraid not. Every lead is being followed up and the constable in Dartmouth has been visiting door to door after the theft of your handbag.'

'There is one more thing, sir. This was left for Kitty the other day at the Dolphin by a woman.' Matt passed over the note Kitty had received and gave the inspector the description of the woman that Kitty had obtained from Mary.

'I shall inform Pinch of this immediately. I'll see what news he has from his search in Exeter. I take it that you are concerned this woman may have been Hammett's sister?' the inspector asked.

Kitty nodded. 'It was my first thought when I read the note and Mary's description seemed to tally with what little I know of Esther.'

'Her house is being watched, but of course she is a free agent to go where she chooses. I'll speak to Pinch and see what he has to say on the matter.' The inspector's face was sombre.

'Thank you, sir. Kitty and I both very much appreciate your efforts.' Matt extended his hand to the policeman as he and Kitty rose ready to leave.

The inspector escorted them back to the front desk where they took their farewell of the desk sergeant.

'Oof, fresh air,' Kitty exclaimed as they walked back to her car. 'I don't know how the inspector stands it in that office.'

Matt smiled. 'I suppose he is used to it. Shall we call in at my office before we go back to Dartmouth?'

Kitty agreed and tucked her arm in his. 'We may as well walk. It's not far and I feel as if I need the air.'

They set off along the street towards the busier part of the town. As they drew nearer to the main shopping area the pavements grew more crowded and Matt found he had to steer Kitty through the throngs to avoid being jostled.

They had almost reached his office when Kitty stopped in her tracks. 'Matt, look, over there.'

Matt looked in the direction Kitty had indicated and saw Doctor Marsh, smartly dressed as usual, making his way at a rapid pace along the street.

'I wonder where he's going?' Kitty released his arm before he could protest and turned back the way they had just come.

'Kitty!' His words fell on deaf ears. She was already in pursuit of her quarry.

CHAPTER TWELVE

With his much longer legs, Matt soon caught her up and fell into step beside her. 'What are you doing?'

'He seems in a tearing rush. It may be nothing, but it would be interesting to see what is so urgent.' Kitty kept her gaze firmly locked on her target.

Doctor Marsh stopped abruptly outside a small shabby tea room and appeared to look in through the window before he pushed open the door and entered inside.

'I think he is meeting someone,' Kitty said.

The tea room was not one she was familiar with. Its frontage was small and unprepossessing with a dirty window and battered signage.

'Come on.' She tugged at the sleeve of Matt's overcoat, eager to cross the street to take a peek inside.

'Kitty, do be careful,' Matt warned as he followed her across the road.

'I'm not going to go inside. I just want to take a look through the window and see who he's meeting,' she reassured him.

Once on the same side of the street as the tea room Kitty walked along to the window and peeped inside, pretending to study the menu that was displayed behind the grimy glass. The interior of the tea room was gloomy, and it took her a moment before she could locate Doctor Marsh.

He was seated with his back to the window at a small table at the rear of the room. A woman sat opposite him, but Kitty couldn't make out her features. She dared not risk standing there for much longer so swapped places with Matt who was waiting patiently outside the neighbouring tobacconist's shop.

'He's at the back talking to a woman, but I can't see properly. It could be Sister Carmichael,' Kitty reported back to Matt.

'Why would he need to meet her in a café? He can talk to her privately anytime at the home.' Matt gave her a quizzical look.

'Well, you go and take a look then,' Kitty urged.

Matt sighed and walked the few steps along the pavement to peer in through the window. He was back within a few seconds.

'It's definitely not Sister Carmichael. It could be his wife, of course. Didn't Mrs C say he was married when she said he was over-familiar with Sister Carmichael?' Matt asked.

'Yes, Doctor Carter said so too but that is not the kind of tea room a man like Doctor Marsh would take his wife,' Kitty replied with a sniff.

'Hmm, well we can't go in there. It would be too obvious, and it looks as if they will be there for a while. They've only just poured their tea. Let's carry on to my office as we planned, it's too cold to stand around here waiting for them to come out, and there is nowhere else we can wait.'

Kitty sighed but could see that Matt was right. The doctor had been in London when Nurse Hibbert had died and Mrs Pearson had been killed. The man could just be a philanderer with a variety of paramours for all they knew.

Reluctantly she turned around and they made their way once more back towards Matt's office above a gentleman's outfitters.

Kitty scooped up Matt's post from the doormat while he busied himself lighting the fire in the grate and putting the kettle on to boil on the small electric plate. She placed his mail on his desk and shivered as she waited for the fire to begin to generate enough heat to warm the room.

The watercolour picture of Dartmouth that she had given him for Christmas was hung above the fireplace and Kitty thought it made the room seem more furnished and professional. Matt set out two teacups before disappearing across the landing to his neighbour's business to borrow some milk.

He was back in a moment bearing a small full jug. 'Here we are. There are some biscuits in the tin there, Kitty.'

She shook her head at his housekeeping and opened the tin of shortbread to extract a biscuit.

'I take it you intend to visit Nurse Hibbert's family?' Matt asked as he set a cup of tea before her.

'I shall go and offer my condolences. I'm not hopeful that she will have said anything much about what was troubling her but perhaps I might pick up a clue.' She took a bite of her biscuit, relieved to discover that it was crunchy and had not gone stale in the tin.

'I suppose it's worth a shot,' Matt conceded as he helped himself to a biscuit.

'What are your plans?' Kitty asked. 'Will you return to Elm House to see what you can find out there?' It really was too frustrating that she was forbidden to go back, but she would not upset her grandmother by going against her wishes. At least, not on this matter. She had caused Grams too much worry and concern over the past twelve months with the other cases they had been involved in.

'I'd like to talk to Sister Carmichael and to that Dodds fellow. He always seems to be hanging around. I might try and speak to Doctor Marsh and the gardener if I can too.' Matt munched thoughtfully on his biscuit.

'I wonder where Doctor and Mrs Marsh live?' It suddenly occurred to Kitty that the doctor must reside somewhere not far from Elm House. He didn't live-in, only the nursing staff and a couple of the domestic staff had rooms according to young Dolly. They were in a wing at the rear of the building up on the top floor.

'That would be interesting to discover. He has a flat in London still you said. That's where he must stay when he goes to do his teaching sessions with the medical students, according to Sister Carmichael's information.' Matt brushed a few stray crumbs from the front of his jacket.

'So, we are agreed then. I shall go and visit Brixham, and you will go and see what you can unearth at Elm House.' Kitty grinned at him. It still felt as if he had potentially the more interesting part of the deal but at least she could do something.

Kitty had decided she would call at Nurse Hibbert's family home the next day. She persuaded the hotel chef to make her a small sponge cake, which she carefully wrapped to take with her as a gift.

The address Inspector Greville had given her was in a respectable part of the town away from the harbour and its environs. She managed to find a place to park where she wouldn't be blocking the narrow lane, then walked back along looking for the house number.

It was a cold, bright day with a stiff wind blowing from the direction of the sea. The lane where the Hibberts lived was comprised of whitewashed workers' cottages, hunkered down under uneven tiled roofs as if trying to shelter from the winter weather.

The Hibberts' cottage was on the end. The front gate was well maintained with fresh looking black paint and the doorstep looked clean and scrubbed. Kitty raised a gloved hand and knocked at the front door. She hoped the family wouldn't feel her visit was too obtrusive at what must be a time of great personal grief.

As she waited for a response to her knock, she heard footsteps inside the house coming along the hallway. The door opened and a plump, grey-haired older woman in a floral pinafore stood before her. The woman's eyes were rimmed with red and shadowed underneath as if she hadn't slept.

'Mrs Hibbert? I'm so very sorry to intrude on your grief but I knew your daughter and came to express my condolences at your loss.'

The woman blinked. 'You'd best come through,' she said in a dull tone. She turned and led the way inside the house. Kitty followed her, being careful to wipe her feet on the mat.

Mrs Hibbert led her into a tiny parlour that was clearly reserved for best. The air smelt of beeswax and it was stuffed full of furniture and Staffordshire pottery.

'Please have a seat, Miss…?'

'Underhay, Kitty Underhay. I brought a sponge cake as I thought you might have a lot of callers and not feel like baking.' Kitty perched on the edge of the floral chintz covered sofa and handed over the cake.

'Thank you, that's very kind. I'll just fetch the tea.' The woman disappeared towards the rear of the cottage and Kitty looked around the room with interest. There were framed pictures of people who Kitty guessed must be the rest of the family. Parents with Eloise and two small boys, taken when they were children. In pride of place was a larger picture of Nurse Hibbert in her uniform. A black crepe bow adorned one corner.

Mrs Hibbert returned bearing a small tray, which she set down in front of Kitty. 'It's very good of you to call, Miss Underhay. How did you come to know my Eloise?'

'I met her at Elm House; she has been caring for a family friend. I saw her shortly before the incident.' Kitty watched as Mrs Hibbert poured them both a cup of tea into what appeared to be the best Royal Albert china in the Art Deco style with a triangular handle.

'Oh, that place.' Mrs Hibbert sniffed as she handed Kitty her cup of tea.

'Eloise seemed unhappy there,' Kitty said carefully.

Nurse Hibbert's mother shrugged. 'She were all right there at first. Excited to have a job nearer home and pleased with her room.'

'I got the impression that Sister Carmichael was difficult to work for.' Kitty took a tentative sip of tea.

'Our Eloise did all the work, dressings, medication, answering the bells.' Mrs Hibbert paused and shook her head. 'That there orderly used to worry her, always following her about, he was. Said he made her uneasy, like as he were spying on her.'

'Have you heard from anyone at Elm House, since the incident?' Kitty wasn't sure how to phrase her question. She wasn't at all certain if Inspector Greville had suggested to her mother that Eloise may have been murdered.

'*She* come yesterday afternoon. All done up like a dog's dinner. All fur coat and no knickers that one. For all she's married to Doctor Marsh, I knows what she is.' The venom in Mrs Hibbert's voice took Kitty by surprise.

'Mrs Marsh visited?' she asked. It struck Kitty that few people ever mentioned Mrs Marsh and yet the doctor was supposed to have only married a few months ago.

'Oh yes. Her ladyship called to say as how our Eloise's death was clearly a tragic accident and as how the home was in no way to blame for it. Pah.' The woman set down her cup, slopping a little of her tea into the saucer. She fumbled in the front pocket of her pinny for her handkerchief.

'Oh dear, that's awful.' Kitty's mind raced as she considered this new information.

Mrs Hibbert blew her nose. 'Offered me a token amount towards the cost of the funeral and to compensate me for the loss of my girl.'

Kitty's mouth dropped open in surprise and she was temporarily speechless at this callous approach from Nurse Hibbert's erstwhile employers.

Mrs Hibbert sniffed. 'I told her to keep her blood money. I can afford to bury my child without any help from her.'

'Do you know Mrs Marsh? Have you met her before?' Kitty asked. The woman seemed very vehement in her dislike of the woman. She was sure Doctor Carter had told Matt that the Marshes had married in London. How could Mrs Hibbert know her?

'Oh yes, I knows her. I reckon most of the men folk hereabouts knows her too. At least them who spend their money on drink and loose women at her knocking shop. Pretending she's all high and mighty and respectable now she's married to a doctor. She doesn't fool me.' Mrs Hibbert gave a sniff.

Kitty felt a little dizzy. Surely this couldn't be the connection between Elm House and the Hammetts?

'Doctor Marsh's wife owns a house of ill repute?'

Mrs Hibbert suddenly appeared to recollect who she was speaking to and a ruddy colour crept into her cheeks. 'Begging your pardon, miss. I hope I haven't shocked you or spoke out of turn, but yes. That woman has a few such so-called businesses hereabouts around the bay.'

Kitty set down her tea unable to drink any more. She felt slightly nauseous. 'I don't suppose you would know if Mrs Marsh is connected with the address on Prospect Road where that wanted man shot at the police a week or so ago?'

Mrs Hibbert nodded. 'The very same, miss. He's related to her that man; she was Hammett before she married. Shady people that doctor and his missus. Our Eloise were proper bothered by it. Last time she come home she said she were going to take some advice.'

'When was that, Mrs Hibbert?' Kitty asked.

'A few days before she died, miss. I don't know the ins and outs of it as she wouldn't tell me. Now I wish she had.' A tear leaked from the corner of the woman's eye and ran unchecked down her cheek. 'She were so clever, our Eloise. We were so proud of her. She worked so hard to become a nurse…' Her voice tailed away for a moment as she gazed at the photograph on the side table. 'And all that for nothing. Somebody did this to my girl, it weren't no accident and she would never have harmed herself, never in a thousand years.' Mrs Hibbert wiped her cheek with the back of her hand.

'I really am so very sorry for your loss, Mrs Hibbert. You must let me know when the funeral is to be held.' Kitty rummaged in her bag for one of her calling cards. 'Eloise was well thought of by the patients she cared for at Elm House. They all spoke very highly of her. She'll be greatly missed.'

Mrs Hibbert took the card and tucked it away inside the pocket of her apron. 'Thank you, miss, it was kind of you to come.'

Kitty rose and Mrs Hibbert walked with her to the front door to see her out.

'Thank you again for coming. It was nice to hear that our Eloise was appreciated by them that mattered to her, her patients.' Mrs Hibbert closed the door and Kitty made her way back along the lane to her car.

She sat for a moment in the driver's seat thinking about all she had just learned. It seemed impossible that Esther Hammett was also the mysterious wife of Doctor Marsh. Why did the police seem unaware of this connection if Mrs Hibbert knew? Or had Mrs Hibbert only learned of it when Esther had called on her?

No doubt it would have suited the Marshes if Nurse Hibbert had committed suicide. She would have had the blame for Mrs Pearson's death. Was it Esther that the doctor had been meeting in that seedy little tea room when she and Matt had followed them? It would make sense if they were attempting to conduct some kind of shady business. Perhaps they had been expecting someone else to join them there.

Kitty drummed her fingers against the cold, hard rim of her steering wheel. Doctor Marsh wasn't living in Exeter. He couldn't be, he would need to be closer at hand to Elm House, yet the police were keeping watch on an address there where Esther had claimed to be resident.

A shiver ran along her spine. It seemed no one was where they had claimed to be. Esther was not in Exeter, Ezekiel could be at any of Esther's properties, and they had no proof that Doctor Marsh had been where he had said during his mysterious alleged visit to London.

Kitty started her car and pulled away, suddenly anxious to be out of Brixham. It all felt dangerously close to Esther and Ezekiel Hammett.

*

Matt had set out on his own mission to uncover more information about both Nurse Hibbert's death and that of Mrs Pearson. He pulled the Sunbeam to a halt on the gravel forecourt in front of Elm House and gazed up at the building.

From his vantage point he could clearly see the flat area of roof near the turret with its low guard rail where Nurse Hibbert had plunged to her death. The gravel gave way to a stone flagged pathway that led around the home and he guessed that must have been the area where she had landed.

Matt stowed his gloves in the pannier of his bike. Before attempting to enter the home, he walked along the path, studying the ground for clues. A dark stain on the pale flagstones and footprints in the soft earth at the edge of the path gave him the landing point for Nurse Hibbert's body. He looked up at the spot on the roof immediately above and could see that anyone up there at that point would have been partially hidden by one of the chimneys.

An elderly man pushing a wheelbarrow laden with tools was visible on the narrow path leading down the hill near one of the flower beds. Matt walked down to meet him, hoping this would be the gardener who had discovered Eloise.

'Mr Johns?' Matt asked.

'I might be, depends who's asking.' The man pushed back the brim of his cap with a grimy hand and squinted suspiciously at him.

'Inspector Greville said that you discovered Nurse Hibbert's body the other day, after her accident?' He hoped the man wouldn't ask too many questions about who he was or why he was asking about the incident.

The man gave a sniff and returned to his task of unloading the barrow. 'I might have.'

'Did you hear her fall? Or see anything or anyone?' Matt asked.

The man peered warily at him. 'I told that policeman everything. No, I didn't see nor hear anything. I'd been working on the other side of the house, right at the bottom of the gardens. 'Tis steep there and I has to be careful not to slip so it takes me all my time watching as I don't break my neck. I finishes up my jobs and then as I brings my barrow up top ready for my tea break, I spies her, poor lass. She were just lying there on the floor all crumpled up and still.'

'The inspector said Doctor Marsh arrived at that point?' Matt was keen to discover what had happened in the aftermath of Eloise being discovered.

The gardener scratched his head. 'I could see right off as there weren't anything to be done for the girl. I was about to go inside the house to get help when the doctor's big black motor pulls up on this side of the forecourt. He sees me and gets out the back and comes running over here. Next thing I knows is Sister Carmichael is outside giving her orders and that Bowkett woman has called the police. 'Tis all in my statement for the inspector.'

'I know, sir, but we do have to check up on these things. Some-times people recollect things after the fact that they didn't think to tell us on the day.' Matt hoped the gardener would assume he was somehow connected with the police. He suspected the man would not be quite so forthcoming if he knew Matt was a private investigator.

The man muttered something unintelligible under his breath and tugged a weed out by its roots, tossing it into the barrow.

Matt tried another tack. 'Was anyone missing or late appearing when the alarm was raised?'

The gardener straightened and stood for a moment; his brow furrowed in thought. 'Miss Bowkett come first, I expect she would be closest being on reception like. And then Sister come out, then one of the domestics. She run back inside screaming. Mr Dodds, he were the last to get there. Now you come to mention it, that's a bit of a rum do, that is.'

'What makes you say that, sir?' Matt asked.

The old man snorted and returned to his weeding. 'Because that Cyril Dodds would get where castor oil can't get. He's usually the first anywhere, he is, sticking his nose in other folks's business. A regular tattletale. Always sneaking about the place looking busy and doing nothing he is.'

'Thank you, Mr Johns, you've been most helpful.' The old man had certainly given him plenty of food for thought. Matt turned to walk back towards the front entrance.

'Hey, who did you say you were? Police, was it?' Mr Johns called after him.

Matt turned to give the man a cheery wave. 'That's right.' It was only a little white lie.

CHAPTER THIRTEEN

Matt braved the icy glare of Miss Bowkett at the reception desk and set off in search of Mrs Craven. He discovered her busy practising her walking using her cane in the corridor leading to the lounge.

'Matthew, good afternoon, where is Kitty?'

'Mrs Treadwell doesn't wish Kitty to visit again at the moment. She is worried it may be dangerous.' Matt opened the lounge door and waited for Mrs Craven to precede him into the room.

'Pah, fiddlesticks. Trust Gwen to be overcautious. She panders to that girl far too much. She made the same mistake with Elowed, but will she listen to me? No.' Mrs Craven flopped down onto a nearby armchair, her stick clattering onto the floor.

Matt decided it would be diplomatic not to respond to Mrs Craven's criticisms of her oldest friend. He collected her stick and propped it against the side of her chair.

'How has everything been here since Nurse Hibbert's death?' he asked in a low tone, taking a seat on the vacant chair beside her.

'Well, Doctor Marsh returned from London, as you probably know. I believe he and Sister Carmichael had words. The dear general heard raised voices coming from the office and sister looked very flustered and pink when she came out.' Mrs Craven nodded sagely. 'His wife is back on the scene too now, you know. I expect Sister Carmichael has had her nose put out of joint. There was definitely something going on between the doctor and Sister Carmichael. I wouldn't fancy her chances if Mrs Marsh got wind of it. No woman likes to have her husband's former paramours hanging around. I've only seen that Mrs Marsh a couple of times, but she seems a hard-faced woman. Rather common, for all her airs and graces.'

'Where does the doctor live?' It occurred to Matt that he and Kitty seemed to have neglected finding this out and it might be important.

'I believe they have a place just along the road. Some kind of apartment. She doesn't spend much time there apparently, which is odd for a couple only married a few months ago. I overheard Sister Carmichael saying something about it to the orderly, that Dodds fellow.' Mrs Craven shifted in her seat and arranged her foot in a more comfortable position.

'Have you heard any rumours or overheard anyone talking about Nurse Hibbert's death? Any of the other staff or residents?' Matt glanced around the room to ensure no one was in earshot.

The room was fairly empty with just a couple of elderly men playing chess together at the table in the window. For once there was no sign of Cyril Dodds lurking around.

'Sister Carmichael was hinting that Nurse Hibbert had made an error with the medication which led to poor Mrs Pearson's death. I think she was implying that Nurse Hibbert may have taken her own life. Nonsense, of course.' Mrs Craven pursed her lips in displeasure.

'Why is it nonsense?' Matt asked. He was curious about the firmness of Mrs Craven's statement.

'It's Sister Carmichael that puts up the medicines, she used to give it to Nurse Hibbert to administer, but she was the one who had charge of it all. I think she made the error and spied the opportunity to blame that poor young girl.'

Matt made a mental note. 'Hmm, do you know where everyone was when Nurse Hibbert died?'

'No, I was with Lottie, she'd brought me the most beautiful box of chocolates and we were just sampling them together when we heard the commotion outside. That Bowkett woman was trying to stop one of the domestics from screaming. The woman was hysterical. It was so loud we heard her inside the home and it seemed to go on for ages. I think Sister Carmichael may have slapped her to bring her to her senses. We all tried to make our way into the reception area to find out what was going on, but Doctor Marsh came inside and sent us all back into here.' Mrs Craven frowned as she tried to recall the event.

'Did you see Mr Dodds at all?' Matt asked.

'Not until much later. He came in with young Dolly, she had a tea trolley, and he was assisting her to dispense drinks and biscuits. A spot of medicinal brandy in our tea. For shock presumably. We were all most upset. Nurse Hibbert was a great favourite.'

Mrs Craven's account appeared to support the information they had received from Inspector Greville and from Mr Johns, the gardener. He was contemplating going in search of Sister Carmichael when the orderly entered the room pushing a tea trolley.

Matt waited until the man had served the chess players and had approached the table where he was seated with Mrs Craven.

'Mrs Craven, a cup of tea?' the orderly asked.

'Yes, please.' Mrs Craven watched him pour her a cup from the large silver coloured pot.

'Sir?' Dodds enquired, holding the teapot over a cup.

'Not for me, thank you,' Matt declined. 'How are you and all the staff after the terrible events of the last few days?' he asked.

The orderly's expression remained unreadable, betraying no emotion. 'We are all deeply shocked, sir. Thank you for your concern.' He set down the teapot and went to push the trolley away.

'It must be difficult having the police asking you all so many questions?' Matt asked.

The orderly paused and Matt thought he detected a slight stiffening in his frame. 'These things are indeed most unpleasant.'

'Yes, I believe that the police are not satisfied with either death.' Matt kept his tone casual to see if the other man would take his bait.

'Mrs Pearson's death was most regrettable. Poor Nurse Hibbert will be much missed by everyone. A terrible accident.'

'I heard that the police don't believe her death was an accident. I expect they will be checking where everyone was within the home at the time of her death. When was Nurse Hibbert last seen alive? Does anyone know?' Matt watched the man carefully.

'I can tell you that, Matthew. Lottie arrived at two thirty and Nurse Hibbert had been assisting with the medication at two o'clock. She was discovered at about two fifty, I believe.' Mrs Craven looked triumphant.

'Then I'm afraid that I cannot help either yourself or the police any further. I was busy putting things away in the supply cupboard at the time the alarm was raised and I had been there since one thirty after lunch had been cleared.' The man gave a slight smile and went to continue on his way.

'And yet you were the last member of staff to arrive on the terrace and were noted to be out of breath.' Matt made the last bit up, but he wanted to rattle the man to see if he could shake more information from him.

'The supply cupboard is on the top floor. I was only alerted to the accident by the sound of one of the domestics screaming. It takes time, even when one is hurrying, to get downstairs.' Dodds looked almost smug as he replied, and Matt could see the man thought he had avoided Matt's trap.

'Hmm, I see, so you were nearer to the roof than anyone else then. Did you see or hear anyone go by? Not even Nurse Hibbert herself?' Matt saw a flicker of alarm in the man's eyes.

'No, sir, unfortunately not. As I said, I was inside the cupboard unpacking boxes.' The orderly gave a forced smile. 'If you will excuse me, sir, the other residents will be expecting their tea.' Dodds made good his escape.

'What did you make of that?' Mrs Craven leaned forward in her seat, a gleam of excitement in her eyes.

'I think he isn't telling us everything.'

'Well, leave it to me. I shall endeavour to discover as much as I can.' Mrs Craven settled back in her chair and surveyed Matt smugly over the rim of her teacup.

'Mrs Craven, do not put yourself in danger. Mrs Pearson and Nurse Hibbert were murdered, and it seems likely that Lady Wellings and Miss Wordsley may also have been victims. Maybe Mrs Palesbury too. I have no wish for you to join them.' Matt made his tone as stern as possible, but he suspected he was on a hiding to nothing.

'I can assure you, Captain Bryant, that I can take care of myself. You need have no fears for me.' Mrs Craven took a sip of her tea and he could see that nothing he said would alter her opinion. He just hoped Inspector Greville would be able to arrest the murderer before Mrs Craven was added to the list of victims.

He had hoped to see Sister Carmichael before returning to Dartmouth to update Kitty but the door to her office remained firmly closed and there was no sign of her in any of the public rooms.

Matt made his way back to the reception area to sign out.

'And how are you, Miss Bowkett? It must have been the most terrible shock for you the other day with the discovery of poor Nurse Hibbert?' Matt switched on as much charm as he could muster. He knew Miss Bowkett had not been happy with either him or Kitty when they had forced their way into the home when Mrs Pearson had been killed.

The older woman gave him a suspicious look. 'It was most upsetting. Nurse Hibbert was very well thought of by everyone.' She swallowed. 'Such a terrible tragedy.'

'I can imagine, and then having the police here asking questions. Most difficult for everyone,' Matt said in a sympathetic tone. 'Especially for someone as refined and upstanding as yourself.' He wondered for a second if he had ladled it on a little too thickly, but the woman seemed to soften.

'Exactly, I mean what will people think? It's really not nice feeling as if one's colleagues are under suspicion. This was always a very respectable place.'

'Have you worked here for long, Miss Bowkett?' Matt asked.

'Three years. I stayed on when Doctor and Mrs Marsh bought the place. I should have left then. But they do say as hindsight is a wonderful thing.' Miss Bowkett sniffed.

'I heard that things had been, well, rather strained since the Marshes bought the home, despite them spending a lot of money on the refurbishments.' Matt leaned in on the counter in a confiding, gossipy way.

Miss Bowkett nodded. 'Indeed. All the old nursing staff left, and Sister Carmichael came into post. She appointed Nurse Hibbert, the other nurses just do odd days here and there. Mr Dodds came with Doctor Marsh, he used to work for Mrs Marsh, or so I believe. There have been some very undesirable people coming here since then. It's not at all like it was before. We have always catered for the better classes and the gentry.'

'I understand that Roderick Harmer and Leonard Pearson are both very good friends of Doctor Marsh.' Matt waited to see if this brought a response.

'That is exactly what I mean. Undesirable the pair of them, gamblers and philanderers both. Always huddled in corners with either Doctor Marsh or Cyril Dodds. Still, it won't be any of my concern soon.' She drew herself up and closed the visitors' ledger.

'Oh?' Matt asked.

'I've given my notice. I shall be leaving at the end of next week. I have a nice post waiting for me with my sister at the post office in Babbacombe.'

'I'm sure you will be greatly missed,' Matt assured her and earned himself a rare smile.

'Captain Bryant.'

Matt turned around at his name to be confronted by Doctor Marsh and Sister Carmichael. Neither of whom looked particularly pleased to see him.

'Good morning,' he returned civilly, whilst mentally bracing himself for what he felt certain would be a tricky conversation.

'If I might have a word in Sister's office?' Doctor Marsh looked at Sister Carmichael who promptly walked away.

Matt followed the doctor along the corridor to the small office that Inspector Greville had occupied only a few days earlier. Once inside the room Doctor Marsh took a seat behind the sister's small rosewood desk and indicated that Matt should take the seat opposite him.

'I see Miss Underhay is not with you this morning?' The doctor took Matt slightly by surprise with his opening.

'No. I believe she is busy on hotel business. Mrs Craven seems to be recovering well and Kitty and her grandmother are very much hoping she will be able to return home soon.' Matt leaned back in his chair and crossed his legs, determined to show a cool and relaxed exterior while he waited for Doctor Marsh to come to the point.

Doctor Marsh appeared to hesitate for a moment, eyeing Matt as if weighing up his words before he spoke. 'You are aware, of course, that the police are investigating the sad demise of Mrs Pearson, although I am confident that they will discover no evidence of wrongdoing by anyone here at the home. However, with poor Nurse Hibbert's terrible accident occurring so soon afterwards questions are bound to be asked.' His eyes narrowed.

'So, I'm given to understand. Your point, sir?' Matt asked.

'My point, Captain Bryant, is that it is the role of the police to ask such questions. I will not have my staff, or my patients, upset by amateur detectives poking their noses in affairs which do not concern them.' The man's voice had lost its usual silky-smooth tone and had hardened almost to a snarl.

Matt gave him an amused smile. 'Then it is indeed fortunate for you that I am not an amateur. I would think too that anyone that might be upset by questions about Mrs Pearson's death or the murder of Nurse Hibbert may well have something to hide.'

He noted the sudden rigidity in Doctor Marsh's shoulders when he mentioned the word murder. 'I see that you are choosing to ignore my friendly request, Captain Bryant. Very well, I shall be more explicit. Neither you nor Miss Underhay are welcome here at Elm House.'

Matt gave a slight shrug. 'My business here is almost concluded, Doctor Marsh. As for Miss Underhay, she was only ever here to visit her grandmother's oldest friend.' His instinct was to protect Kitty as much as possible and to deflect any animosity towards his own direction rather than hers.

He rose from his seat. 'By the way, I understand you arrived by car at the same time as poor Nurse Hibbert's body was discovered. Had you come directly from the station, sir?' He had nothing to lose by asking questions. Whether the doctor would choose to answer them was another matter.

Doctor Marsh had followed his lead and had also stood, no doubt intending to escort him from the premises.

'Not that it is any of your concern, but I have nothing to hide. Yes, my wife had organised a car to meet me and bring me here directly. Sister Carmichael had pressed for my early return from London after Mrs Pearson's death.'

Matt had his hand on the handle of the door. 'Sister Carmichael and Mr Dodds both worked for you previously, I believe?'

'I think you'll discover that is a matter of public record. Sister Carmichael worked for me in London for some five years and Dodds for my wife for several years. I am fortunate in having a loyal and highly trained staff. Now, if you have no further questions, I would be obliged if you left, Captain Bryant.'

Matt favoured the man with another smile. 'Of course, sir, and thank you. You have been most helpful.' He raised his hat slightly, opened the door and strolled leisurely back along the corridor to the reception whistling to himself.

He waved to Miss Bowkett and stepped outside the home into the weak wintery sunshine. After retrieving his leather gauntlets from the pannier of his bike he sat astride the vehicle for a moment looking up at the home.

There was a movement in one of the upstairs windows and he saw that Sister Carmichael and Dodds, the orderly, were both watching him. Unable to resist, he gave them a cheeky salute before firing up his engine and driving off from the forecourt in a spray of gravel.

CHAPTER FOURTEEN

Kitty had not been idle on her return to the Dolphin. She telephoned Inspector Pinch at Exeter Police Station immediately. The inspector was not available, however, to take her call and she was forced to leave a message with the desk sergeant telling him of her discovery of the link between Esther Hammett and Doctor Marsh.

She also telephoned Torquay Police Station and left the same message with the desk sergeant for Inspector Greville. It was a relief when Matt arrived safely at the hotel. Ever since her conversation with Mrs Hibbert it had worried her that he might be walking into some sort of trap at Elm House.

She sent for coffee and installed Matt in her office before eagerly telling him all she had discovered from Mrs Hibbert about Esther. His expression was sombre when she finished her story.

'This is an unexpected turn of events. Have you alerted Inspector Pinch?' he asked.

'I had to leave a message for him at the police station but, yes, I telephoned as soon as I returned, and I've left the same message for Inspector Greville. Now, tell me what you have learned at Elm House?'

Matt told her of his conversations with the various parties.

'So, it seems that Dodds would have had opportunity to murder Eloise or he may know who killed her and is shielding them. His story of not hearing or seeing anyone is a little thin. He was the only person on that top floor. Sister Carmichael also has no alibi, we only have her word that she was in her office. It might be worth checking on Doctor Marsh, and now Esther, to find out if the doctor really did arrive on the London train if you say the gardener saw them pull up at the time he found Eloise.' Kitty frowned.

'We also need to discover the motive for Eloise's death and, for that matter, Mrs Pearson's. If we run with the theory that Marsh is somehow murdering some of his patients for profit, then why was Mrs Pearson killed when he was not there to issue the certification of the cause of death?' Matt drummed his fingers lightly on the edge of the desk. 'It doesn't make sense.'

'Unless they believed that people were already becoming suspicious. Perhaps after hearing that Lady Wellings's death was being looked into they may have wished to try and place the blame elsewhere. The coroner would no doubt have been in touch with the home. Nurse Hibbert perhaps would have seemed the perfect person to take the blame. Then they could arrange for Mrs Pearson to die while Doctor Marsh couldn't possibly be implicated as he was away in London,' Kitty said.

'They probably also didn't realise that Doctor Carter would be the one doctor in the whole of Torbay, apart from the coroner, who had already been alerted to the possibility of murders at Elm House.' Matt looked thoughtful.

'Yes, that would be bad luck on their part,' Kitty agreed. 'I wish I knew what it was that Nurse Hibbert wanted to tell us. She could have worked it all out I suppose.'

'I know, all we have at the moment is speculation and an idea with no real proof.' Kitty could see that Matt was as frustrated as she was with the situation. 'And we are not welcome at Elm House.' He grinned as he added the last phrase.

'Well, Grams will be relieved at that news at least. Not that I intend telling her. It would only serve to make her even more worried.' Kitty wasn't sure if she planned to share her discovery that Esther Hammett was in fact Mrs Marsh with her grandmother.

The black telephone on her desk rang as she finished speaking and she picked up the receiver to take the call.

'Inspector Pinch, thank you for telephoning. I take it my message reached you?' Kitty looked at Matt as she greeted the inspector.

'Indeed, thank you for the information, Miss Underhay. I have spoken to Inspector Greville and he will immediately post a watch on the address in Torquay.' The inspector sounded uncomfortable.

'How did no one notice that Esther Hammett wasn't residing at the Exeter address? Was she not seen entering or leaving or not being there at all?' Kitty asked. It seemed to her that there had been some huge error on the part of the Exeter police.

Inspector Pinch coughed. 'I can only offer my unreserved apologies to you, Miss Underhay. The member of the force tasked with watching the premises has been removed from his post with immediate effect.'

'I take it that the focus of the search for Hammett must now shift to Torbay? It all appears to confirm that Hammett's sister is somehow involved in sheltering him.' Kitty could only hope that both the inspectors were now finally taking her theory that Hammett had been behind the break-ins at both the Dolphin and Matt's home seriously.

'We shall be deploying as many constables as possible to the area and I believe Inspector Greville is going to visit Mrs Marsh to ask further questions as we speak.'

Kitty knew that the inspector's offer was as good as she was likely to get. 'Thank you, Inspector.'

'If there is any news of a capture, I shall of course inform you immediately,' Inspector Pinch assured her.

The call ended and Kitty replaced the receiver in the cradle. 'I take it that you heard all of that?' she asked Matt.

He nodded. 'I'm sorry, my dear.'

'It sounds as if the constable charged with observing the Hammett house in Exeter was either lazy or corrupt.' Her voice trembled, she was still angry that the police had not identified Esther Hammett and Doctor Marsh's wife as being one and the same person.

How had it been missed? Or did the Hammetts web of corruption have a much wider reach than any of them had realised. Was this why the coded pages were so important? She suddenly realised that it all made it much harder to know who she could trust.

A shiver ran down her spine and she hoped that Mrs Craven would remain unharmed for the remainder of her stay at Elm House. Matt's description of his encounter with Doctor Marsh had seriously alarmed her and she knew the Hammetts to be ruthless.

'I wish we knew more about Sister Carmichael's role in all of this. Mrs Craven definitely seemed to think there was, or had been, a liaison of some kind between her and Doctor Marsh. If so, then why would Esther permit her to continue working with him?'

'And then there are those mysterious nocturnal visitors to Elm House,' Matt added.

'Hmm, so where do we go next?' Kitty's mind raced. 'I wonder if Inspector Greville intends to search Elm House or the Marshes' apartment?'

Matt's gaze locked with hers. 'I take it the idea of sitting back and doing nothing while we wait for the police to act does not sit well with you?'

Kitty smiled. 'It concerns me that the police do not appear to have been terribly successful so far in either capturing Hammett or even in acting on the information we gave them about Mrs Craven's concerns at Elm House. What do you propose we do? I have to say that I have a few ideas of my own.'

Her pulse quickened at the idea of doing something. There was no way she intended to wait passively for the police to act. If the corruption amongst the constabulary ran as deeply as she feared there would be no guarantee that the police would ever manage to capture Hammett. That to her was unthinkable.

Matt's grin widened. 'That's my girl, what were you thinking?'

'It strikes me that if the inspector is likely to wish to search Elm House, and if something or someone is concealed there that the Marshes do not wish to be discovered, then they will need to move quite quickly. I also fear that someone is likely to tip them off and the police will discover nothing useful when they do carry out a search,' Kitty said.

'Go on,' Matt said.

'How do you feel about a little night-time observation tonight?' Kitty asked.

'At Elm House?' Matt's eyes twinkled.

'If Mrs Craven's observations of the mystery visitors are correct, and if the police are likely to raid the home, then it seems plausible to me that if we keep watch tonight, we may very well learn something more about whatever is going on there.' She waited for Matt's response.

'I agree. What is your proposition?' Matt asked.

Kitty spent the remainder of the afternoon preparing her plans. If Mrs Craven and her friend's information was correct, the mysterious activities at Elm House usually commenced at around eleven thirty and ended between midnight and one.

She had arranged to call for Matt just before nine. Mickey insisted on walking her to her car after she had confided her plans in him and sworn him to secrecy. She could tell he wasn't happy, but she needed him to cover for her if her grandmother should ask where she was.

'You have a care, Miss Kitty, and Captain Bryant an' all. That Hammett is a dangerous bloke and he's carrying a gun. He didn't think nothing of shooting at those constables in Brixham t'other day.' Mickey locked her shed back up for her and returned the key through the car window.

'I promise we shall be very careful. Our plan is simply to park nearby and keep watch. That's all, nothing dangerous,' Kitty reassured him.

'If you'm not back by four a.m. then I shall instruct the night porter to telephone the police and tell them where you are,' he warned her.

'Very well. We should be back well before then.' Kitty gave him a cheery wave and set off for the ferry. The crossings were less frequent at night and she didn't want to miss the boat.

Matt was ready and waiting for her when she pulled up outside his house. Like her he had dressed in warm, dark, comfortable clothing.

'Brr, it's turning cold; at least it isn't raining,' he said, taking his place beside her.

'I have come prepared,' she assured him. 'Take a look on the back seat.'

He leaned around to take a peep as she steered her car towards the old toll house on the edge of the common.

'Well done, I see you have thought of everything.' She caught a brief glimpse of his smile in the moonlight.

A low mist followed them as they drove on towards Torquay and Kitty could see her breath in front of her face.

'I hope that if these visitors do come tonight that they will be prompt. The night porter will alert Inspector Greville if I'm not back at the Dolphin by four, before the dairy delivery arrives.' She changed gear ready to start the steep climb up towards Elm House.

She parked her car near where she had dropped Dolly off only a few days earlier and turned off her lights.

'You do realise that if a policeman happens by, I shall receive a fine for not displaying my night light.' She smiled at Matt as she started to pull her things from the back seat. 'Here, I have filled the foot warmers with hot water for our feet. There are rugs for our knees, and I have a flask of cocoa and some biscuits.'

Once the metal bottles swathed in wool were under their feet and they were ensconced in the rugs they settled down to watch and wait. Kitty had selected a spot where they had a clear view of the entrance to Elm House. Her own car was parked a way back. It was partially concealed from the casual observer by some hedging, now bare of its leaves, that hung over the garden wall of a nearby house.

The road was quiet and still. Clouds flitted across the face of the half-moon giving flashes of illumination. No one passed by either on foot or in a vehicle. Kitty shivered and snuggled down under her rug. She was aware of Matt next to her, taut as a coiled spring in his seat despite his casual demeanour.

'Matt, look.' She prodded him in his ribs.

In the turret at the top of Elm House a yellow light appeared. It flashed off and on three times, then was extinguished.

'It looks like a signal.'

'Stand by.' Matt pushed his cap back a little way on his head and they continued to wait.

She had just started to lose the feeling in the tips of her toes when they heard the unmistakeable rumble of an approaching car engine. Matt placed his hand on her knee in silent warning and they ducked down as low as they could get behind the dashboard while still being able to view the road.

There was a glimmer of headlamps for a second as the car crested the hill. Then the driver turned off his lights and the car moved almost imperceptibly through the open gates into Elm House's forecourt.

'All right, let's give them a few minutes and then we'll move,' Matt murmured.

Kitty was already poised to go. She moved her warmer and rug to one side and had her hand on the door handle. At Matt's signal she quietly opened her door at the same time as him. Once out, she pushed it back closed so it was barely latched, wincing at the slight click of the catch.

They moved together along the footpath towards the home, pausing at the entrance to ensure the coast was clear. As they waited, she heard faint sounds of movement and muffled conversation at the rear near the tradesmen's entrance where Dolly had let Kitty in a few days earlier.

Matt moved in close to Kitty, his breath warm on her cheek as he murmured in her ear. 'Keep close to the wall or the gravel will give us away. Follow me round and we can get onto the paved area. Stay low.'

She felt something hard in his coat pocket bump against her hip and she knew he must have brought his gun. This both frightened and reassured her at the same time. She followed his lead, slipping into the dark shadows thrown by the laurel bushes as they crept along the boundary as close to the wall as they could get until they reached the path.

The home was in darkness, the only light showing had been a lantern next to the closed front door. Kitty crouched down to keep as low as possible behind the rough stone wall which formed the edge of the first tier of the garden. The scent of damp earth tickled her cold nose.

Once they had rounded towards the back of the home they paused to listen again.

'Give us a hand. This is heavy.' A male voice, rough, low and grumbling, accompanied by scraping and bumping noises.

Kitty risked a quick peep over the top of the wall. The large black car they had seen earlier was pulled up close to the door with its lights off and doors open. A glimmer of light spilled out from inside the home through the open back door giving some faint illumination.

Two men, both clad in dark clothes, were hauling a couple of large boxes to strap onto the luggage bar at the rear of the car. Another man, shorter, with a slight limp stepped out of the shadowy back door of the home to join them.

She ducked back down again and became aware that Matt had crept further away from her in order to get closer to the men.

'Is this the last lot?' a different male voice asked.

'That's the last of the packages. We've had to make new arrangements for landing and distributing the next shipment. It's too risky here now with the police poking about and that private investigator sticking his oar in.'

'And whose fault is that?' the other voice complained.

'Shut your pie hole and get that lot secured. Scotland Yard are onto us an' all now. We can't afford to hang about. This whole place will be swarming with police tomorrow. I've had a tip off.'

Kitty's heart thumped as she heard this. She was right. Someone inside the police force was warning the Hammetts to help them to stay ahead of the police. Something about that third man made her stomach clench.

She lost sight of Matt as the moon went behind a cloud and she wondered where he had gone. She sucked in a deep breath to calm her nerves.

'That's the last one then now, guv, all tied on and ready to go.' It sounded like the first man again.

'You know where we're going? There's a boat waiting to receive these and move them on round the coast. It's too risky to send them the usual route.'

'Yes, guv.'

She heard the click of a car door opening and she started to edge back the way she had come. If she could get to the entrance quickly enough, she could attempt to see which way they were going and try following them in her car.

The low rumble of voices was barely audible when she reached the boundary wall of the home once more. Her pulse raced as she heard the car engine start up. Taking a chance, she darted out of the entrance of the home and ran to her car. She flung herself inside and pulled the door closed as the black car reappeared at the gateway of the home, its headlamps once more unlit.

'Matt, where on earth are you?' Kitty muttered as she waited for the black car to roll out of sight down the brow of the hill before starting the engine of her own car ready to follow them.

She had barely driven forwards a few yards when Matt sprinted out of Elm House's entrance and scrambled into the passenger seat beside her.

'Come on then, Kitty. Follow that car.'

Kitty set off in pursuit, making certain that she hung back far enough so the occupants of the black car would be unlikely to notice her. She turned on her headlamps once on the main road and there were a few more vehicles about.

'Which direction do you think they are taking? I heard them say that there was a boat waiting,' Kitty asked.

'It looks to me as if they are headed towards Exeter, if it's Hammett that's with them, and I think it may be, then we know he has plenty of hiding places around there. The waterfront with all the warehousing would be a good choice for them,' Matt said. 'I tried to get close enough to get a look at their faces, but it was very dark, and they had mufflers pulled up.'

'I wonder what's inside those boxes?' Kitty slowed down to allow the black car to pull further ahead. Another car was now in between them so she felt a little more confident that they wouldn't notice her. Although she started to wish that she had chosen a less distinctive colour for her car.

The car that had been travelling between them turned off towards Newton Abbott and Kitty allowed her car to fall back further. Suddenly, without warning the black car accelerated away.

'We're losing them,' Matt cautioned.

'Do you think they've noticed us?' Kitty pressed her foot down harder on the accelerator aware that her little Tourer was nowhere near as powerful as the vehicle they were pursuing. There was a sound from the car ahead. It came and went so swiftly she barely registered what it might be, the exhaust backfiring perhaps.

The sound came again. 'Maybe, or they may just be in a hurry now they're on an open road.' Matt had barely finished speaking when he grabbed at her steering wheel. 'Kitty, pull over, quickly.'

Shaken by the urgency in his tone, she obeyed and pulled her car to a stop on the grass verge at the edge of the road.

She released a breath she hadn't realised she'd been holding. 'What's wrong? What happened?'

'They shot at us. I saw the glint of the gun barrel appear through the back window of the car when I grabbed your wheel.' Matt slumped back in his seat. 'Did you not hear the shots?'

Kitty nodded. 'I heard something like an exhaust backfiring, but I was so busy concentrating that I didn't realise that's what it was. Ezekiel knows that I have a red Morris Tourer. They must have recognised the car.'

'Thank God they missed us. Come on, we'd better turn around and head back. It's much too dangerous to try and continue. Are you feeling all right to drive?' he asked, concern showing on his face.

She nodded. 'Yes, I'm all right.'

'You know that if you don't return by four the night porter will alert Inspector Greville.' Matt reached across and patted her hand. She guessed he was trying to lighten the seriousness of what could have happened if the shots had reached their target.

Kitty blew out a breath and her free hand crept up to her neck to check that her mother's precious little suffrage brooch was still secured on the silver chain Alice had given her for Christmas. She had put it on before leaving the hotel to bring her luck. She liked to think her mother had been watching over her.

'As a matter of interest, how do we present this escapade to Inspector Greville?' she asked as she turned the car around to head back towards Torquay.

Matt gave a low chuckle. 'I fear he will not be very impressed with either of us. Especially when we tell him that Hammett shot at us. I think we had better brace ourselves for a scolding.'

Kitty drove Matt back to his home before heading back to Dartmouth where she managed to cross the river after some bribery of the ferrymen. She parked her car in the street near the Dolphin. It was too late, and she was too weary to take it inside the garage. She decided to go and get some sleep and move it later when it was daylight, and more people would be about.

The night porter was looking out for her and let her inside promptly when she appeared at the front door.

'I'm right glad to see you back, Miss Kitty, else Mickey would've had my guts for garters,' Bill said as he secured the door behind her.

'Thank you for looking out for me.' She stifled a yawn and made her way up the stairs to her bed, conscious that she would only get a few hours' sleep at best before her grandmother would expect her to be at work.

CHAPTER FIFTEEN

Matt telephoned the police station in Exeter and told them about the latest incident. He suggested they increase their patrol by the waterfront immediately for the next few hours as that was where he thought the black car might be headed.

'We believe the men to be armed so please ensure the constables are made aware.' He hoped that he had done enough to ensure that no one else was hurt and that they were right in their guess of where Hammett might have a boat waiting.

As he replaced the telephone receiver back in its cradle, he wondered if he was doing the right thing. There was a real risk that the web of corruption within the force that seemed to serve Hammett and his sister might mean his message was not passed on. Or that he might be placing honest men in the path of danger.

He and Kitty had been certain any waiting boat would be unlikely to be at a harbour. The time of day would mean any unusual activity would be noted by the fishermen who would be setting out to sea at that time.

The waterfront in Exeter was as familiar to Hammett as the back of his own hand and a boat receiving parcels there would be unlikely to attract much notice. It also meant Hammett could disappear into one of the many tunnels or escape routes like a rat up a drainpipe. In the meantime, the boat and the mysterious parcels could be away in no time.

Despite his weariness, Matt had difficulty falling asleep. Something that he knew rarely augured well. When he woke a few hours later, his body was sheathed in sweat and his head was still ringing with the sounds of a war long since finished that had haunted his dreams.

He lay still for a moment waiting for the ghosts of the past to dissipate in the cool morning air. He became aware of a pain in his hand and, glancing down, he saw spatters of blood on his sheets coming from a gash on his knuckles.

Warily, he pushed himself upright to discover how much damage he might have done during the night terrors that plagued him from time to time. A constant, ugly reminder of his past. To his relief the furniture in his bedroom was still in place and the only casualty appeared to be a small round mirror on a metal stand, which he sometimes used whilst shaving that now lay shattered on the bedroom floor.

Matt fell back against the cooler linen of his pillows and studied the injury to his hand. Fortunately, the wound did not appear too deep and the bleeding had halted. He roused himself and got out of bed to start his morning.

He had just completed his morning ablutions and dressed for the day when there was a heavy pounding at his front door. Alarmed by the force of the knocking he hurried down the stairs.

'Inspector Greville!' He noticed the inspector appeared far from pleased to see him, and he was accompanied by the two men he and Kitty had seen at the police station. 'Good morning.'

'Is it?' the inspector retorted.

Matt's brows raised. It was too early for this after a bad night's sleep and he was in need of a cup of tea. 'Please come in, gentlemen. I'll make us some tea.'

He showed them into his sitting room and left them to themselves while he waited for the kettle to boil. Luckily his housekeeper always kept a tea tray set up ready, so it was only the matter of minutes before he returned to his guests.

'Now, gentlemen.' He set out the cups and poured the tea. 'To what do I owe the pleasure of this delightful early morning call?' He had a very good idea why they were there. Or at least why Inspector Greville might be there. He was uncertain about the Scotland Yard connection. Unless it was to do with the snippet of conversation he and Kitty had overheard a few hours ago.

'Captain Bryant, may I introduce Chief Inspector Flynn and Inspector Sutton from Scotland Yard.'

Matt shook hands with both men who continued to regard him with steely stares.

'I'm delighted, I'm sure. Please do help yourself to biscuits.' He indicated the decorative metal tin on the table.

'I expect you know why we are here?' Inspector Greville asked. Matt guessed it must be something very serious as the policeman had not so far succumbed to a biscuit. He could only hope that no one had been killed trying to capture Hammett.

Matt took a sip of his tea before answering. 'I can only assume this is something to do with Ezekiel Hammett and Elm House.'

'You placed a telephone call to Exeter Police Station a few hours ago?' Inspector Sutton, a large man with eyes like two dark currants set in a pale, doughy face consulted a small black notebook that he had drawn from his pocket.

'Yes, that's correct.' Matt helped himself to a biscuit. If no one else needed one, he certainly did. If it had not been so early, he might have added a nip of Scotch to his tea.

'In that call, you said you suspected Ezekiel Hammett and two others were en route to Exeter in a black car containing some kind of contraband and that Hammett was armed,' Inspector Sutton continued to read from his notes.

'That's correct, sir, yes.' Matt popped the rest of the biscuit in his mouth and chewed. He was starting to feel a little better now he had taken some sustenance and had time to wake up a little more.

'May we ask how you came by this information?' Chief Inspector Flynn asked.

Like his colleague, Chief Inspector Flynn was also a large man, with a bend to his nose that suggested a history in the boxing ring.

'Ah.' Matt had known that he and Kitty would have to own up to their nocturnal activities and he knew that the three policemen seated on his sofa were unlikely to be pleased. He took a deep breath and told them everything, including the shots that had been fired at them when they had attempted to follow the car.

Inspector Greville's complexion slowly turned a darker shade of puce during Matt's story. As soon as Matt finished speaking, he exploded into speech.

'What on earth did you and Miss Underhay think you were doing? Why didn't you consult me before undertaking such a foolhardy adventure? You could both have been killed and could have derailed a national police investigation in the process.' He glowered at Matt.

'In normal circumstances, sir, we would of course have alerted you. However, we have reason to believe that there may be officers stationed both here in Torquay and at Exeter who are reporting to Hammett and his network,' Matt explained.

The Scotland Yard men leaned forward in their seats. 'May we ask what led you to believe this?' Inspector Sutton asked.

Matt explained what had happened with the constable who had been tasked with allegedly watching Esther's Exeter address and the comment he and Kitty had overheard about a tip off.

'We raided Elm House at dawn this morning. Our birds had already flown the coop.' Inspector Greville looked exasperated.

'What happened at Exeter, sir?' Matt asked. He had known that they would find nothing at Elm House. Hammett had been one step ahead of the police there.

'Two constables were sent to keep watch down at the waterfront. They had strict instructions not to intervene in any way but to simply observe and make notes.' Chief Inspector Flynn sighed and set down his empty cup. 'A car fitting the description you gave was seen being unloaded. A note was made of the boat and the car registration.'

'And Hammett?' Matt asked.

'Only two men were observed, neither fitted the description of the wanted man.' Inspector Sutton looked grave.

Matt muttered a curse under his breath. 'He escaped again. The man is slippier than an eel. What happens now then, gentlemen? Am I permitted to know more about this secret operation? I can assure you I have the highest credentials and have signed the Official Secrets Act.' Matt leaned back in his armchair.

The policemen exchanged glances. 'There is growing alarm at the highest level about the increased supply and use of cocaine, both within the capital and beyond. We have for some time been using undercover detectives to try and infiltrate the supply network to discover how it is being brought into the country and distributed. We have been able to discover the small fry at the end of the chain, but it has been much more difficult to discover who is at the top of the pile. It now seems that Elm House and its proprietors are at the top of the chain,' Chief Inspector Flynn explained, having clearly made the decision to trust Matt with the story.

'How did you make the link to Devon, sir?' Matt asked.

'Via one of the patients at Elm House. A young lady called Veronica Wordsley. She had managed to wean herself from her addiction and had approached us to help others who wanted to break the habit. She provided us with the key information we needed that helped us to track some of the suppliers higher up the chain. We were concerned that she may have placed herself at risk of retaliation and her guardian agreed that she should come to Elm House to rest and recover before she followed up on her plans to move abroad.' Chief Inspector Flynn frowned as he spoke.

'Let me guess. There was a leak, and someone not only found out about Miss Wordsley's involvement, but inadvertently placed her not in a place of safety but right in the heart of the vipers' nest.' Matt felt sick. It certainly explained what had been behind the unfortunate girl's death.

Inspector Sutton nodded. 'So it would seem. Unfortunately, poor Miss Wordsley died before we could act to protect her. However, it did draw our attention to Doctor Marsh and his so-called wife.'

Matt picked up on the inspector's comment. 'I don't understand, sir, we were led to believe that Esther Hammett was married to Doctor Marsh?'

'She tells everyone they are married but Marsh is merely one of the surnames she uses. If she has entered into a marriage with Marsh, it would be bigamous, as she was married before and there is no record of a divorce or death of her first husband. Esther seems to conveniently ignore her first marriage and always goes by her maiden name. It would seem from what we know that they are more business partners than husband and wife. When we unravelled some of Esther's business activities it seems that she was the one who put up most of the money for the purchase of Elm House,' Inspector Sutton explained. 'The papers Miss Underhay supplied were very useful to us. I wish we could locate the original notebook.'

'Kitty discovered them hidden in a box she received in the autumn, we have no idea where Jack Dawkins may have acquired them or why. I assume that I am able to share this information with Miss Underhay? You may rely on her discretion. I wouldn't want her to be placed in any danger due to her not fully understanding all of the particulars of this matter.' Matt hoped the men would understand from the firmness of his tone that he intended to tell Kitty everything whether they agreed or not.

Their recent stay at Enderley Hall had been rendered both dangerous and complicated by his not being permitted to share information with Kitty.

'Very well, but we must urge you both to step away from this case and tell no one of any of the facts that we have just shared with you. We have the rest of this ring to round up.' Chief Inspector Flynn fixed his steely gaze in Matt's direction.

'What about Hammett, sir? He must be caught soon. Every moment that he remains free poses a danger. We believe he recognised Kitty's car last night as he has been observing her movements.' Matt's main concern was for Kitty's welfare.

He had no doubt that as the Scotland Yard men uncovered more of Hammett's operations the motives for Nurse Hibbert's death would also become clearer, along with the name of her murderer. Was she killed for discovering the cocaine smuggling operation or for concerns over what seemed to be the lucrative sideline of dispatching patients for financial reward?

The two London policemen exchanged glances. 'We would recommend Miss Underhay to remain at the Dolphin Hotel and not to leave Dartmouth. Greville, can you station a trustworthy constable to watch out for Miss Underhay's safety until Hammett is caught?'

'Yes, sir. I'll arrange it. The local constable in Dartmouth is a good officer and can be trusted,' Inspector Greville agreed.

Matt was relieved but at the same time he knew Kitty would not be happy at all with Scotland Yard's recommendations.

'I see you have injured yourself, Captain Bryant?' Inspector Sutton looked at the dressing on Matt's knuckles.

'An accident here at home,' Matt reassured him. He hoped the policeman hadn't formed the impression that he had been in a fight.

'We have a very good idea who some of the people are that may have been feeding information to Hammett. Plans are afoot to swoop very soon both on them and on those involved in the cocaine supply chain. The boat, car and drivers are all being followed as we speak. Once we have our evidence, then rest assured, we will have them.' Inspector Flynn clenched his fist as he spoke.

*

While Matt had been busy with the police Kitty had been woken by Alice, who had knocked on her door just before nine.

'Miss Kitty, I've got you a cup of tea here and some toast.'

Kitty rubbed the sleep from her eyes and groaned when she saw the time on her little Black Forest wall clock. She slipped out of bed and padded over to her bedroom door to let her friend in.

'You'd best shake your feathers, miss, your grandmother is already asking where you are as you'm not at your desk.' Alice bustled into Kitty's room bearing a small tray set with tea and a plate of buttered toast.

Kitty tugged on her warm red flannel dressing gown and took a seat in one of her fireside chairs as Alice set the tray down before her on the side table and closed the bedroom door.

'Thank you, Alice, this looks delicious.' The smell of the hot toast and the little dish of strawberry jam was making her mouth water.

Alice perched herself on the end of Kitty's bed. 'Father has set off to Elm House to fetch our Dolly and her box and bring her back home.'

Kitty looked up from where she had been pouring herself a cup of tea. 'Really? What has happened?'

'The police was there before it were light this morning. Searched the place from top to bottom they did. Our Dolly telephoned here and left a message for me. When I come on shift at half seven, I saw it and sent young Albert, the kitchen boy, with a message to Father. I didn't want our Dolly there a minute longer. Not after what you'd said the other day, and now this.' Alice picked at the stitching on the side seam of her apron.

'I can't say that I'm not relieved, Alice. I feel terrible for poor Dolly, but Elm House is not a good place to be.' Kitty took a reviving sip of tea.

'Father was going to make certain as they paid our Dolly her wage afore she left.' Alice frowned.

'I should jolly well hope they would. I hope Mrs Craven will leave there today too if she can. I doubt that many patients will remain unless they are too sick to go elsewhere.' Kitty applied jam generously to her slice of toast.

'Hmm, and what exactly were you and Captain Bryant up to last night, miss? Bill said as you come home just ahead of the milk cart and your motor car is parked up the side street.' Alice's lips pursed and her eyes narrowed as she waited for Kitty's response.

'Honestly, Alice, it was like one of your films.' Kitty took another sip of tea and told her maid everything that had happened.

The girl's complexion paled, and her eyes widened when Kitty told her about being fired at. 'You could have been killed, miss. You'd best hope as your grandmother don't get wind of it.'

Kitty hastily swallowed the rest of her tea. 'Yes, I'd better dress and get downstairs. You know what Grams is like. She'll be certain to smell a rat if I don't hurry up and put in an appearance.'

Alice jumped to her feet. 'Go and get washed, miss. I'll get your things ready.' She shooed Kitty off to the bathroom.

With Alice's aid, Kitty was soon dressed and downstairs.

'Good morning, Kitty dear, you're a little late today?' Her grandmother was at the reception desk with Mary. She surveyed Kitty's appearance with a searching glance.

'I haven't been sleeping well so I stayed in bed a little later today.' Kitty smiled and kissed her grandmother's delicately powdered cheek.

'You have looked a little peaky these past few days,' her grand-mother conceded. 'All the more reason to simply focus on your work here instead of gallivanting around the bay playing at being a detective.'

Kitty flushed at her grandmother's rebuke. 'I always get my work here done, Grams.'

'I know, I'm sorry, Kitty darling. It's simply that until this ter-rible man is caught, I feel quite on edge. Mary has just informed me that the police were at Elm House again this morning. I have telephoned and spoken to Sister Carmichael to ask that Millicent come here to stay until she is well enough to go home.'

'I've allocated Mrs Craven the Princess suite, Miss Kitty,' Mary said.

Kitty managed to suppress a groan at the idea of having Mrs Craven actually residing at the Dolphin for a while. The Princess suite was usually kept for honeymooning couples and distinguished visitors, but no doubt Mrs Craven would find some cause for a grumble. 'Excellent, Mary, thank you.'

Kitty went to unlock the door of her office ready to start her day when there was a commotion at the hotel entrance and Mrs Craven's piercing tones cut the air.

'My cane, please, Mr Potter, and do be careful with the luggage.'

Mrs Treadwell went to greet her friend while Kitty exchanged a sympathetic smile with Mary before escaping into the safety of her office. Mrs Craven had not lost any time in departing from Elm House. She wondered what time Matt would arrive and if he would have any news about Ezekiel Hammett. The police might have captured him already if their idea that he would head back to the quays at Exeter was correct.

She opened her accounts ledger and tried to concentrate on the neat columns of figures that persisted in dancing in front of her eyes. There seemed an uncommon amount of hustle and bustle in the lobby with new arrivals, judging from her limited view through the small stained glass porthole office window.

There was a knock on her door as she was about to give up and go on a quest for a reviving cup of coffee. To her surprise General Ackland stood before her, leaning heavily on his cane.

'My apologies, Miss Underhay, for disturbing your work, but I wondered if I might have a word?'

'General Ackland, please do come in and take a seat.' Kitty stood and pulled a chair forward.

The elderly man lowered himself down carefully as Kitty closed the office door to ensure their privacy.

'May I offer you some tea or coffee, sir?' Kitty asked.

He dismissed her offer with a wave of his hand. 'It's quite all right, my dear, I have no intentions of disrupting your morning. I'm sure you are surprised to find me here, but I felt it prudent to leave Elm House and I am not yet recovered enough to return to my home. Mrs Craven suggested that as she would be staying here, I might care to join her.'

'We are delighted to have you here, sir.' Kitty privately wondered how many other patients from Elm House might decide to complete their recoveries by staying at the Dolphin. It was always nice to have more business, but she wouldn't wish to see the hotel turn into some kind of makeshift nursing home.

The general's eyes twinkled, and Kitty suspected that he had guessed her thoughts.

'I thought you might like to learn what went on this morning at Elm House?' He rested his hands on the silver top of his walking stick and looked at her.

'I heard the police arrived before dawn and conducted a thorough search but found nothing,' Kitty said. 'My friend, Alice, has a sister who works there.'

'Ah yes, that would be young Dolly, serves the tea and fetches and carries for the kitchen.' General Ackland nodded approvingly.

'Yes, her father has gone to fetch her home. I suspect there will not be many people remaining at Elm House soon.' Kitty wondered if there was anyone left there at all.

'Indeed. Most of the patients have gone. The few who were very ill are being collected by ambulance and taken to other homes within the bay, or so I believe,' the general answered her unspoken question.

'I take it the police are gone now?' Kitty asked.

General Ackland nodded. 'They all left immediately after the search. By then the home was in chaos, of course. Patients packing, their families arriving to collect them.'

Kitty's curiosity was piqued. 'Who was there when the police came, sir?'

The general's bushy brows beetled together in concentration. 'Dodds, the orderly, Sister Carmichael, Doctor Marsh was on the scene pretty smartish too. I rose as soon as I heard all the palaver so I took as much notice as I could of what was going on.'

'No sign of Mrs Marsh?' Kitty asked.

General Ackland rubbed the end of his nose. 'No, my dear. There were people rushing about all over the shop by then, but I can't say I noticed her amongst them. She was never a frequent visitor.' He pushed himself up from his seat. 'I'd better get back to the lounge. Mrs Craven is expecting me for a game of cards.' His sudden smile made him appear almost boyish although Kitty wondered how Mrs Craven could possibly have that effect upon someone.

Kitty rose and opened her office door to see him out. 'Thank you for giving me some of the details about what happened this morning, sir. It all seems very extraordinary.'

After the general had gone, she took her seat back at the desk once more. She could imagine the chaos and disruption during the police search. Now it seemed the home was to close. Where would Doctor Marsh and Esther go? If the police had managed to find the men who had shot at her then they might well be taken in by the police for questioning.

Kitty drummed her fingers on the edge of the desk as she thought about what the general had told her. There were so many unanswered questions running around inside her head.

Another knock sounded on her door and Alice appeared, her cheeks pink with excitement.

'Miss Kitty, can you spare a minute?'

'Of course.' The words had scarcely left her lips when Alice hurried in, closely followed by Dolly. The younger girl appeared flushed and out of breath as they closed the door.

'Do take a seat, Dolly, are you all right, my dear?' Kitty asked.

'She's a bit out of breath, miss, on account of her having run all the way here,' Alice explained.

Dolly nodded vigorously. 'I come as soon as I could, miss.'

'Has something else happened? General Ackland has just been here and told me all about the police raid. Alice said that your father had gone to collect you to bring you home.' Kitty could see the girl obviously had something she thought was important to tell her.

Dolly's breathing began to settle, and she launched into her tale. 'It were while I were waiting for Father, miss. The police had finished and had questioned everybody. I'd spied my chance earlier to ring here and leave a message for our Alice, so I'd packed my box and were just keeping out of the way. Cook had packed her box and was after her wages. Sister Carmichael were proper flustered as people were telling her as they were leaving, and Miss Bowkett weren't there yet to take any telephone calls and that.' She paused to catch her breath.

Dolly's description combined with the general's information was giving Kitty a very clear picture of the events unfolding at Elm House.

'Go on, Dolly,' Alice urged.

'Well, Mr Dodds were being kept busy answering various bells with people wanting help packing their stuff and I just kept taking cups of tea round, laying low like. The telephone was ringing, and Doctor Marsh was going about to various patients trying to reassure them and persuade them to stay. Proper rattled he were and not at all happy. The police had kept him for half an hour answering questions before they went.'

'Tell Miss Kitty what you heard.' Alice nudged her sister.

'I was agoing to.' Dolly glared at her sister.

'Dolly?' Kitty asked encouragingly.

'I'd gone back to the kitchen. Cook had gone upstairs to her room to finish off the last of her packing. Said she weren't making no breakfasts and Sister Carmichael could do as she'd a mind. Well, I thought as I'd at least wash up the cups and put the place to rights as I didn't want them to have no excuse for not giving me my wage. I were bending down by the sink as I were after some fresh cloths out the basket there when I heard voices outside the back door. I reckoned as they hadn't seen me because I were bent down.'

'Who was it?' Kitty asked.

'The doctor's wife and Mr Dodds. I were surprised because she hadn't come a nigh while the police had been there. She had the doctor's car waiting for her with the motor running and the chauffeur sat inside. I couldn't hear that well over the car engine, so I crept up a bit closer by the back door.'

Kitty could picture the girl hiding with her ear pressed to the woodwork.

'I risked a peek. Mrs Marsh were giving Mr Dodds some kind of orders and I could see as he didn't care for what she were saying by the look on his face. Then he said something back to her and she raised her hand and clocked him one, right across his face. Near knocked him off his legs she did, as he weren't expecting it.

I ducked down right quick as I didn't want her a catching me and having her try to box my ears.'

'Did you hear anything of what was being said?' Kitty asked, shocked by the girl's story of what she'd witnessed.

'I only caught a few bits. Mrs Marsh said as she were leaving before the police came back again. It looked as if she were asking Mr Dodds to do something for her and he didn't want to and that were when she hit him. When I risked another peep, Mr Dodds were rubbing the side of his face and Mrs Marsh had a bundle in her hand. Something wrapped up in what looked like a scarf. I heard her say, "Take it or it'll be the worse for you. Then wait for my instructions. You're in too deep to get out now." I ducked down again as I were proper scared of them catching me.' Dolly halted her narrative and looked at Kitty with round, frightened eyes.

'You did very well. That was terribly brave of you,' Kitty said.

'Thank you, miss. The car drove off then and I crept back to the kitchen door and made like I was just coming in when Mr Dodds rushed in from outside. He looked a bit took aback when he saw me and put the hand with the bundle behind his back before hurrying off into the house.' Dolly's cheeks had pinked again at Kitty's praise.

'You didn't see what the bundle might have contained I don't suppose?' Kitty asked.

Dolly shook her head, her auburn curls dancing against her face. 'If I had to guess though, miss, given the size and the shape I would wager it were a gun, like what you see in the films.'

CHAPTER SIXTEEN

'What shall we do, miss?' Dolly asked. 'Should we let the police know?'

'I don't know. Do you think Mr Dodds might still be at Elm House?' Kitty asked. Her mind was whirling.

'When Father come to fetch me home, most everyone else had already gone. Miss Bowkett were there with Cook collecting their money from Doctor Marsh. Father made me wait outside while he collected my money. Sister Carmichael was with Doctor Marsh, but I didn't see where Mr Dodds had gone.' Dolly screwed up her face as she tried to recall where everyone had been.

'Do you know if Mr Dodds had a vehicle of any kind? A motor car or bicycle? I assume he lived-in like Nurse Hibbert? Do you know much about him at all, Dolly, that might give us a clue to where he might be?' Kitty suddenly felt a tide of fear rising inside her as she wondered what Esther's instructions may have been to the orderly. Someone else could be in mortal danger and it might even be her or Matt if Ezekiel had somehow managed to get a message to his sister about the night-time pursuit.

The creases on Dolly's brow deepened. 'He didn't have a car or anything and he lived-in like the rest of us, but his room was in a different part of the house. The women's part were separate from the men. There would be different people come to see him sometimes when he was supposed to be on duty. I used to make a cup of tea and put it outside with a couple of biscuits for Mr Johns, the gardener, on an afternoon. I wasn't supposed to but it was cold, and I felt sorry for him. That's when I used to see Mr Dodds talking to these different men. He were never outside for long and I didn't get much of a look at them. I thought as perhaps they were family or something.'

'Do you know where Sister Carmichael might be now? Did you hear her say anything about her plans?' Kitty asked. She thought that she was starting to understand Dodds's role in all of this, but she still wasn't sure about Sister Carmichael. Where did she fit in?

'Just after the police had gone, I overheard her asking Doctor Marsh what she should do. She were quite upset and he told her not to get hysterical and that he would sort things out, something about London. They might have said a bit more but then he noticed as I were nearby, and I hurried off before he could shout at me.' Dolly looked at Kitty.

Kitty picked up the telephone and dialled Matt's number. It rang out unanswered so she tried the number at his office in case he might have gone there. There was still no reply.

'Right, it seems that Matt must be out and about. He could have gone to the police station in Torquay or be on his way here. I don't think we can afford to wait.' She scribbled a message for Matt to leave for him at the reception desk and collected her coat from the stand.

'I'm going to go to Elm House. I doubt there will be anyone still there, unless Sister Carmichael is still around, but I might learn where Mr Dodds might have gone, and I can try to get to the bottom of Nurse Hibbert's and Mrs Pearson's murders.'

'Then you're not going by yourself, miss. 'Tis too dangerous,' Alice declared.

Dolly nodded her agreement. 'Best if I come along an all, miss. I knows where the nurse's bedroom was and how we can get inside if Sister has gone already and the place is locked up.'

Kitty could see that both the Miller sisters were determined to accompany her. 'Your parents will kill me.'

Alice grinned and ran off to collect her hat and coat before all three girls hurried out to where Kitty's car was parked. Kitty hoped that they might see Matt's Sunbeam on the road as they crossed the Dart and headed towards Torquay.

Instead, the road was quiet with only a few vehicles making their way in the soft, drizzly mist that clouded the landscape.

'What's the plan, miss?' Alice asked as they followed the road along the coast, the sea no longer visible through the thickening cloud.

'If Sister Carmichael is still within the building then we will try for entry. We can find an excuse, I'm sure. I want to ask her about Mrs Pearson and Nurse Hibbert. I also want to know where Mr Dodds and Doctor Marsh may have gone.' Kitty changed gear with a slight crunching sound as they started up the hill towards Elm House.

'If she's not there then I knows how we can get inside,' Dolly said, leaning forward from her seat in the back to raise her voice over the noise of the engine.

'I'd like to look in Nurse Hibbert's and Mr Dodds's rooms if possible to see what we might find. Has Nurse Hibbert's room been emptied yet, Dolly?'

'No, miss, I heard Sister say to Mr Dodds as how the doctor's wife had been to see Nurse Hibbert's family, but nobody hadn't packed up her bits as the police had been through her stuff.' Dolly hung on to her hat as Kitty took a sharp bend.

They were cresting the brow of the hill now and were almost at the entrance to Elm House. The mist had thickened further into low cloud, reducing visibility and shrouding the outside world in a blanket of dull, grey fog. Kitty was forced to use her windscreen wipers to sweep drops of moisture from the glass.

She pulled her car to a halt outside the front entrance of the home feeling a little guilty that she was breaking her promise to her grandmother to stay away from Elm House. No other vehicles were parked on the forecourt. The building loomed above them, dark and unlit in the murky gloom. The front door was closed and there were no signs of life.

'It don't look as if there's anyone home,' Alice remarked as she scrambled out of the passenger seat.

Dolly hopped out after her sister and eyed the front of the building. 'I can't see any lights on.'

Kitty locked her car doors and adjusted her gloves before smoothing down her coat. 'Let's find out.' She marched up to the front door and pulled on the cast iron chain of the bell pull. A sonorous jangling came from inside the home.

'No excuse for not hearing that if anyone is in,' Alice remarked as they waited on the step for someone to answer.

After waiting for a minute, Kitty tugged it once more. 'We'll try around the back if no one answers. Dolly, you said you thought we could get inside?'

'Yes, miss. I knows a trick with the back door. I saw Mr Dodds do it once when he was locked out.'

The building remained dark and silent, so they walked around the side of the building to the tradesmen's entrance. Dolly pressed her nose to the glass pane of the scullery window and peered inside.

'No sign of anyone here, either, miss. I reckon we might be too late, and they've all gone.'

'If we get caught doing this, then it's my fault. Neither of you is to take the blame,' Kitty warned as Dolly plucked a hairpin from her hat and slid it into a crack between the frame and the door.

After a few jiggles, she straightened up, smiled triumphantly and turned the handle.

'There we are, miss.' She pushed the pin back into her hat.

'Thank you, Dolly. If you ever wish to change career then burglary may be your thing.' Kitty grinned at her.

She took a deep breath and led the way into the deserted scullery. A few cups and saucers stood draining next to the sink and a white tea cloth lay abandoned on the worktop.

They made their way through the kitchen and along the corridor to the servants' stairs. Dolly then took the lead to show them the way up to Nurse Hibbert's room first.

'Did Sister Carmichael have a room here too?' Kitty asked.

'Yes, miss. She were at the far end.' Dolly led them up another flight of stairs to what must have originally been the servants' quarters when the house had been a private residence. 'Here, this one was Nurse Hibbert's room.' Dolly halted in front of a plain cream painted door.

Kitty had half expected the door to have been left locked but to her surprise it opened as soon as she turned the handle. It was easy to see that the room had been searched. Drawers lay half open, the meagre contents, stockings, undergarments and personal items all on show.

'Poor Eloise,' Kitty murmured as she stepped inside the room. It was obvious they would find nothing there. No evidence of a diary or letters of any kind. Even the cheap black imitation leather handbag held nothing more than a purse, comb and handkerchief.

'Nothing here, miss.' Alice closed the wardrobe door.

'Right, let's try Mr Dodds's room next. You said he lodged on a separate landing, Dolly?' Kitty led the way out of the bedroom.

'Yes, down along here, miss.' Dolly took the lead once more and they walked along to where the corridor took a sharp turn towards a small set of steps leading to what must have once been the attics.

Again, the door at the top was unlocked and opened immediately. Mr Dodds's room was surprisingly spacious and tucked under the eaves. A narrow iron-framed bed was neatly made with a dark green satin eiderdown. The kidney shaped dressing table was bare of personal items and only a small lamp stood on top of the locker beside the bed.

'The wardrobe is empty, miss,' Dolly announced as she checked it.

'And the chest of drawers.' Alice had opened and closed each drawer in turn.

Kitty opened the drawer of the bedside locker. 'Nothing.' Frustrated, she closed it again. It looked as if they were too late in finding Mr Dodds too.

'Here, miss, I don't know if this is anything?' Dolly had retrieved a small wastepaper basket and was unfolding a crumpled scrap of paper. She passed it to Kitty.

Kitty frowned as she tried to make out the untidy scrawl. 'Maria, 12 o'clock Tor.'

'A meeting?' Alice peered over Kitty's shoulder. 'A woman?'

'It's a shame it's ripped,' Dolly said. 'Torquay? Torre? The station, perhaps?'

Kitty shook her head. 'No, if it's what I think it is, Maria is a boat. He's headed to the harbour.'

Alice looked at her watch. 'It's just after eleven now. We can catch him.'

'Let's have a quick look in Sister Carmichael's room first and then get going.' Kitty's heart thumped as they hurried back the way they had come with Dolly again in front to show them the way.

However, as they rounded the corner back onto the main landing Dolly suddenly halted causing Kitty and Alice to bump into her. Ahead of them, blocking the way stood Sister Carmichael in person. Even worse, she was holding a small service revolver, which she had trained on them.

'Miss Underhay and friends.' She looked at Dolly. 'So, you were one of the spies, were you, Dolly Miller? Going somewhere, ladies?'

'We came to collect something Dolly had forgotten this morning when she packed,' Kitty said. 'We rang the bell, but no one came.'

'The back door was open, and we were just on our way out.' Alice placed a protective arm around her younger sister's shoulders.

'I don't think so.' Sister Carmichael took a few steps closer. 'I heard you opening and closing doors and drawers. Snooping.' She spat the last word out.

'Where is Doctor Marsh?' Kitty asked.

'Gone. He'll be in London by now, away from this place. I told him not to take this on.' Sister Carmichael steadied the gun, so it pointed directly at Kitty.

'Will you be joining him?' Kitty asked. 'Or will his wife object to that?' She knew it was probably foolhardy to provoke a woman with a weapon but the more she could keep her talking, the better their chances of getting out of Elm House alive.

'She's not his wife, not legally, despite them marrying. She's still married to somebody else, although she thinks I don't know that. She just calls herself Mrs Marsh because she thinks it makes her respectable. I'll be joining Clive as soon as I've finished up here. I'm the one he really cares about, not her.' The nurse's eyes hardened. 'She's already taken off, looking to save her own skin.'

'I'm afraid that you'll find that they've both hung you out to dry. The perfect person to take the blame for Mrs Pearson's murder and Nurse Hibbert's death while they disappear,' Kitty said. 'A nice little scheme, getting rid of wealthy elderly people with grasping relatives who would be generous if their family member were to conveniently pass away. What went wrong? Did Nurse Hibbert find out? Is that why she had to die?'

'I'm not responsible for any of that. Don't try to put that on me.' Sister Carmichael's hand wobbled and the gun wavered around causing Dolly to flinch and cuddle closer to Alice.

'You dispensed the drug that killed Mrs Pearson.' Kitty kept her voice as matter of fact as possible even though her pulse was racing.

Sister Carmichael shook her head in denial. 'No, that was that idiot, Dodds. He had his own supply of morphine. Clive only agreed to help people out, you know, hurry things along a little bit, after Esther put pressure on him. A nice donation from a grateful relative for services rendered was another source of income. She knew his weakness, you see, that's how she got him to marry her.'

'Weakness?' Kitty realised what Sister Carmichael was implying. The smuggling and the parcels made sense. 'He had a cocaine habit himself?'

'That's why Clive left London. It had become harder to hide his problems. Dodds was trying to cut Clive out of the arrangements with the families to take a cut of the money. He was the one who killed Nurse Hibbert too. Esther's orders, she wanted a scapegoat. This was a nice set up here, too good to lose without a fight.'

Kitty moved forwards and the nurse turned to keep the barrel of the gun pointing at her.

'Keep still or I'll shoot.'

'And where is Dodds now? Another one making a getaway and leaving you behind? Did you get any of the money from the drug smuggling operation that was being run from here?' Kitty kept carefully edging forward, forcing the woman to turn to keep the gun trained on her and away from Dolly and Alice.

'I don't know or care where he is, the slimy double-crossing layabout. He worked for her, so I expect he's gone wherever she's sent him.' Kitty could see spittle forming at the corners of Sister Carmichael's mouth.

Before Kitty could say anything more Alice sprang forwards. Sister Carmichael had no chance to react before Alice had cuffed her hard up the side of her head with her handbag, temporarily stunning their captor. The gun clattered to the floor and Dolly scrambled forward to grab it.

'What on earth do you have in that bag?' Kitty asked as the nurse clutched the side of her head as she leaned against the wall.

'Four tins of sardines, for the hotel cat.' Alice grinned at Kitty.

With the tables turned, Sister Carmichael stumbled forwards, still dazed as she made a feeble attempt to get away. Kitty promptly stuck out her foot and tripped her, bringing the woman to her knees. She moved swiftly to snatch the bunch of keys from the nurse's waist.

'I think it best you remain here until the police come to collect you.' She bundled the protesting woman into Dolly's old bedroom and locked the door.

'What time is it now?' Kitty asked Alice as they hurried away down the stairs, ignoring the angry thumps and bangs coming from the locked room on the top floor.

'Eleven thirty, we need to hurry if we are to get to the harbour in time,' Alice replied.

'Dolly, would you please stay here and telephone the police. If Matt arrives, tell him we've gone to the harbour and ask him to meet us there.' Kitty tossed the bunch of keys across to the young girl.

'Here, take the gun with you, miss.' Dolly passed the firearm over, clearly relieved to have it gone from her possession and Kitty stowed it safely inside her bag.

'Hurry, Alice, and let's hope that we're in time.'

CHAPTER SEVENTEEN

Matt's housekeeper arrived not long after the police had gone. She soon had order restored in his bedroom and, after tutting over the injury to his hand, insisted he ate breakfast before setting off to see Kitty.

He wasn't looking forward to informing her that the police wanted her to remain at the hotel. He knew how much she liked to be in the thick of things. The quest to capture Ezekiel Hammett was deeply personal as she hoped he might provide answers about why and how her mother had been murdered all those years ago.

The common was shrouded in fog when he finally managed to get his motorcycle to start. The damp weather appeared to have adversely affected the Sunbeam and the engine coughed and spluttered in protest as he made his way to Dartmouth.

Mary appeared unsurprised to see him as he entered the hotel lobby.

'Miss Kitty's gone out, sir, with Alice and her sister. She tried to telephone you, sir, but couldn't reach you, so she left this message for you.' The receptionist handed him a small envelope with his name on the front. His heart sank when he opened it and read the contents

Matt,

Gone to Elm House to find out where Dodds and Sister C have gone. Believe Dodds has a gun given to him by Esther.

Kitty

'What time did she leave?' Matt stuffed the note in his pocket.

'About an hour ago, sir.' Mary's eyes rounded as he muttered an oath under his breath and hurried back out to his motorcycle.

It took another couple of precious minutes of coaxing to get the engine to fire and he set off once more through the murky morning back over the river to Torquay. He cursed himself as he rode for not having telephoned Kitty immediately after the police had left his home. The only reason he hadn't was because he had thought Kitty might be late rising after their busy night and that he would arrive before she had time to go anywhere.

He had forgotten that now she was a motorist, the Red Peril meant she could take off under her own steam. She no longer had to rely on Mr Potter's taxi.

Elm House was shrouded in mist when he pulled up outside the entrance. The light was on however next to the front door, but there was no sign of Kitty's red motor car. He hesitated for a moment wondering if there was any point in even trying the bell or if anyone inside would give him any information.

He decided that he had nothing to lose and he might at least manage to discover if Kitty had been and gone already. To his surprise when he approached the front door, he discovered it was slightly ajar. He pushed it open and found Dolly sitting behind the front reception desk. Above his head in the distance he could hear shouting and the faint sound of someone hammering on wood.

'Dolly, where is everyone? Where's Kitty?'

'Miss Kitty has gone with Alice to the harbour in Torquay. They're looking for Mr Dodds. I'm waiting here for the police to come.' Dolly appeared remarkably calm and matter-of-fact.

'What's happened?' He hoped Kitty had not gone racing into danger.

'We locked Sister Carmichael in my old bedroom after she pulled a gun on us. Kitty and Alice took the gun with them as we think as how Mr Dodds has a gun as well what Mrs Marsh give him,' Dolly replied.

Matt groaned, so much for Kitty being sensible and staying safe. 'Are you all right to stay here? Are the police on their way?'

'Yes, sir. Mr Dodds was meeting a boat at the harbour at twelve o'clock, Miss Kitty has gone to try and stop him.' Dolly's eyes were bright with excitement despite the anxious expression on her face.

'When the police arrive, tell them where we've gone and get them to send a car to the harbour,' Matt instructed as he hurried back out to his bike.

Thankfully the Sunbeam's engine caught at the first attempt and he roared off back down the hill towards the harbour passing Inspector Greville's black police car on the way. He had his own service revolver in his pocket. He hoped as he sped along the road towards the boats bobbing in the murky distance that he wouldn't have to use it.

Kitty's car was parked at a slight angle by the side of the road near the harbour wall, arguing a rapid exit from the vehicle. He pulled the Sunbeam into an empty space at the kerb nearby raising the ire of another motorist who he had deprived of the spot. Ignoring the shouts and raised fists he hurried away towards the quayside looking for Kitty.

*

Kitty and Alice had made their way onto the quayside. The mist that had been so dense around Elm House was slightly lighter nearer the sea. Even so, it still floated across in drifts making it difficult to read the names painted on the sides of the brightly painted boats moored in the harbour.

'Watch out for the ropes, miss, you'm liable to turn an ankle.' Alice clutched at her arm as they tried to dodge the iron rings set in the stone flags and tangle of ropes that secured the boats to their mooring points.

'This is like looking for a needle in a haystack.' Kitty paused for a moment next to a large stack of ancient, weed-covered lobster pots which exuded an odour of bracken water and long dead fish.

'There's some men over there that look like fishermen.' Alice pointed towards a couple of men wearing knitted hats and heavy sweaters who appeared to be unloading nets from a small boat.

'Be careful, Alice, they could be the ones providing Dodds with his passage,' Kitty cautioned as they hurried over to them.

'Morning, ladies.' The younger man, clad in rough working trousers and a thick navy-blue jumper with a ragged hole at his elbow, winked at them as they approached. 'We've already sold our catch if you'm after fresh fish.'

'Thank you, but we're actually looking for a boat called the *Maria*?' Alice said, her cheeks turning pink under the man's bold gaze.

'That sounds like one of the pleasure craft. They'm moored further along toward the end. Try there, miss, you might have more luck.'

'Thank you.' Kitty tugged at Alice's sleeve and they scurried along the quay.

'What time is it now?' Kitty asked. She could hear male voices up ahead in the mist and saw the shadowy figures of a couple of men moving about.

'It's almost twelve now, miss. What are we going to do? We can't run straight into them. That's how people get killed in the films.' Alice skidded to a halt.

'Over here.' Kitty, like Alice, kept her voice low and they crept forward a few more yards to crouch behind yet another large stack of stinking lobster pots.

'Do you reckon as that's them?' Alice leaned out to take a better look.

'We need to get as close as we can, follow me and stay low.' Kitty's heart thumped as she edged nearer to the figures beside the boats, taking care to stay close to the lobster pots and nets. It dawned on her that she hadn't really thought her plan through properly about how she intended to stop Dodds from fleeing.

'We need to get going soon or we'll miss the tide.'

Kitty didn't recognise the male voice. Whoever it was had a local accent and she surmised it was probably one of the crew members.

'We'll go in a minute, once our passenger here has handed over his fare.' Another local voice, male and rough.

Alice squeezed Kitty's arm, her freckles suddenly bold against the pale skin of her face. Kitty placed a gloved finger against her lips indicating to her friend to stay silent.

'You need not fret. Here's your money, all counted and ready. The boss lady put it in there herself, you'll get the rest from the delivery man in Dieppe.'

Kitty's breath caught in her throat. That was definitely Dodds speaking, she recognised his voice, and he had to be referring to Esther. The mist was making it difficult to see what was happening and she wished she could see more clearly. However, it also had the added benefit of hiding her and Alice from the view of the *Maria's* crew. They would not have been able to get so close otherwise as Dodds and the others would have seen them immediately.

'All right, looks as if it's all in order. You'd best get on board then. We should be good to make it to the French coast. The radio report said the weather should be clearer once we're at sea.' This sounded like the man who had demanded the money.

Kitty tried to get a better look to see what was happening. She moved further around the lobster pots, but the mist suddenly swirled and moved leaving her and Alice's position exposed.

'Hey, who's that? Who's there? Show yourselves,' the crewman demanded. He peered in their direction.

Kitty gave Alice a firm shove back towards the safety of the fishermen they had passed earlier further down the quay. 'Run, Alice!'

Alice let out a frightened squeak and stumbled away, her heels tapping on the stone of the quay as she ran.

'It's that blasted interfering woman. The one who came to the home with the private detective.' Dodds scowled at her and Kitty stepped back fumbling with the catch on her bag as she moved ready to grab the gun.

'Hurry up and cast off! Dodds, get on board. If she's here the police won't be far behind her.' A burly great bear of a man started hurling the ropes onto the deck of a medium sized blue and white painted boat.

Dodds jumped down onto the deck of the *Maria*, a sneer on his face. 'Too late, Little Miss Nosy.'

To her horror he produced a gun from inside the breast pocket of his jacket as the final rope was released and the other crew member jumped on board as the engine roared into life.

Kitty's hand tightened around the handle of the gun in her bag and she placed her finger in readiness on the trigger.

'Maybe this will teach you to mind your own business. Goodbye forever, Miss Nosy Parker!' Dodds took aim, and Kitty pulled the gun free of her bag ready to return fire. The mist moved again temporarily closing off her view of the boat and his grinning face.

There was a loud bang, just as someone tackled her from behind pushing her down hard onto the stone floor of the quay. Her gun was sent skittering along the flagstones. Her knees hurt and she pressed her hands to her ears as another loud bang sounded close by. Whoever had knocked her down was covering her, shielding her with their body. She smelled the familiar scent of bergamot and a tiny trace of old tobacco and leather.

'Kitty, are you all right? Did he hit you? Are you hurt?' Matt's voice, as he pulled her hands from her ears and helped her back to her feet.

'What happened? Where is Dodds?' Shouts were coming from the direction of the sea, but the engine of the *Maria* sounded further away. The fog obscured her view, and the boat was already gone from her sight. Behind them, back by the harbourside, came the wail of a police siren, mournful in the thickening mist.

'I think I may have winged him.' Matt held her close in his arms. His body heat a warm and solid reality.

Shock started to set in, and she began to tremble uncontrollably. Her legs had turned to rubber and for a moment she was incapable of movement.

Alice came running back towards them, emerging out of the fog with her hat slightly askew and her face pale with fear. 'Miss Kitty, are you all right? What happened? I heard shots.'

'I'm all right, Alice, honestly. He missed me. I'm just annoyed that they seem to be getting away.' Kitty was conscious that she had skinned her knees and ruined her stockings when Matt had forced her to the floor. 'Goodness, I must look quite a fright.' Her voice shook and she had a horrible feeling that she had landed in a pool of fishy water.

Alice picked up the gun from the flagstones as the two fishermen they had met earlier came running to meet them, accompanied by a rather breathless Inspector Greville. Matt had discreetly tucked his own gun out of sight back inside the deep inside pocket of his leather greatcoat.

'Miss Underhay, Captain Bryant, what exactly is going on?' The inspector bent forward, his hands on his knees his breath coming in great gasps as he spoke.

'Dodds is getting away on a boat called the *Maria*, they're headed for Dieppe. He shot at me.' Matt continued to hold Kitty steady as she spoke.

'I returned his fire. I think I may have hit him but in the fog with a moving target it's hard to be certain,' Matt added.

'I'll alert the harbour master, sir. He can put the message out to look out for the *Maria*,' the younger fisherman spoke up and, receiving a nod of approval from the inspector, he and his mate left on their errand.

'With the harbour master alerted the French authorities will be asked to watch out for the *Maria* and her crew. They won't get away.' Matt looked down at Kitty.

'Dodds murdered Nurse Hibbert and Mrs Pearson, that is if Sister Carmichael is to be believed.' Kitty swayed on her heels and would have fallen if not for Matt's support.

'Is Dolly all right?' Alice asked. 'Has someone been to Elm House?'

Inspector Greville held out his hand to take the gun that Alice was still holding. 'Yes, Miss Miller, your sister is quite safe, and Sister Carmichael has been taken to the police station in Torquay. I should tell you, Miss Miller, that she is alleging that you assaulted her and, along with Miss Underhay, held her prisoner.'

Kitty could see a twinkle in Matt's eyes as he looked at her. 'Kitty?'

'She did pull out that gun the inspector is holding and point it at us first,' Kitty said. She saw the inspector's moustache twitch.

'And I didn't hit her so very hard. It was the sardine tins in my bag,' Alice protested.

'I suggest that we all adjourn to the police station and discuss this further.' The inspector began to lead the way back along the quay towards the waiting police car.

'Are we in trouble?' Alice asked in a low voice. 'Mother will die of shame and Father will be furious if me and our Dolly get arrested.'

'It will all be fine,' Matt assured her with a smile. 'Sardines?'

'For Tiddles, the kitchen cat at the Dolphin,' Kitty explained.

*

Dolly was waiting for them at the police station, seated on one of the bent wood chairs under the watchful fatherly gaze of the desk sergeant. As soon as she saw Kitty and Alice she ran to her sister and burst into tears as Alice hugged her tightly.

Inspector Greville left them in the waiting area and went off in search of a suitable room since it was clear they would not all fit in his office.

'I'm so glad as you're both safe.' Dolly fished a white cotton handkerchief from her pocket and blew her nose. 'Sister Carmichael has been took to a cell. And there's some policemen from London wants to speak to us.'

Inspector Greville reappeared and lifted the hinged section of the sergeant's desk so they could follow him along the whitewashed corridor into the heart of the police station.

'Chief Inspector Flynn and Inspector Sutton from Scotland Yard will be joining us shortly.' Inspector Greville led them past his office to an area of the station where Kitty had never been before. It turned out to be the canteen area. A large room containing several scrubbed pine tables and dining chairs. The room smelt of stale cabbage and disinfectant and Kitty wrinkled her nose in distaste.

'Please have a seat, ladies, and Captain Bryant.' The inspector indicated the chairs and they all dutifully sat down. Kitty wished she could have gone to a washroom first and tried to clean herself up. She suspected the additional odour of fish she had noticed was emanating from her direction.

A tray of tea arrived carried in by the desk sergeant. A large brown Betty teapot and a random assortment of utilitarian china cups. Kitty thought she'd never seen such a welcome sight.

The two policemen from London arrived as Alice was pouring the tea and took their places next to Inspector Greville. Kitty sipped her tea as the visiting inspectors shared all the information they had previously given to Matt.

She was pleased to see that the tea had returned the colour to Alice and Dolly's pale faces, although she could tell they were both still concerned that they might be in trouble.

'Now, Miss Underhay, perhaps you would care to give us your version of what happened and what Sister Carmichael said. We already have Miss Dolly Miller's version.' Inspector Greville looked at her. Kitty told the policemen what had happened at Elm House and then the later events at the harbour.

Alice added additional details and confirmed everything that Kitty said.

Inspector Sutton's eyebrows rose to almost meet his hairline as she described what happened at the quayside.

'And you heard them say they were headed for Dieppe?' he asked.

'Yes, although I suppose it's possible that they may change their plans if Matt did succeed in injuring Dodds.' Kitty set her empty cup back down on its saucer. She felt better for having had a hot drink, it had been a long time since her hurried breakfast of tea and toast.

'We've telephoned London and we have men out looking for Doctor Marsh. Inspector Pinch is leading a team in Exeter to arrest various people there and with luck we should get hold of Mr Dodds and the crew of the *Maria* soon.' Inspector Sutton set down his notepad.

'What of Esther and Ezekiel Hammett?' Kitty asked.

'Vanished, the pair of them,' Inspector Greville said in a gloomy tone.

'There seems little doubt from your evidence and the information we uncovered that there were two operations going on at Elm House. The smuggling of cocaine, landed at various local harbours and then distributed into a vast network of contacts. That seems to have been Esther's business, using Doctor Marsh and his contacts to provide a respectable veneer to the operation. Then Doctor

Marsh, aided by his lover, Sister Carmichael, seem to have found a sideline in assisting people to depart this earthly life in return for a financial gift from the departed's relatives.' Inspector Sutton glanced at his superior officer.

'This came unglued when Dodds, who was in Esther's pay, no doubt to keep an eye on Doctor Marsh and Sister Carmichael, decided to go into business for himself,' Inspector Greville chipped in.

'He murdered Mrs Pearson while Doctor Marsh was away to collect a payment from Leonard Pearson, except it all went wrong when Doctor Carter refused to certify the death.' Kitty shivered.

'And poor Miss Wordsley was killed for giving information to the police about the cocaine smuggling operation.' Inspector Greville drained his tea.

'I fear Dodds must have overheard Nurse Hibbert when she came outside to arrange that meeting at the tea rooms with me. He must have guessed that she was about to blow the whistle. She had obviously realised something was very wrong at Elm House and the death of Mrs Pearson must have frightened her. She must have realised then that it had to be either Dodds or Sister Carmichael who were responsible. I don't think she was involved at all in the smuggling or the deaths, was she, Inspector?' Kitty asked.

'No, I think she was entirely innocent, poor soul. She was intended to be the scapegoat for Lady Wellings and Mrs Pearson's deaths,' Inspector Greville confirmed.

Dolly looked distressed by this revelation and Alice gave her younger sister a hug. The canteen door opened, and the desk sergeant re-entered. He passed a slip of paper to Inspector Greville.

The inspector read it. 'The *Maria* has been intercepted. They tried to return to port further along the coast. It appears Dodds was hit in the shoulder and had lost quite a lot of blood. The *Maria's* crew it seems draw the line at murder.'

Matt snorted. 'They didn't stop Dodds's attempt to kill Kitty.'

'Miss Underhay, we would still advise you to be very careful over the next few days. We don't know the Hammetts whereabouts and they may hold you responsible for their misfortune. The same goes for you, Captain Bryant,' Chief Inspector Flynn warned.

Kitty saw Alice and Dolly exchange worried glances. 'Please don't worry, sir, I think I've had quite enough excitement to last me for a long time. I just want to see the Hammetts behind bars where they can't hurt anyone else.' And the sooner that happened the happier she would be.

CHAPTER EIGHTEEN

Alice and Dolly returned to Dartmouth by taxi, while Matt and Kitty decided to walk back through the town to collect Matt's motorcycle and Kitty's car. Kitty did her best to clean up her hands and knees in the police station toilet before setting off. Although the police station's carbolic soap and water appeared to do little to diminish the odour of dead fish emanating from her coat.

'I must admit I'm glad it's still foggy. Hopefully no one will notice the deplorable state of my stockings.' Kitty had her arm linked through Matt's as they made their way back towards the seafront.

'I'm sorry about that. My main concern was to remove you from Dodds's line of fire.' Matt smiled apologetically at her.

She grinned back up at him. 'I think I've rather lost track of the number of pairs of stockings I've ruined since I met you.'

'It's a good thing we know how they were spoiled, or your reputation would be as ruined as your stockings.' He ducked away as Kitty released his arm and pretended to hit him.

'I hope the Hammetts are caught soon.' She rested her hand back on the crook of his arm once more.

'I must confess I shall be much happier myself when they are both behind bars. I had thought Ezekiel was the worst of the two, but after everything we've learned today, I fear it is Esther that we need to worry about more.' It occurred to her that the EH who had signed the note at the hotel could have been Esther acting on her own behalf, rather than Ezekiel as she had assumed.

They halted at the kerb and prepared to cross the road to reclaim their respective vehicles. As they approached the sea, the mist swirled and parted momentarily. Suddenly Kitty clutched at the sleeve of Matt's greatcoat.

'Matt, look over there by the railing. It's that boy again. The one I thought was following me, Alice and Dolly the other day when we went to the cinema.'

The lad was skulking near her car, leaning against the rails. She recognised him at once due to his distinctive headwear and worn clothing. Matt followed her gaze.

'Come on, let's see if we can catch him and find out what he's up to.' Matt started across the road towards the lad.

Kitty hurried after him, but as the boy saw them approaching through the mist he took off at a run, ducking and diving back up towards the high street. He plunged through a small group of people leaving one of the shops and scurried up a side street. Matt pursued him for a while leaving Kitty behind.

He returned to her a few minutes later, breathless and empty handed. 'I lost him in the fog amongst the crowd. I suspect he knows all the shortcuts like the back of his hand. Sorry, old thing.'

'How very vexing. I suppose that's one mystery that will have to wait until another day.' Kitty stopped at the side of her car.

'Are you feeling all right to drive?' Matt asked, a tender note in his voice.

'I'm perfectly fine now, thank you. I think the shock of being shot at yet again has finally worn off. Shall I see you back at the Dolphin later? We have to update Mrs Craven and General Ackland with everything that's gone on. I shall also have to smooth down my housekeeper, Mrs Homer's, feelings as she has been missing a chambermaid all day.' Kitty also hoped that her grandmother would not be too distressed when she learned of their adventures.

Although if Mrs Homer had already reported Alice's absence then she wasn't at all hopeful on that score.

Matt bent his head to kiss the tip of her nose, sending her pulse skittering about with delight. 'Go back and have a rest. If you feel up to it let's go out for dinner tonight. I'll book a table for somewhere nice in Dartmouth.'

Kitty grinned. 'So long as you promise not to fall asleep in your soup.'

'I can see I shall never live down our cinema date.' Matt held her car door open for her as she climbed into the driver's seat. 'Take care, darling, and I'll see you later.'

Kitty smiled and gave him a cheery wave as she pulled away into the fog. Matt followed behind her on his motorcycle as she drove back along the coast road. He turned off as they reached the common and she continued to follow the road down to Kingswear and the ferry station.

*

Matt whistled merrily to himself as he tied his bow tie. He was looking forward to a quiet evening out with Kitty. Dinner at one of the smaller rival hotels in Dartmouth, followed by an evening dancing on the pocket-sized dance floor. A chance to forget all about crime and murder, time to celebrate being alive and with Kitty.

The telephone rang as he reached the bottom of the stairs.

'Matthew, I'm terribly sorry to trouble you but may I ask if Kitty is with you?' Mrs Treadwell's voice, slightly reedy with anxiety.

'Has Kitty not returned home?' He tried to keep his tone calm so as not to alarm his elderly caller, even though his internal alarm bell was clanging a warning.

'No, she went out with Alice and Dolly this morning and telephoned from somewhere this afternoon to say not to worry about her and she would be back around teatime. With this dreadful fog and it being so dark now, well it's getting late and it's not like Kitty to not let me know where she is.'

Matt thought quickly. 'I met her in Torquay and followed her back on my bike as far as Windy Corner on the common. Alice and Dolly had gone home by taxi, so she was on her own. Perhaps she's got car trouble. Please don't worry, Mrs Treadwell. I'll go out and look for her in case she's had a puncture or something.' He hoped it was a puncture or a mechanical problem, but by now there had been plenty of time for Kitty to have walked down into Kingswear or even back up the hill to his home to obtain help.

'Oh, would you, Matthew, that would help put my mind more at ease.' Kitty's grandmother sounded relieved at his reassurance and offer of assistance.

Matt replaced the telephone receiver and tugged on his leather greatcoat and cap. All thoughts of his pleasant carefree evening had vanished from his mind, replaced by anxiety for Kitty's welfare. Where was she? What on earth could have happened to her on that short drive from the common down to Kingswear?

The fog enveloped him in an icy blanket as soon as he left the cosy comfort of the house. In the distance came the low mournful warning wail of the shipping siren. He threw the tarpaulin off his motorcycle and pulled on his gloves. If Kitty's motor had broken down in this weather and she was still with her car, she would be freezing.

The yellow light of his headlamp made little impact on the dense mist and he crawled slowly along the narrow road alert for any sign of Kitty and the Red Peril. No other vehicles appeared to be abroad, and on such a foul night he didn't blame them.

The poor visibility meant that he kept his engine idling as he crawled along the lane expecting at any moment to encounter the red Morris Tourer and a cold and indignant Kitty. The road grew steeper shortly after the turn to Coleton Fishacre before dropping down to take the bend towards the river inlet.

Visibility now was down to just a couple of feet and even the puttering of the motorcycle engine seemed muffled. The moisture in the air settled and clung to the exposed skin of his face and he was thankful for the protection of his coat and cap. Anxiety mounted in his stomach, where was she? Had she crossed the Dart on the ferry and gone on to somewhere else?

He dismissed the thought as swiftly as it had entered his head. No, Kitty was in trouble, he was sure of it. It occurred to him that if there continued to be no trace of her on the road he could continue on to the river and enquire from the ferrymen if they had seen her.

Matt was about to kick up the accelerator of the motorbike to do exactly that when something caught his eye. A small thin branch from one of the scrubby bushes at the side of the road gleamed white in the light from his headlamp. It was freshly broken right beside the concealed open entrance to a field.

His heart hammered against the wall of his chest as he took a chance and steered his bike into the field opening. A collapsed old wooden five bar gate leaned drunkenly against the hedge, leaving just enough room for a car the size of Kitty's to have squeezed through the gap.

Matt halted and felt inside the breast pocket of his coat for the small flashlight he kept there. He shone it down on the muddy entrance to combine with the light from his headlamp. He was certain there were tyre tracks there that could have been made by a car and not just tractor marks in the churned-up grass.

He stowed the torch away once more and drove the Sunbeam further into the field, wincing a little as driving across the rough tussocky grass jarred his shoulder aggravating his old war wound. He continued to scan the ground as he rode slowly forward looking for any indication that Kitty's car might have passed that way.

The grassy ground suddenly curved away from him as the field followed the line of the hill down towards the creek. It was virtually impossible to pick anything out now in the dense fog, but he was sure there were tyre tracks in the grass.

As he crested the brow to descend the steeper part of the field, he thought he saw a dark shape and a faint gleam of light up ahead. Unwilling to take the motorcycle any further for fear of becoming mired down he stopped his engine. He retrieved the flashlight once again from his coat pocket and set off to investigate on foot.

He tripped on a clump of grass as he hurried as swiftly as he dared towards the faint gleam of light. He could also hear the faint rumble of a car engine growing louder the closer he got. As he drew nearer, he made out the familiar shape of Kitty's car resting at a strange angle against the slender trunk of a solitary tree.

Matt ran the final few yards to approach the car and wrench open the driver's door. Kitty was slumped forward in the driver's seat, her head on the steering wheel. The car engine was still running, and he automatically reached for the key to turn it off.

He pulled off his gloves and touched Kitty's cheek, discovering the flesh was ice cold beneath his finger. He thought for a moment that his heart would stop with fear.

'Kitty!'

She made a tiny moaning sound, and he drew in a deep breath as he offered a silent prayer of thanks to whichever of her guardian angels was on duty. Dizzy with relief, he steadied her head and neck as he moved her tenderly, so she was off the steering wheel and supported by the seat. He ran the flashlight over her, thankful to see no visible signs of blood or injury. Only a large and ugly contusion forming on her brow.

'Kitty my darling, it's all right. I have to go for help. I won't be long.' He reached into the back seat and pulled out the blankets she had stowed there from their surveillance at Elm House. He wrapped her up to keep her warm then ran, stumbling over the tussocky ground, back to his motorcycle.

*

Someone somewhere was beating a very large gong with a hammer and Kitty wished they would make it stop. Her limbs lay heavy on something as if they had been weighted down. Along with the gong she could hear voices, dim and distant, none of the words making any kind of sense. Almost as if they were being spoken in some foreign tongue.

She was aware that she was somewhere bright. The white light seemed to be trying to force its way underneath her closed eyelids. She didn't want to open her eyes. Instead, she wanted to retreat back into that dark, warm, dim, twilight world she had been so cosily inhabiting.

Kitty tried screwing up her eyes to block out the irritating brightness but that made her head hurt and she became aware that there was something on her head.

'Kitty, Kitty, can you hear me, my dear?'

Her grandmother's voice seemed to penetrate into her consciousness piercing through the fog. Fog, there had been something about fog, she thought. Something cold.

'Kitty.' The voice was insistent. A different female voice, sharper.

She tried to say something to make them stop and leave her to sleep but her voice didn't seem to be working properly and all she managed was a kind of croak. Immediately she sensed a buzz of chatter and activity around her.

'Kitty.' Her grandmother's voice once again.

'Gwen dear, move aside and allow me to try. Kitty, for heaven's sake, open your eyes!'

Kitty groaned; she would know that voice anywhere, but why on earth was Mrs Craven telling her to wake up? She risked a peep at the bright, white world and caught a glimpse of her grandmother's pale anxious face.

'Oh, Kitty, thank heavens. Nurse, quickly, she's awake.'

Her grandmother moved out of her line of vision and the next thing she knew, someone was pulling up her eyelids and shining something in her eyes. Instinctively she tried to push them away as the brightness seemed to make the thudding noises in her head even louder.

Her pillows were plumped, and she was placed in a more upright position. She opened her eyes and squinted at her surroundings.

'Where?' Her voice cracked and her grandmother pressed a glass to her lips.

'Take a sip of water, dear. You're at the cottage hospital.'

Kitty obeyed her grandmother. Her lips felt dry and cracked and the water tasted warm and fusty. She licked her lips as her grandmother removed the glass. Her focus seemed to be fuzzy and everyone had a shadowy outline surrounding them. It all felt like a very bad dream.

She swallowed, blinked and looked around again. The room smelled of disinfectant and flowers. Her grandmother and Mrs Craven were sat on chairs beside her bed looking expectantly at her.

'How?' She tried to formulate her thoughts into words.

'You had an accident in your car in the fog coming back home. You went into a field and banged your head.' Her grandmother bit her lip and occupied herself with twitching the bedcovers straight.

Kitty closed her eyes again for a moment and tried to remember. Fog and cold, she had been cold.

'I knew it was a mistake having that car,' she heard her grand-mother mutter to her friend. Kitty wanted to argue but she was simply too tired.

When she opened her eyes again the room was darker and a lamp beside her bed threw a pool of golden yellow light over the pale green bedcovers. She looked around and saw that her grandmother and Mrs Craven had gone. Instead, Matt and Alice occupied the visitors' chairs.

Alice's pale face was wreathed in worry. Matt appeared haggard with fine stubble covering his jaw and dark circles beneath his eyes.

'Miss Kitty.' Alice leaned forward and took hold of her hand as she peered anxiously into her face. 'Oh thank heavens, I were so afraid.'

'Kitty.' Matt's eyes were fiercely blue and rimmed with red as if he hadn't slept for a long time.

'Please can I have a drink.' Her voice came out as a whisper, but she was pleased that she sounded more coherent this time.

Alice immediately held the water glass to her lips and this time Kitty drained the glass. 'Thank you.'

Alice retook her seat. 'You've been out cold for ages, miss. We was all really worried about you.'

'I can't remember…' A tear rolled unbidden down her cheek.

'You were in a motoring accident. After we left Torquay, I followed you on the Sunbeam until I reached my house. It was very foggy.' Matt leaned forward to explain.

'I can remember the fog and being cold.' She frowned and winced as it made her head hurt.

'Be careful, miss, you've had a right old bang on your head,' Alice said anxiously.

'You were going back home to the Dolphin and we were going to go out for dinner,' Matt continued.

Kitty tried to think.

'When you didn't arrive, your grandmother telephoned me, and I went to look for you. You had gone off the road and come to a halt in a field.' Matt's voice was gentle.

Kitty was puzzled. 'Why would I do that? I'm a good motorist.' Despite the ache across her temples, she was vexed.

'Someone had sabotaged your car, miss. Robert and Captain Bryant had your car fetched out of the field and brung to the garage in Dartmouth. The mechanic there says as the brake cable had been cut,' Alice explained.

Kitty licked her lips and tried to process what Alice had said. 'Somebody tried to kill me again?'

'I'm afraid so, Kitty. I must confess when I first found you slumped over the steering wheel so cold and still, I feared they had succeeded.' Matt's expression was grim.

Her eyelids fluttered shut again as she tried to recall anything about the crash. She remembered the afternoon. Going to Elm House with Dolly and Alice. Sister Carmichael and the gun. Dodds fleeing on the *Maria* and the gunshots. Then they had gone to the police station.

She opened her eyes. 'The boy. The one with the cap.'

'Inspector Greville has him in the cells,' Matt reassured her.

'My poor car.' Another tear leaked out as she thought of her little red motor.

'The Red Peril was far less damaged than you, old thing. Please don't worry. The garage says it will be as good as new in a couple of days.'

Alice passed her a handkerchief from her bag and Kitty blew her nose. The movement made her wince and Alice and Matt's outlines flickered in the most alarming way before becoming steady once more.

'We'll have to go in a minute, miss. We shouldn't be here now, but Captain Bryant bribed the sister with a box of chocolates for the nurses.' Alice smiled at her.

'I'm so happy to see you both.' Kitty smiled back.

Alice stood and kissed her cheek. 'I just need to step out for a minute. I'll see you tomorrow, miss.'

'Thank you, Alice.' Kitty knew her friend was being tactful to allow Matt time alone with her.

He slid onto Alice's recently vacated seat and took hold of Kitty's hand, lifting it tenderly to kiss her fingers. 'I thought you were a goner, Kitty.'

'I'm so sorry.' Her heart tore at the pain in his eyes. She knew what he had gone through with the loss of his wife and baby.

'Don't be silly. It was hardly your fault some homicidal maniac decided to try and kill you.' The corners of his lips twitched upwards.

'I suppose not, but even so.' Her words trailed off.

'Even so, it made me realise even more how much I've come to care for you, Kitty. I don't want to lose you.'

Her heart lifted.

'Come along, now. Visiting time was over long ago. Out you go.' A plump, cheery woman in a navy dress with white starched apron and cap bustled into the room and fixed Matt with a steely glare. 'This young lady has concussion and needs her rest. No excitement. Be off with you now.'

Matt rose reluctantly and kissed Kitty briefly on the lips. 'Good night, darling.'

He bade the sister a good evening and walked out of the room.

After her visitors had departed, the sister checked Kitty's temperature and pulse before straightening her bedcovers and pillows. Kitty settled back and closed her eyes as the nurse completed her tasks and left the room. Her head ached now from the strain of holding a conversation, but her spirits felt lighter for having seen Alice and Matt.

The sister returned with some tablets for her head and Kitty dropped off into a light doze. Outside on the main ward the sounds grew less as the hospital quieted and settled down for the night.

It was dark in her room when Kitty woke again, and she wasn't sure at first what had disturbed her. She kept her eyes closed as she listened and tried to orientate herself. There was a faint click of a door latch and the eerie sensation that she was no longer alone.

CHAPTER NINETEEN

She lay still and focused on keeping her breathing even so whoever it was would assume she was still asleep. It wasn't one of the nurses, Kitty was sure of that. Even when she had been barely awake and confused, she had realised that they made different sounds when they moved. Their aprons crackled and they moved briskly with a bustle to their steps.

Whoever this person was didn't want to be noticed and was moving slowly and stealthily inside her room. The hairs on the back of Kitty's neck prickled and she wished the night light beside her bed had been left on as she risked a quick peek from under her lashes.

The room was dark and shadowy. Kitty braced herself, something was wrong, she knew it. There was a few seconds pause then something soft was pressed hard against her face. Her nose and mouth were covered as she was pushed down onto the mattress of the bed. She tried to fight back and call for help but to no avail. Panic set in as she fought for her breath.

She struggled against the pressure of the pillow but then, fighting every instinct for survival that she had, she allowed herself to grow limp. The pressure immediately relaxed for a split second. Kitty pushed upwards and sideways with all her strength, wriggling out from under the stifling weight of the feathers and linen.

'Help!' Her voice sounded surprisingly loud in the small room.

The pressure was suddenly gone completely. She heard a muttered curse in the darkness as she kicked out at the shadowy figure beside her bed. The door of her room flew open with a bang as her attacker ran out. A dark male silhouette showed briefly against the pale white night lights of the ward.

The main light switch for her room was clicked on and she held up her hand to shield her eyes from the dazzling brightness of the overhead light. She gasped as she sat up in her bed, sucking in air.

'What is it? What's happened?' A young police constable appeared in the doorway next to the startled night nurse in charge of the ward.

Kitty's hand shook as she pointed to the pillow lying on the floor next to her bed where it had fallen. 'Someone just tried to kill me.'

*

Matt attended the police station in Torquay early the next morning as soon as he received Inspector Greville's telephone call. He accepted one of the inspector's cigarettes as he listened with alarm to the report on the latest attempt on Kitty's life.

'How did the assailant manage to gain entry to her room? I understood that a constable was to be posted outside the door of the ward until Kitty was discharged in order to prevent any possibility of just such an occurrence?' Matt's hand shook slightly as he drew on the cigarette. He had thought he had lost Kitty once already when he had found her so cold and still inside her car. The hospital should have been a much safer place for her.

'The constable was distracted into assisting one of the porters who was trying to transport a load into the elevator. The attacker took advantage of his absence and managed to gain access to Miss Underhay's room.' Inspector Greville's moustache drooped, and his tone was grim.

'Did Kitty say if she saw who it might have been?' Matt asked, annoyed that the constable had been so incompetent to leave the room unguarded.

'A man in dark clothes. She only saw his outline as her room was in darkness.' The inspector blew out a thin plume of cigarette smoke. 'My men are out in force in Dartmouth going from house-to-house.'

'Thank God she wasn't harmed.' Matt stubbed out his cigarette in the overflowing ashtray on the inspector's desk. 'Have you managed to get any information yet from the boy?'

'The lad is one Tommy Coombs; he's well known to my men. Petty crimes and a regular nuisance. He often hangs about around the harbour looking for odd jobs.' Inspector Greville's tone was disparaging.

'Do we know anything about why he was watching Kitty or who he may have been reporting to?' Matt asked. 'He could well have been the culprit who tampered with Kitty's car or have knowledge of who may have done it.'

'He has refused to speak. I intend to talk to him again, perhaps you might care to sit in?' The inspector rose at Matt's nod of acquiescence and the two men made their way out of the office and on down the short flight of concrete steps to the cells. Somewhere that brought back unhappy memories for Matt when he had been incarcerated there himself for a short time in the autumn.

The custody officer produced a large iron ring of keys and opened one of the dark green painted metal cell doors. Matt followed Inspector Greville inside, recollections of his own stay in the same cell still playing on his mind. The feelings of powerlessness and entrapment, while confined in a small space. He had a hatred and fear of confined spaces and being inside the cells brought him out in a cold sweat. To his relief the inspector left the door open with the custody sergeant standing watch outside.

The scruffy lad lolling on the wooden bench eyed them warily from distrusting eyes. Matt realised that the boy was older than he and Kitty had thought. Now he was no longer wearing the oversized cap he appeared to be closer to fifteen or sixteen rather than the eleven or twelve years they had taken him for.

The boy's shoulders were hunched in a gesture of defiance although Matt could tell he was trying to appear nonchalant in front of the inspector.

'Now then, my lad, Captain Bryant and Miss Underhay saw you hanging about near Miss Underhay's car besides the harbour the other evening. That same evening Miss Underhay was almost killed when her car crashed whilst she was driving back to Dartmouth.' The inspector looked at the lad.

The boy shrugged. 'Weren't anything to do with me. I don't know no Miss Underhay or her motor. There was a few cars parked by the harbour, like always. I was just there to see what all the ruckus was about.'

'You ran off when I chased you,' Matt said. He had stayed near the entrance to the cell where he could step outside if it became too claustrophobic.

'I didn't know you or what it was as you wanted. Why was you after me anyhow?' The boy scowled.

'Miss Underhay and her friends had seen you previously, following them in the town and loitering around the entrance to the picture house.' Matt deliberately kept his tone mild.

'Ain't anybody allowed to walk into town now or to see a picture if they want? No law against that, is there?' Tommy retorted.

'Someone attempted to murder Miss Underhay again last night. They broke into the hospital in Dartmouth and tried to suffocate her with a pillow.' The inspector's eyes narrowed as he looked at the lad.

The boy snorted. 'Well, that weren't me, was it? Not when I'm banged up in here. Strikes me as you should ask her who she's annoyed if people am trying to kill her.'

'We know you were watching Miss Underhay. Someone was paying you to do so, and you know what happened to the brakes on her car.' Matt found his fists were unconsciously clenching as he questioned the lad.

'Don't know what you mean. Her having an accident weren't nothing to do with me. I'm often down by the harbour. I sometimes get work off the boats, you can ask anybody.' The boy looked quite cocky as he replied.

'I suggest that you tell us who was paying you to observe Miss Underhay or the inspector will have no option but to charge you with her attempted murder for tampering with the brakes on her car.' Matt knew what he was saying was a complete bluff. There was not enough evidence to link the boy to Kitty's accident. He just hoped that the lad might not know that.

'There ain't anything to say it was me touched them brakes. I didn't do nothing. I just kept watch.' Tommy sat up straight. Matt's statement had clearly alarmed him.

'Kept watch for who?' Inspector Greville pounced immediately. The boy stayed silent.

'Perhaps you had better charge him, Inspector,' Matt said.

The boy scowled. 'The doctor and his missus.'

The inspector exchanged a glance with Matt.

'Doctor Marsh?' Matt asked. 'Was he there yesterday? Who tampered with the brakes? The doctor or his wife? Or was it you after all acting on their instructions?'

Tommy looked shifty and Matt could see the boy was regretting letting slip the information.

'I suggest you answer, or I will have to charge you as an accessory to attempted murder, if not the attempted murder of Miss Underhay.' Inspector Greville's voice and expression was stern.

Matt saw the Adam's apple in the lad's throat bob as the boy swallowed nervously. 'Will I be free to go if I tell you?'

'I'll decide if you have a case to answer depending on what you tell us.' Inspector Greville's eyes gleamed and Matt could see the policeman was keen to follow up the chink in Tommy's armour.

'Doctor Marsh was in the town with his missus. I saw them a coming out of the bank and said as how I'd just seen that red car pull up quick at the harbour with two ladies in it. I said how there had been a shooting or something on a boat. I thought there might be a bob or two in it for me like as Mrs Marsh had paid me before to keep an eye out.' Tommy paused and a flicker of fear showed in his eyes. 'Mrs Marsh it was wanted to know what the pretty blonde lady were doing.'

'Carry on,' Inspector Greville pressed.

'Mrs Marsh was proper agitated, something about the China-man, you know that orderly, after I'd told her there had been the kerfuffle with a gun. Anyway, she gives me a few bob, and tells me to stay and keep watch. Doctor Marsh comes along to the harbour with me and, well, he done something to the car. The blonde lady and everybody had gone off in the police car so there weren't many people there by then once the fuss had died down. He went off to meet his missus and told me to wait and see if the lady come back.'

'Presumably that's what you were up to when Kitty and I returned from the police station and saw you,' Matt said.

The boy nodded. 'So, I didn't do nothing. I just watched is all. See, you can let me go now.'

'Do you know where Doctor Marsh and his wife were going after they had tampered with Kitty's car?' Matt asked.

Tommy shook his head. 'I dunno, I didn't hear them say. I think as they were going to travel separate though as Mrs Marsh told him to make sure as everything was took care of local like before he come back to her. They drove off together but it sounded as like her was setting him down somewhere.'

A cold, hard ball of anger settled in Matt's stomach as he heard the boy out. The something Marsh was to take care of must have been Kitty. It would explain how Kitty's assailant had known the layout of the hospital and been able to enter so easily. Doctor Marsh would have been there before several times, probably to see patients who were intending to recuperate at Elm House.

Once he had learned that the attempt to kill Kitty by tampering with her car had failed, Marsh must have decided to take more direct action. Sister Carmichael had either been mistaken or had deliberately lied when she had said that the doctor had gone to London.

Matt had to step outside the cell. The enclosed space and his anger at the Marshes and Tommy were threatening to overwhelm him. He heard the inspector asking a few more things of Tommy before Greville came to join him.

'Since we are unable for now to talk to Doctor and Mrs Marsh, I think we have more questions to ask of Sister Carmichael,' Matt said as the custody sergeant relocked Tommy's cell door, whilst ignoring the boy's loud shouts of protest.

The inspector nodded his agreement. Together they followed the sergeant along the small row of cells to the end one where he selected another key from the ring and unlocked the door.

Sister Carmichael looked up as they entered. She had removed her cap, apron and cuffs and was seated on the edge of her bed looking a very different woman from the one Matt had encountered at Elm House. Her brown hair had come loose from its bun and hard lines marred the corners of her mouth. She had a small cut and blue bruising to her temple that Matt suspected had been inflicted by Alice's handbag.

She scowled when she saw Matt accompanying Inspector Greville. 'What are you doing here? Come to gloat?'

'No, I feel sorry for you. You have been abandoned to take the blame for some heinous crimes by a man who doesn't deserve a single shred of your loyalty.' Matt chose his words carefully. He wanted to find out the truth from her this time.

Sister Carmichael glared at him. 'I had nothing to do with the deaths at Elm House. That was all down to Dodds.'

'That's not true though, is it? Yes, Dodds killed Mrs Pearson and Nurse Hibbert, but what of Miss Wordsley and Lady Wellings? You could be charged with their deaths, not to mention the cocaine smuggling.' Matt glanced at the inspector.

Sister Carmichael's complexion paled. 'No, I had nothing to do with any murders. The smuggling, yes, I knew about that.'

'Your lover, Doctor Marsh, is still with his wife. He and Esther have gone away together. He never intended to leave her for you at all. Theirs is not just a financial arrangement as he led you to believe. No, you were intended all along to be their scapegoat, left to hang or rot in prison while they get away together to live the high life on the proceeds of their crimes.' Matt wondered if he had overdone it slightly. He wanted to push the woman into telling everything that she knew and her passion for Doctor Marsh had to be the key.

'No, that's not true. He only agreed to marry her for the money and the business. He was forced into it after she found out he was dependant on cocaine. It wasn't a real marriage; her first husband is still alive.' Sister Carmichael shook her head causing more of her hair to become unpinned to fall wildly about her face.

'They were together in Torquay making their plans after you had been arrested. They were seen collecting their money from the bank,' Inspector Greville added, backing up Matt's statement.

'No, that's not true. He was going to London. She'd already left and gone back to Exeter. I was going to meet him at the Albion Hotel. We h-had tickets to g-g-go to France.' The woman broke down in tears.

Inspector Greville looked at Matt and they withdrew from the cell as the sergeant relocked the door. It seemed Sister Carmichael could tell them little that they did not already know.

'What now, sir?' Matt asked as he ascended the stairs with the inspector.

'I think it's clear that Marsh was responsible for the other deaths, no doubt at Esther Hammett's instigation. It certainly appears that he is behind the attempts on Miss Underhay's life.' Inspector Greville reopened the door of his office. 'I'll alert the police stations to look out for him and have the railway stations watched.'

'Thank you, sir. Let us hope he is caught soon and his so-called wife too.' Matt was thoughtful as he bade farewell to the inspector. Where had Marsh gone?

*

Kitty insisted on discharging herself from the hospital after lunch and returning home to the Dolphin, much to her grandmother's distress.

'Darling, you are still unwell, and someone tried to smother you. Please reconsider staying at the hospital. The constable is there to guard you.'

'I can rest just as well in my own bed. The constable can accompany me to the hotel and stand outside my door there as easily as he does here. I feel much better now, Grams, and I'm sure I shall be perfectly safe at home.' Kitty's head still ached but she was determined that if her assailant were to try again, she would rather be in her own room with a better chance of defending herself. 'I promise I shall rest.'

She complied with her grandmother's wishes and went straight to bed on her return to the Dolphin. The round-faced young constable who had received a tongue-lashing from his sergeant about exposing Kitty to the risk of attack at the hospital stayed on guard outside her room.

Kitty longed for Matt to visit her; she wanted to know if they had determined who her assailant might have been and if he had been captured. She also wanted to know if he would have more to say about his feelings towards her after their interrupted conversation the previous night.

It irked her enormously that she was confined to bed while everything appeared to be happening without her. She longed to be up and about looking for clues to ensure that the Hammetts were finally caught.

Matt eventually arrived at the hotel shortly before tea. Alice accompanied him to Kitty's room and joined her to listen intently to everything Matt had learned on his trip to the police station.

'Inspector Greville has men looking everywhere for Doctor Marsh and Esther Hammett.' Matt rubbed his face with his hand as he finished speaking.

Kitty could see how tired he looked. 'So, it was Doctor Marsh who tampered with my car and tried to smother me? All at Esther Hammett's behest?'

'They clearly blame you for all their misfortunes,' Matt said.

'Blimey, miss, I hope they catch him soon. He's a proper madman.' Alice's eyes were like saucers after listening to Matt's tale.

'Are you feeling any better now, Kitty?' Matt asked.

'The bandage is off my head and my headache has eased. I am much happier to be back home. I just wish I could do something to catch Doctor Marsh. Where on earth could he have gone?' Kitty asked. 'Has anyone checked with the ferrymen to see if he has crossed the river?'

'The police have checked but he could have taken a small boat, or of course have gone round by road,' Matt said.

'It beats me how nobody in town has seen them Hammetts, let alone Doctor Marsh. Everybody is talking about it and the place is a crawling with policemen.' Alice moved around the room as she spoke, tidying Kitty's things.

'Where would I hide if I were Doctor Marsh?' Kitty mused aloud, thinking of all the possibilities open to him. London, Exeter, Esther's many properties, or somewhere much more obvious, right under their noses. Somewhere he could lie low until all the attention had died down.

Kitty jumped out of bed. 'Alice find me my dark blue dress.'

Matt stared at her. 'Kitty, what are you planning?'

She shooed him out of the room. 'Wait for me downstairs and call Mr Potter. We need a taxi to Torquay.'

Alice helped her dress even as she scolded her. 'Your grandmother will have my guts for garters. What about that policeman? What are you going to do with him?'

Kitty grinned and hugged her friend. 'No blame will be attached to you. As for the constable, I have an urgent errand for him to attend to.'

'Well, I'm coming an all, Miss Kitty, you'm not shaking me off so easy. You shouldn't even be out of bed, let alone gallivanting about trying to catch a murderer.' The young maid's expression was determined.

'Very well.' Kitty gave way. 'Now, help me get out of the hotel without Grams discovering that I've gone.'

The constable was dispatched back to the police station amid much protestation with instructions and Alice assisted Kitty downstairs and into the back of the taxi next to Matt. Alice jumped in beside her and they set off.

Kitty was unsurprised to discover that it was Robert Potter rather than his father who was their driver. Something that brought a deep pink blush to Alice's cheeks.

'Where exactly are we going?' Matt asked once they had crossed the river. 'I presume you've had one of your brainwaves?'

'Back to Elm House.' Kitty settled back in her seat and wished the motion of the car would stop making her feel so nauseous.

CHAPTER TWENTY

Robert stopped the taxi further along the street on Kitty's instructions, near where she had parked previously for their nocturnal observations.

'What makes you think he will be here?' Matt asked as they stared at the red brick and glass turret of Elm House, silhouetted against the crisp blue of the winter sky.

'It's deserted. It's been searched already by the police during their first raid, and again after we captured Sister Carmichael. There is no reason for anyone to come back here. It is a large building with plenty of places to hide. There is still food in the larder and beds to sleep in,' Kitty said.

'And a telephone connection to make and receive messages,' Alice added, her expression thoughtful as she considered Kitty's logic.

'The constable has gone back to the station to alert the police to our errand. Inspector Greville and his men should arrive anytime soon.' Kitty looked at Matt. 'Now, we need to get inside and flush him out.'

'We can get in through the back door, miss. Where our Dolly showed us.' Alice looked at Kitty.

Matt sighed. 'I don't suppose there is any point in wasting my breath trying to persuade you to wait for the police?'

Alice opened the car door and she and Kitty got out.

'I'll watch the front of the home, sir, in case he makes a run for it through there.' Robert's gaze met Matt's.

'Hurry,' Kitty urged as Matt joined them on the pavement and they headed in through the gated entrance and made towards the back of the home.

As on their last visit, the house appeared empty and deserted. The windows blank and devoid of light or life. A chilly breeze whipped around the corner of the building as they gathered around the back door and Kitty shivered.

Matt produced his lock kit from his pocket, and, like Dolly, he soon had the kitchen door open.

'Alice, stay here and guard the back.' Kitty didn't want her friend exposed to any danger. 'Stay out of sight, we don't know if he has any kind of weapon.'

Alice nodded and Kitty and Matt left her to watch the rear entrance.

'I think we should try the turret,' Kitty whispered. 'I believe that is where we will find him. Hopefully he won't have taken much notice of the taxi arriving in the street. I think he will be waiting for nightfall and a boat to make good his escape. Where we got out of the car would be shielded from his view by those overhanging bushes and there's no view of the back of the home from the tower. The glass is all at the front to give the view of the bay.'

She led the way up the servants' stairs to the top floor. Matt followed close on her heels. Everywhere remained silent and still. Her heart thumped and she wondered if she had been mistaken and had dragged her friends on a wild goose chase. Or even worse, right into the lion's den.

'How do we get into the turret?' Matt whispered, his breath warm on her ear.

'Mrs Craven's famous cupboard, it has to be. There must be a concealed entrance, we just have to find it.' Kitty crept across the landing past what had been Mrs Craven's room to the cupboard door at the end of the landing. She held her breath as she tried the handle, half expecting it to be locked to prevent admission.

To her surprise it clicked open, exposing the seemingly empty store cupboard, painted white and lined with bare shelves. She raised her hand to feel along the shelves the way she had seen Sister Carmichael do so just a few days earlier.

Within a few minutes her questing fingers discovered a notch under the shelf and as she pressed, the entire section of shelving swung open revealing a tiny room with a narrow flight of stone stairs leading upwards.

Matt caught hold of her coat sleeve preventing her from doing anything else while they waited and listened for any signs of life. For a moment all she could hear were the sounds of her and Matt's breathing and the distant cries of the seagulls wheeling somewhere in the sky above the home.

Then she heard a faint scuffling sound on the boards from somewhere up above their heads. Matt's grip tightened on her arm and she knew he'd heard it too. He placed a finger on his lips indicating she should be quiet as he reached into his coat pocket and drew out his gun.

Kitty swallowed, the gleam of light on the gun barrel and Matt's grim expression underlining the possible dangers ahead of them. Matt walked in front of her and she followed behind as they made their way slowly and silently up the narrow stairs towards the turret room. Outside, they heard the unmistakeable sound of a motor car crunching onto the gravel forecourt of the home followed by muffled male voices. This event caused a rapid scuffling just ahead of them.

Doctor Marsh suddenly appeared before them, clearly about to attempt to flee down the stairs only to discover Matt and Kitty blocking his exit. The doctor's elegant suit was dirty and his tie askew. His usual debonair demeanour ruffled.

Matt pointed the gun at him. 'Going somewhere, Doctor?'

Doctor Marsh darted back up the staircase with an oath and Matt sprang up quickly after him. Kitty followed hard on his heels to see them scuffling together in the small square turret room.

The brass telescope she had seen before from outside the building was knocked from its stand in the melee. Kitty hung back near to the head of the stairs blocking the exit as she looked for a way to help Matt.

The room was bare apart from the telescope and no immediate weapon seemed available to her. The doctor, fighting with all the strength of a madman, broke loose from Matt's grip. He pushed Matt down hard onto the floor where he landed on his damaged shoulder jarring the gun free from his hand. Kitty rushed forward to pick it up from where it had skidded under the remains of the telescope stand.

Doctor Marsh took advantage of the situation to open one of large windows and scrambled out onto the flat roof ledge, guarded by a low iron railing that had been so fatal to Nurse Hibbert. Kitty heard shouts from the men down below. They must have seen the doctor emerge onto the roof and she guessed that Inspector Greville and his men had surrounded the home.

'Come back inside and give yourself up!' Kitty ran to the window and pointed the gun at the doctor. Behind her she heard Matt groan in pain as he struggled to his feet.

Marsh turned to face her, his expression a mask of fury, the pupils of his eyes wide and dilated. 'What for? To face the hangman's noose? I have a better way out.'

He paused, the corners of his mouth tipping upwards in the mockery of a smile.

'Kitty!' Behind her, Matt, on his feet once more rushed to her side, grabbing her and pulling her away so she was shielded from the sight as Doctor Marsh took his plunge from the roof.

She stifled a sob and buried her face in the comforting warmth of Matt's woollen overcoat as Inspector Greville arrived, panting and breathless into the room. The cries and whistles from down below carried on the air telling their own tale.

'Too late,' the inspector muttered, shaking his head as he surveyed the scene.

Matt discreetly reclaimed his gun, tucking it back inside the pocket of his overcoat. Kitty trembled and her head pounded as Matt steadied her.

Alice and Robert were waiting for them when they made their way back out of the home into the fresh, clean outside air. The inspector hurried off to issue instructions to his men. Alice was white-faced and anxious with Robert's arm about her waist.

'The doctor's dead, miss. Broke his neck when he jumped.'

'Are you all right, Alice?' Kitty asked anxiously. She hoped her friend had been spared the sight of the doctor's plunge from the roof.

Alice nodded. 'Yes, miss, I was back here with Robert. When the police arrived, he rushed around here to be with me, so we didn't see when he did it. At least he can't hurt no one else no more, miss.'

'It was still a horrible thing. I had hoped that we might learn where his wife had gone,' Kitty said.

'He was out of his mind. You noticed the white powder on the windowsill of the turret room?' Matt asked.

Kitty nodded. She had barely registered the implications of its presence when she had been looking for a weapon to aid Matt. 'Some of the cocaine from the last parcel of drugs, no doubt, retained for his personal use.'

'There is nothing more to be done here. The inspector will no doubt wish to speak to all of us later to take our statements. Kitty, you need to rest, you look all in. I suggest we all return to the Dolphin,' Matt said.

Kitty agreed, aware that her legs were still shaking and the terrible headache she had so recently got rid of was threatening a permanent comeback. They made a silent return to the taxi and remained so during the journey back to Dartmouth. The light was fading rapidly now as the sun sank in the sky.

Once outside the hotel, Kitty and Matt got out as Alice said goodbye to Robert. She stepped out onto the pavement after promising to meet her beau later. Robert waved farewell and drove away in the taxi.

'Alice, do go inside and get yourself a cup of tea. You must be exhausted.' Kitty was concerned for her friend's welfare and felt enormously guilty that Alice had exposed herself to so much danger recently.

'I'll get a tray ready for you as well, miss.' Alice stepped inside the hotel, leaving Kitty alone with Matt.

Kitty stood for a moment outside the Dolphin. The lights were on inside the lobby and the curtains had not yet been drawn against the cold. Matt placed his arm around her waist.

'Are you all right, darling girl?'

He so rarely called her darling it always pierced her heart, knowing that this was when his feelings for her were most on show.

'Perfectly. It was just such a shock when he jumped. I hadn't anticipated such an outcome.'

'I don't believe he was in his rational mind. Don't feel bad about him, Kitty. Remember, he would happily have seen you dead and he was responsible for the deaths of several other innocent people.' Matt gave her a tender squeeze.

'I know. You are right.' She smiled at him to show that she was recovered from the shock. 'I only wish that we could have found Hammett and his sister.'

'Inspector Greville and his men are on the case. They will soon run out of places to hide. Their empire is crumbling around them and, from my experience, there is no loyalty amongst thieves and villains,' Matt said.

She shivered as a cold draught hit them from the direction of the river. 'Let us hope so. At least I feel safer knowing Doctor Marsh is no longer a threat.'

'I think it would take a man braver than Hammett or his sister to make an attempt here again.' Matt's expression sobered, and she knew he was recalling his discovery of her inside her car after the crash.

'Let's not think of them any more for now. We have more pressing concerns, I'm afraid. I think we had better go inside and face the music.' She inclined her head towards the diamond paned leaded windows of the lobby where she could see her grandmother, Mrs Craven and General Ackland had all gathered and were clearly waiting for them.

Matt smiled back at her and gave her another gentle hug. 'I don't know who to fear most, your grandmother or Mrs C.' He moved his arm from her waist to take hold of her hand.

Kitty's own smile broadened, and she squeezed his fingers. 'I think if we face them together then we will be just fine.'

His eyes twinkled at her, and they walked into the lobby of the Dolphin side by side.

A LETTER FROM HELENA

I want to say thank you for choosing to read *Murder at Elm House*. If you enjoyed it and want to keep up to date with all my latest releases, just sign up at the following link. Your email address will never be shared and of course you can unsubscribe at any time.

www.bookouture.com/helena-dixon

If you read the first book in the series, *Murder at the Dolphin Hotel*, you can find out how Kitty and Matt first met and began their sleuthing adventures. I always enjoy meeting characters again as a series reader, which is why I love writing this series so much. I hope you enjoy their exploits as much as I love creating them. I am always being asked by my nursing and medical colleagues to write a book in a medical setting, so I decided to oblige. I'm not sure that this is quite what they had in mind, but I hope that they and you have enjoyed reading it.

I hope you loved *Murder at Elm House* and if you did, I would be very grateful if you could write a review. I'd love to hear what you think, and it makes such a difference helping new readers to discover one of my books for the first time.

I love hearing from all my readers – you can get in touch on my Facebook page, through Twitter, Goodreads or my website.

Thanks,
Helena Dixon

nelldixonauthor

@NellDixon

www.nelldixon.com

ACKNOWLEDGEMENTS

I would like to thank all my friends in Torbay who have given me so much support and information to assist me with *Murder at Elm House*. My medical and nursing colleagues who remain slightly baffled about why I write books but cheer me on and support me anyway. My fabulous and wonderful friends from all over the world, including the Bat Cave, the Tuesday group, and the Coffee Crew.

Many thanks also to all the staff at White Hill Country Park who are endlessly helpful and supportive.

A special shout-out to Julian and everyone at Torbay Old Wheels. Julian very kindly spent a delightful morning giving me a tour of his personal cars and all kinds of information so that my descriptions of Kitty's car and the terms used were as accurate as possible. I am so grateful for his assistance.

I love writing about Kitty and Matt and sharing their world and I couldn't do it without all of the brilliant team at Bookouture, especially my fabulous editor, Emily Gowers. And also my lovely agent, Kate Nash.

Many thanks to all of you. Your support is appreciated so much.

Made in United States
Orlando, FL
08 July 2022

19533563R00143